P9-CEB-009

From the seamy prisons of Mexico to the glamorous movie sets of L.A. and the lush and exclusive resorts of Santa Fe, Ed Eagle and his team of private detectives must hunt or be hunted. . . .

Ed Eagle—the six-foot-seven, take-no-prisoners Santa Fe attorney—is no stranger to murder, corruption, or organized crime—both north and south of the border. His home in Santa Fe, a picturesque desert town where the wealthy enjoy the good life, seems like a welcome retreat from the grit and crime of big cities.

But looks can be deceiving.

A puzzling murder in a golfer's hacienda brings in a new client for Ed, but while his time is spent unraveling a complex web of sex, money, and false identity, a much more dangerous threat lurks. A ruthless and implacable enemy who has proved more than a match for him in the past has returned to Santa Fe, and this time she wants nothing less than all-out retribution.

continued . . .

Dirty Work

"High on the stylish suspense." —*The Santa Fe New Mexican*

The Short Forever

"A tight mystery right up to the end . . . good-guy charm."
—*The Palm Beach Post*

Praise for Stuart Woods's
Holly Barker Thrillers

Hothouse Orchid

"Filled with plenty of local color, eccentric characters, and plenty of twists and surprises." —*Midwest Book Review*

Iron Orchid

"A page-turner." —The Associated Press

Blood Orchid

"Suspenseful, exciting . . . sure to please Woods's many fans."
—*Booklist*

Orchid Blues

"Mr. Woods, like his characters, has an appealing way of making things nice and clear." —*The New York Times*

Praise for the Other Novels
of Stuart Woods

Beverly Hills Dead

"Snappy dialogue, lively characters, and a story that moves along at a brisk clip . . . a lot of fun." —*Booklist*

The Prince of Beverly Hills

"A taut thriller." —*The Cincinnati Enquirer*

BOOKS BY STUART WOODS

FICTION

Lucid Intervals[†]

Kisser[†]

Hothouse Orchid[*]

Loitering with Intent[†]

Mounting Fears[‡]

Hot Mahogany[†]

Santa Fe Dead[§]

Beverly Hills Dead

Shoot Him If He Runs[†]

Fresh Disasters[†]

Short Straw[§]

Dark Harbor[†]

Iron Orchid[*]

Two Dollar Bill[†]

The Prince of Beverly Hills

Reckless Abandon[†]

Capital Crimes[‡]

Dirty Work[†]

Blood Orchid[*]

The Short Forever[†]

Orchid Blues[*]

Cold Paradise[†]

L.A. Dead[†]

The Run[‡]

Worst Fears Realized[†]

Orchid Beach[*]

Swimming to Catalina[†]

Dead in the Water[†]

Dirt[†]

Choke

Imperfect Strangers

Heat

Dead Eyes

L.A. Times

Santa Fe Rules[§]

New York Dead[†]

Palindrome

Grass Roots[‡]

White Cargo

Deep Lie[‡]

Under the Lake

Run Before the Wind[‡]

Chiefs[‡]

TRAVEL

A Romantic's Guide to the Country Inns of Britain and Ireland (1979)

MEMOIR

Blue Water, Green Skipper (1977)

[*]A Holly Barker Novel   [†]A Stone Barrington Novel
[‡]A Will Lee Novel   [§]An Ed Eagle Novel

SANTA FE EDGE

STUART WOODS

A SIGNET BOOK

SIGNET
Published by New American Library, a division of
Penguin Group (USA) Inc., 375 Hudson Street,
New York, New York 10014, USA
Penguin Group (Canada), 90 Eglinton Avenue East, Suite 700, Toronto,
Ontario M4P 2Y3, Canada (a division of Pearson Penguin Canada Inc.)
Penguin Books Ltd., 80 Strand, London WC2R 0RL, England
Penguin Ireland, 25 St. Stephen's Green, Dublin 2,
Ireland (a division of Penguin Books Ltd.)
Penguin Group (Australia), 250 Camberwell Road, Camberwell, Victoria 3124,
Australia (a division of Pearson Australia Group Pty. Ltd.)
Penguin Books India Pvt. Ltd., 11 Community Centre, Panchsheel Park,
New Delhi - 110 017, India
Penguin Group (NZ), 67 Apollo Drive, Rosedale, North Shore 0632,
New Zealand (a division of Pearson New Zealand Ltd.)
Penguin Books (South Africa) (Pty.) Ltd., 24 Sturdee Avenue,
Rosebank, Johannesburg 2196, South Africa

Penguin Books Ltd., Registered Offices:
80 Strand, London WC2R 0RL, England

Published by Signet, an imprint of New American Library, a division of Penguin
Group (USA) Inc. Previously published in a Putnam edition.

First Signet Printing, April 2011
10 9 8 7 6 5 4 3 2 1

Copyright © Stuart Woods, 2010
Excerpt from *Strategic Moves* copyright © Stuart Woods, 2011
All rights reserved

 REGISTERED TRADEMARK—MARCA REGISTRADA

Printed in the United States of America

This book is for Bonnie Piceu and Paul Dietz.

1

Ed Eagle sat at his breakfast table and watched his new wife, Susannah Wilde, cook his breakfast. He was a lucky man, he thought.

She set down two plates of huevos rancheros and joined him.

"What are you doing today?" he asked. He was concerned that she might become bored, and he didn't want that.

"I'm having lunch with a producer I worked with a few years back, Dan Karman. You remember that novel I bought a few weeks ago?"

"Yes, sure."

"Danny's written a screenplay based on it, and we're going to talk about shooting it in Santa Fe." Susannah was a well-known actress.

"Sounds great," Eagle replied, and he meant it. He didn't want her spending a lot of time in LA, shooting a movie.

"What are you up to?" Susannah asked.

"The usual. I'm having a first meeting with a man who's been charged with murdering his wife. It happened early this morning."

"You meet such nice people in your work," she said.

"Oh, this one's quite a nice fellow, I'm told, and he might even be innocent."

"I thought all your clients were innocent."

"He's not my client yet," Eagle replied. "If he's not innocent now, he will be by the end of the day."

Susannah laughed. "That's my Ed," she said, pouring him a second cup of coffee. "Do you remember a film producer named James Long?"

Eagle put down his coffee. "I certainly do," he replied. "He's the guy who furnished Barbara's alibi in her trial for murdering those people at the Hotel Bel-Air, when she thought she was murdering me."

"Long has his own production company, backed by inherited wealth, and Danny thinks he might be a good choice to get this film made. How would you feel about that?"

Eagle shrugged. "I don't have anything against the guy," he said. "I suppose he's as much Barbara's victim as I. She drugged him, left the house, shot those two people, then returned before he woke up. He thought she was in bed with him the whole time, and testified to that."

"Long might be the best way to go," she said. "He puts up a big chunk of the production money, then raises the rest from private investors, so he doesn't have to take any crap from a studio."

"Sounds good, but how does he distribute?"

"He has a good track record for making successful films on moderate budgets, so the distributors look on him favorably. Shouldn't be a problem."

"I liked the novel," Eagle said. "I hope you get a good screenplay."

"You can read it tonight," she said, clearing the table.

AN HOUR LATER Eagle sat in the attorneys' visiting room at the Santa Fe Municipal Jail, waiting for his prospective client. He read through a single-page report put together by an associate in his firm.

Terrence Hanks, known as Tip, is a twenty-nine-year-old golf professional, born in Delano, Georgia, a small town, and educated in the public schools and on a golf scholarship at Florida State University. He got his PGA Tour card six years ago and moved to Santa Fe two and a half years ago, building a house out at Las Campanas.

Ten months ago he married Constance Clay

Winston, the ex-wife of another golf pro, Tim Winston. She and Hanks were having an affair while she was still married to Winston.

Yesterday, Hanks returned home after uncharacteristically missing the cut at a tournament in Dallas. His story is that he found his wife in their bed, dead of a gunshot wound to the head. He called 911.

The police found a handgun near the bed that had Hanks's fingerprints on it and charged him with murder. He was referred to you by his personal attorney, Earl Potter, who, as you know, doesn't do criminal work.

Hanks is a relatively successful tour player, earning an average of a little over a million and a half dollars a year since getting his card, so he can afford representation.

Precious little information, Eagle thought, but it was a start. He looked up to see a young man being escorted into the room, and he waited while he was unshackled. He was maybe six-one, a hundred and seventy, tanned and freckled, with a mop of sun-bleached hair that reminded Eagle of a younger Jack Nicklaus.

Hanks stuck out his hand. "I'm Tip Hanks, Mr. Eagle," he said, and his handshake was cool, dry and firm.

Eagle shook the hand. "Call me Ed," he said, "and have a seat."

"Earl Potter speaks highly of you," Hanks said.

"Earl's a good lawyer and a good fellow," Eagle replied. "Tell me how you ended up in here, and please remember, everything you say to me is privileged—that is, I can't disclose what you say to anyone, and no court can force me to do so, unless I believe you intend to commit a crime, in which case I'm bound to report that to the court."

"Earl has already explained that to me," Hanks replied. "I'd like you to represent me, if you're available."

"Did Earl also explain that if you admit guilt to me, I can't put you on the stand to testify that you're innocent?"

"He did, and I understand that, too. For the record, I'm not going to admit guilt, because I'm completely innocent of killing my wife. Will you represent me?"

"Tell me what happened this morning, and then we'll talk about representation."

"I played in a charity tournament in Dallas, starting with the pro-am on Wednesday. I played badly, and I missed the cut. Do you know what that means?"

"Yes, I'm a golfer."

"I had planned to fly home yesterday, but I had a couple of drinks with two other guys who also missed the cut, and that turned into an early dinner. We finished about seven, and I went to my room, called my wife and told her I'd be home around noon today. Then I got into bed and turned on the TV. I woke up about three a.m. with the TV on, and I couldn't get back to sleep. Finally, around four a.m. I got up, got dressed and went to the airport."

"Which airport?"

"Love Field."

"Which FBO?"

"Vitesse."

"I don't know it," Eagle said. "I usually fly into Signature."

"You'll save money on fuel by going to Vitesse."

"What do you fly?"

"A Piper Meridian."

This was a single-engine turboprop, similar to the JetProp Eagle had once owned. "What time did you take off?"

"About five twenty. I was lucky with the winds, and I landed in Santa Fe at eight fifteen. My car was there, and I got home about eight forty."

"Did you notice anything unusual when you arrived?"

"No, everything was normal, except my wife had been shot in the bed. She still had a pulse, but she had taken a bullet to the right temple, and it seemed obvious that she wasn't going to live long. I called nine-one-one, and it took the ambulance about eight minutes to get there. Sometime during that eight minutes, she died."

"Was there anything unusual about the bedroom?"

"It was pretty neat, and my wife's clothes were on a chair."

"Was that where she usually left them when you went to bed?"

"No, she has a dressing room, and she undresses in there, unless . . . we're in a hurry."

"I understand."

"Something else: She was on my side of the bed. I always sleep on the left side, and she sleeps on the right, even when I'm away."

"Had both sides been slept on?" Eagle asked.

"Yes."

"Do you think she started sleeping on her usual side, then shifted to your side?"

"I've never known her to do that," Hanks replied.

"Did you see the gun?"

"Yes, it was on the floor beside the bed, and the bedside-table drawer was not quite closed. That's where I keep the gun."

"Did your wife know it was there?"

"Yes, and she knew how to use it."

"What sort of gun was it?"

"It was a Colt Government .380."

"Loaded?"

"I kept it in the drawer with the magazine in and a round in the chamber, cocked, but with the safety on."

"Were you expecting trouble?"

"I had a burglary right after the house was finished,"

Hanks replied. "I suspected it was somebody who worked on the house."

"Tell me about that."

"It was a Saturday afternoon. I went out to the Santa Fe flea market, gone about two hours, and when I came back I went into my dressing room and found a jewelry box turned upside down. I was missing a Rolex watch, a couple pairs of cuff links and my old wedding ring. I was divorced at the time."

"How did they get in?"

"I believe by the bedroom door opening to the outside. I had put the alarm on but hadn't locked the house. The transom window over the door was open, and it turns out that deactivates that part of the alarm, something I didn't know before. I think the guy came in through that door, went straight to the dressing room, emptied the jewelry box and got out in a hurry. There's a dirt road that cuts across my property behind the house, and he could have driven in there without being seen."

"Any luck on recovering any of the stolen items?"

"None at all. And I believe the man who shot my wife came in and left the same way. If he'd left by the front door I would likely have passed him on the way to the house. As I walked into the bedroom I heard a car drive away behind the house, and when I looked out I saw some dust raised, but the car wasn't in sight."

"Do you know why the police arrested you?"

"They said because my fingerprints were on the gun. But it was my gun, so you'd expect that."

"I'll represent you, Tip," Eagle said, "and I think I can probably get you bail. How much equity do you have in your house?"

"It's paid for. Am I going to be able to continue playing golf? I have to make a living."

"I'll try, but maybe not. But you'll be able to practice. I'll need a retainer of fifty thousand dollars against my hourly rate and expenses."

"I can raise that and reasonable bail," Hanks said. "How much do you think that will be?"

"Maybe a couple of hundred thousand." Eagle looked at his watch. "You'll probably be arraigned within the hour. I'll see you in the courtroom."

The two men shook hands, and Eagle left. This one didn't look so tough, he thought.

2

Barbara Eagle Keeler was taken by a female guard from her cell in the El Diablo Prison for Women, east of Acapulco, Mexico, handcuffed and delivered to the office of Pedro Alvarez, the warden of the facility. It was not her first trip there.

She had been imprisoned now for nine weeks after a trial of one hour and ten minutes and a jury deliberation of half that, and sentenced to twenty-five years to life in prison for each of three attempted murders, the sentences to run concurrently. One of the attempted murders had consisted of Barbara's severing with a straight razor the penis of a young man who turned out to be the nephew of a captain of police in Acapulco. This had proven an unfortunate choice of both victim and technique, and had ensured her conviction by an all-male jury, who, upon hearing the young man's testimony, had, as one man, crossed their legs.

Before leaving the Acapulco jail for El Diablo, Barbara had been raped repeatedly by the captain and a couple of his subordinates, as the nephew had watched, but the young man had not been allowed to cut up her face, as he had wished to do.

"It is more difficult in prison for a beautiful woman than an ugly one," the captain had explained. "You will be avenged often."

The captain had spoken without taking into account the animal cunning that reposed in this particular woman. Barbara had survived an awful second marriage to the murderer of her first husband. She had been convicted as an accessory, though she had not known of the man's intentions, and had served a sentence in a New York State prison, where she had been schooled in female-on-male violence and other criminal activity by other inmates and where she had been interviewed by the Santa Fe attorney, Ed Eagle, on the subject of her criminal sister, who had been married to a Hollywood film producer with a Santa Fe home.

Upon her early release, due to a court order after a lawsuit concerning prison overcrowding, Barbara had made her way to Santa Fe, where she had looked up Ed Eagle and, in fairly short order, enticed him into marriage.

A few months later, she had made off with a large sum of his money, and, after an extensive search by two clever private detectives, she had been lured aboard a yacht in La Jolla, California, and transported to a spot in Mexican waters a few miles off Tijuana, where, by previous arrangement, the police had boarded the yacht and arrested her for the three attempted murders, two of which victimized the private detectives.

Upon transfer to El Diablo, she had established herself among her fellow prisoners as someone who would not be fucked with, as she would have put it, without violence being perpetrated upon her assailant. At the same time she had preserved her appearance and her physical fitness, and she had made it her business to be noticed by the warden, Capitán Alvarez.

Alvarez lived with his very plain wife in an apartment adjacent to his office, and Barbara had learned that the wife sometimes traveled to Acapulco to visit her mother. Twice Barbara had been ordered to Alvarez's office, where he had raped her.

Barbara had accepted this stoically, even letting the man believe she enjoyed it, because she knew that if she fought him, he would kill her—or have it done by the guards. Now his wife was in Acapulco again, Barbara had learned through the prison grapevine, and she was back in Alvarez's office.

The capitán was, perhaps, six-two and three hundred pounds.

"Get naked," he had said to her, forgetting to say "please."

He had removed her handcuffs, then closed and locked his office door. He poured himself what was, apparently, not his first shot of tequila of the morning and sipped it while he watched her undress.

Barbara had done so without hesitation, and had even managed to be alluring during the process. Alvarez had dropped his pants, sat down on his office sofa, taken her by the hair and pulled her to her knees, where she did what was expected of her. Such was her skill that it did not take long for him to reach a successful conclusion. He sagged sideways onto the sofa and, after a few minutes of her caresses, fell asleep, snoring loudly and breathing tequila into the close atmosphere of the small room.

Barbara did not waste time putting on her clothes. She went to the interior door she believed led to his quarters, opened it as quietly as possible and entered the apartment.

It consisted of a living room with a dining area, a bedroom and a bath. There were bars on the windows of the living room and bedroom, but an exploration of the bathroom revealed a small window over the toilet that had not been fitted with bars. She stood on the toilet seat and unlatched the window, which swung outward. She found herself looking a dozen feet down into an alley, which ran off a larger street to her left that a sign revealed to be Camino Cerritos. Directly across the street from the alley was an establishment named, on a large sign, Cantina Rosita.

Barbara closed the window, then inspected the bedroom. Inside a closet she found a wardrobe of dresses perhaps two sizes larger than her own, and shoes slightly smaller than her feet.

She looked through a chest of drawers and a bedside table, hoping to steal money but finding nothing except some awful costume jewelry. There was something else she was very glad to see: a telephone on the bedside table. She closed the bedroom door and found the phone book. Her Spanish was poor, but she managed to divine how to call the United States, so she dialed a number she knew very well, belonging to her dear friend, the film producer James Long.

"Hello?" a sleepy male voice said.

"Jimmy, it's Barbara," she said softly.

"Good God! I read in the paper you were in a Mexican jail!"

"I am—in a prison called El Diablo, in a little town east of Acapulco, called Tres Cruces. Write all this down."

"Okay, I've got a pen."

"Listen to me carefully," she said. "Do you still have the same cell phone number?"

"Yes."

"I have some clothes and some identity documents in a suitcase in the apartment over your garage, remember?"

"Yes, of course."

"I've found a way out of here. Can you come to Acapulco?"

"Yes."

"Charter a small airplane. I'll pay for it. Ask the pilot to wait, for two or three days, if necessary."

"All right, when?"

"Now, today. Book a room at the Acapulco Princess, and check in. I'll call you on your cell when I'm ready. Tomorrow, rent a car from the hotel, drive to Tres Cruces and find Camino Cerritos and a bar called Cantina Rosita. Park near there. There's an alley across the street. I'll call you on your cell, then drive into the alley, and you'll see a small window about ten or twelve feet above the pavement, on your right. Park under the window. Got it?"

He repeated the instructions.

"Buy me some hair dye, auburn, in the hotel shop, and some good scissors."

"Okay."

"I love you, baby," she said. "I'll call as soon as I can." She hung up and returned to the office, where Alvarez still snored away, and began searching the room for useful items. There was a cabinet containing guns, but it was securely locked and grilled with ironwork. There was also a substantial safe with an electronic key-pad lock.

She went to the desk and methodically searched the drawers, but the only thing of use to her was half a dozen of what appeared to be handcuff keys. She took one and put it into her mouth, under her tongue, then she looked at the sides and bottoms of the drawers, finally finding what she was looking for, taped to the bottom of a pull-out typewriter shelf. It was a piece of paper with a six-digit number written on it, and she did not doubt that it would open the safe. She also did not doubt that if she used the code now, it would cause electronic beeping that would wake the warden. She memorized the number.

Alvarez stirred. She ran back to the sofa, sat on the floor beside him and pretended to be asleep.

"Hey, you, girl," Alvarez said, shaking her.

Barbara raised her head. "Hey, you," she said in a low voice.

"You're pretty good, you know?"

"I know."

"Get dressed and get out. I'll send for you again."

"I'd love to see you again," she said. "When?"

"You want some more, eh?"

"Oh, yes," she agreed.

"Maybe tomorrow," he said.

"When does your wife return?" she asked.

"What do you know about my wife?" he demanded.

"Just that she's away."

He looked at her for a moment. "Sunday," he said.

"Then we have tomorrow to play," she said, standing up and slowly putting on her clothes.

"Tomorrow, then," he said.

"Yes, Capitán," she replied. "I will be ready."

He handcuffed her, then unlocked the office door and turned her over to the guard who waited outside.

The guard marched her back down the dirty hallways and put her back in the small cell that she shared with five other women.

"Have a good time?" one of the women asked suggestively.

"Shut up, bitch," Barbara replied, and lay down on her bunk. *Tomorrow,* she thought. Saturday at the latest.

Later, she got up and motioned to the guard in the hallway.

"Eh?" the woman said.

"I can't sleep," Barbara said. "I need something to take."

"Sleep is expensive," the woman replied.

"Twenty dollars American for Ambien or two Valiums."

"Show me the money."

"When I see the medicine."

The woman went away and returned with two yellow pills. "Valium," she said. "See the writing?"

Ten milligrams, Barbara thought. *Ideal.* She retrieved the money from a capsule in her vagina and paid the woman. Now all she had to do was survive tomorrow.

It was nearly noon before the guard came for Barbara in her cell, and she had been getting nervous, thinking something had gone wrong. The guard finally opened the cell door, and she didn't handcuff Barbara.

The guard took her down the corridors, let her into Alvarez's office and closed the office door behind her. Barbara locked it herself.

This seemed to please Alvarez. "Would you like a drink?" he asked.

"Sure," she replied, walking toward his desk, where a bottle of tequila reposed, along with some glasses. "Let me get you one." She was unbuttoning her blouse as she walked.

"Good girl," Alvarez said, unzipping his pants.

Barbara fished the two Valium tablets from her bra

and ground them between her thumb and forefinger into the glass as she poured the liquid. She turned and walked over to Alvarez while reaching behind her and unhooking her bra.

"You're not having one?" he asked.

"Afterward," she replied. "I enjoy it more if I'm sober." She knelt between his legs and began toying with his penis. *"Salud."*

He tossed off the tequila, grabbed her hair and pulled her into his crotch.

She took longer this time, hoping the drug would work quickly, playing with him, bringing him to the brink of orgasm, then backing off. After fifteen minutes or so he came loudly, then sagged sideways on the sofa, as he had done the previous day. She continued to stroke him until he fell asleep.

Barbara walked back to the desk, took a swig from the tequila bottle, swished it around her mouth and spat it onto the floor, then went into the apartment, picked a dress from the closet and put it on. She took a scarf from a drawer to wear over her blond hair, then picked up the phone and dialed James Long's cell number.

"Hello?"

"Where are you?"

"Just driving down Camino Cerritos," he said. "I was delayed by some roadwork."

"Can you be under the window in five minutes?" she asked.

"Yes."

"See you then." Barbara hung up and looked around the room for something else but didn't find it. She walked back into the office and looked around. In a corner was a silver-trimmed Mexican saddle, with a cowboy's rope tied to it. She took the rope and started back into the apartment, then stopped.

She had nearly forgotten the safe. She knelt before it and pressed in the code she had found in the desk. There was a soft click; then she turned the handle and the door swung open. To her delight, the first thing she saw was two stacks of bills, one of dollars, the other of pesos. She took both. On a lower shelf, half a dozen pistols were arrayed. She chose a small Beretta semiautomatic and checked to be sure it was loaded.

At the bottom of the safe she found a cloth bag and put the gun and the money into it and tied it around her neck. She walked back to where Alvarez slept, thought about putting a bullet into his brain, then decided against it. It would just make the authorities angrier and motivate their search for her.

She went back into the apartment and into the bathroom, where she tied one end of the rope around the base of the sink; then she stood on the toilet, opened the window and, with one foot on the sink, raised herself and looked out. A car was just turning into the alley, with Jimmy at the wheel. Perfect.

Barbara tossed the remainder of the rope out the

window, then, pushing off the toilet tank, got her upper half out the window and looked down. The car was directly beneath her.

Holding tightly to the rope, she allowed the rest of herself to fall out the window, breaking the fall with the rope. She landed in a sitting position on top of the car, then let herself to the ground. "Hi, there," she said to Jimmy.

"Hey, babe," he replied, smiling.

She got into the backseat. "Let's get out of here," she said, "but slowly. We have some time, I think."

Jimmy backed slowly down the alley and into the street, then put the car in drive and headed back the way he had come.

Barbara kept her head down until they had cleared the town; then she crawled over the seat and into the front.

"How long until Acapulco?" she asked.

"A little over an hour."

"How long before the roadwork?"

"Half that."

"Stop well before it, and I'll get into the trunk. We don't want the workers remembering a car with a woman in it."

"Good thinking," he said. "How are you? Was it rough?"

"At times, but nothing I couldn't handle."

"What's that around your neck?" he asked.

21

"Ill-gotten gains," she replied.

Twenty minutes later Jimmy slowed the car. "I think the roadwork is just around the bend ahead."

They both got out of the car and checked for traffic. Barbara climbed in the trunk. "I'll let you out when it's safe," Jimmy said, then closed it after her.

He got in and drove away, while Barbara did her best to make herself comfortable. Shortly, the car stopped, then moved forward in little spurts; then they were finally past the work and at speed. Jimmy slowed and stopped again, then helped her out of the trunk.

Barbara put on the head scarf and took Jimmy's sunglasses from him and put them on. "There," she said. "Did you get the hair dye?"

"It's in our suite," he said. "Why don't we go straight to the airport and get out of here?"

"No," she said. "They'll shut that down as soon as I'm missed. Let's go to the Princess. We'll check on the airport tomorrow. I don't care if we have to wait for a few days, until the heat is off."

"I don't think the pilot will wait that long," he said.

"Call him when we get to the hotel and tell him tomorrow. Where's my suitcase?"

"In the suite," he replied. "I had everything in it pressed."

"Good." As they approached Acapulco, Barbara put her head in Jimmy's lap. "Wake me when we're there," she said.

Jimmy drove to the hotel, passing the main entrance, then stopping at a side door. He handed her a key card. "This will let you in through that door and into the suite. It's number nine hundred, ninth floor, turn right out of the elevator. I'll go park the car."

Barbara got out of the car and let herself into the hotel, then followed Jimmy's directions to the suite. It was spacious and sunny, with a terrace overlooking the Pacific. She undressed, went into the bathroom and began applying the hair color. By the time Jimmy got upstairs, she was a redhead. She dried her hair, and when she came out of the bathroom, Jimmy was in bed, naked.

"You deserve a reward," she said, climbing in beside him.

4

When Alvarez awoke it was dark in his office. He stood up and groggily felt for the light switch along the wall above the sofa. Then he took a step and fell heavily on the floor. His trousers were around his ankles.

He pulled them up and buckled his belt, then, holding on to the arm of the sofa, pulled himself to his feet and found the light switch. He was alone in the office. Panicked, he went to the safe and checked the door, but it was locked. Relieved, he sank into his office chair and poured himself a glass of tequila from the open bottle on the desk. Where the hell was the woman? Then he noticed that the door to his apartment was open. Was she in his bed? He'd kill her!

He got up and staggered into the apartment, switching on an overhead light. She was not in the living room, so he went into the bedroom and turned on a bedside lamp. The bed was perfectly made. He tried the bathroom and was stunned to see a rope, one end tied to the sink pedestal, the other end hanging out the window above the toilet. He pulled it in and untied it from the sink, then returned to his office and placed the rope back on his prize saddle. Everything had to be in perfect order when his wife came home.

But where was the woman? He unlocked his office door and stepped into the hallway. No one there. Thank God the guard was gone. He went back into his office and sat down at his desk. She had escaped, and he had to do something, but what? If he sounded the alarm, he would have to explain how she got out of his office. He would be fired out of hand the moment the story hit the papers and TV. What was even worse was that he would have to explain it to his wife.

He looked at his clock on his desk: just after eight p.m. There was a knock on the office door. "Come in!" he called.

The door opened and the guard stood there, looking around the room. "My shift is ending," she said. "Do you want me to return the American woman to her cell?"

Alvarez, borne on a cloud of tequila, improvised. "The American woman has been transferred," he replied.

"Transferred? Where?"

"Who knows? I think the woman has connections in the government. They came; they had the proper papers; they took her away. Now go home and forget about it. If anybody asks about her you know nothing, except that she has been transferred. You don't want to get caught in that particular flypaper."

"That is true," the woman said, and closed the door.

Transferred—that was it! Alvarez mopped his brow and poured himself another tequila. The woman was gone, and good riddance! He would stick to his story. There had been a telephone call from the Ministry of Justice. He was to bring the woman to his office, where she would be collected in due course. They had brought a transfer order, properly signed and stamped, and had taken her away. If anyone asked, he knew nothing further. He drank more tequila.

BARBARA AND JIMMY WERE, at that moment, having a room-service dinner on the terrace of their suite, watching the moon rise over the Pacific. Barbara kept an eye on the TV, waiting for her picture to be displayed, but it didn't happen. What was going on?

"You still looking for yourself on TV?" Jimmy asked.

"Yes, and I don't understand it."

"Maybe the warden is still asleep."

"Possibly," she said, "Or . . ."

"Or what?"

"Alvarez is now in a very difficult position," Barbara said. "I'm gone, and there's a rope hanging out his bathroom window. What does he do?"

"Sound the alarm?"

"I've been gone for hours," she said. "The Valium had to put him down for quite a while, especially when mixed with the tequila."

"Yeah, that would do it, if he drank enough."

"He's a lush. He drinks all the time."

"Then maybe he's still out."

"It's been more than eight hours," she said. "When he wakes up and I'm gone, he's going to have to figure out what to do, and from his point of view, the absolute worst thing he could do is raise an alarm for my recapture."

"Good point," Jimmy said. "You've got that on your side."

"He's in control inside the prison. If I'm gone he can cover it up, at least for a while, but if his superiors know I'm out, all hell will break loose."

"Granted."

"And then there's his wife," Barbara said, smiling. "Word is, he's more frightened of her and her father than of his bosses. She comes home tomorrow morning. If he's smart, and he is, in a kind of reptilian-brain way, he'll cover it up."

"How about the money you stole from him?"

"I'd bet anything she knows nothing about it. It's graft—bribes he's taken over time. There was sixty-one thousand dollars and about twenty in pesos."

"So, only you and Alvarez know about that."

"Right, but if they catch me, everyone will know. Jimmy, we have to get out of here tomorrow morning, first thing. Call your pilot."

Jimmy got out his cell phone. "Hello, Bart? Jim Long. I want to fly back to LA tomorrow morning."

"No," Barbara said, tugging at his sleeve.

"We have to stop somewhere on the way to LA. What's an out-of-the-way airport?"

Jimmy shrugged. "How about Yuma?" he said to Barbara.

"Perfect. Tell him to file for there; then he can drop me and take you back to Santa Monica."

Jimmy passed on the request and hung up. "Bart's good with that," he said.

"How well do you know him?"

"Very well. He's worked on nearly all of my films as a stunt pilot, and ferrying around cast and crew. He can do just about anything, and I put money in his pocket all the time."

"Good, then he won't ask too many questions about me."

"Don't worry about it."

"Tell him I live in Yuma, and my husband doesn't know I've been in Mexico."

"Okay."

"Does he fly to Mexico a lot?"

"All the time."

"Good. You can give him Alvarez's pesos."

The following morning they drove to the Acapulco Airport and onto the ramp, stopping next to the Beech Baron and depositing their luggage with Bart, who seemed to think nothing of taking on an unexpected passenger and dropping her in Yuma.

They took off and climbed to twelve thousand feet, and headed northeast. Barbara opened her suitcase and went through all her ID—credit cards, driver's license and passport, all genuine, all in the name of Eleanor Keeler. Her last husband had been Walter Keeler, who had died in a car crash. She had been left a tightly controlled legacy and suspected Walter's lawyer of having screwed her out of anything more. He had, no doubt, cut off payments when she had been convicted in Mexico, but she still had a fund of several hundred thousand dollars in a San Francisco bank. It would take some doing, but she would get her hands on that.

The airplane landed at Yuma later in the day, and Barbara handed the pilot her passport. "For some reason, they didn't give me an entry stamp when I crossed the border," she said.

"When did you cross?"

"Three days ago. I flew private into Acapulco."

"It'll probably be okay," he said.

She and Jimmy waited next to the airplane. She was nervous, and she looked for a way out of the airport. There was a midsized jet parked next to them with the engines running. Maybe she could hide in the toilet.

Their pilot came walking across the tarmac with a uniformed customs official, scaring her half to death, but the official wanted only to inspect the airplane, which took no more than two minutes; then he left.

"We're cleared," the pilot said, returning her passport. "It was no sweat about your entry stamp, and you're stamped into the U.S. now." He got her bag out of the airplane for her.

She put an arm around Jimmy's neck and kissed him. "I'll be in touch, baby. You just go back to LA and live your life. You know nothing about me."

"Gotcha, kiddo," he said, climbing back into the airplane.

BARBARA SPENT THE NIGHT in an airport motel, then, the following morning, rented a car and drove to Phoenix, ending up in Scottsdale at the Mondrian, a fashionable hotel full of beautiful people.

She had a new life to invent now, and a long shopping list of a car, an untraceable cell phone, clothes and luggage. She started with a day at the hotel spa, including a recoloring and cut of her hair.

That night, snuggling in bed with a business executive she had met at the bar, Barbara thought of Ed Eagle. He was still out there, in Santa Fe, waiting for her.

She wouldn't disappoint him.

5

E d Eagle stopped by the DA's office and asked to see him.

Roberto Martínez rose as Eagle entered, then shook his hand, waving him to a chair. "I've been expecting you, Ed."

"Well, I'm glad I didn't disappoint you, Bob," Eagle replied with an easy smile.

"You ready for arraignment?"

"Oh, I don't think we need to go that far, Bob."

"'That far'?"

"I think we should just settle this here, and get it over with."

"Ed, are you already looking to plea-bargain? That makes me feel even better about our case."

"Bob, I expect you haven't had time to go over the case file," Eagle said, starting to get up.

"Wait a minute," Martínez said, waving him back to his chair. "I've had a look at the summary. It's a good case."

"Bob, Tip Hanks can account for every minute of his time between the hours of four a.m. and when he called nine-one-one. He was in Dallas; he couldn't sleep, so he decided to get up and return home early. His wife wasn't expecting him until noon."

"So, he killed her earlier than planned," Martínez said, leaning his chair way back and putting his feet on the desk.

"No, Bob, whoever she was in bed with shot her, and before Tip's car pulled up to the house, because Tip never heard the shot. The killer heard Tip's car door slam and beat it out of the bedroom door opening to the terrace, then ran down the hill to the dirt road where he'd parked his car. Tip heard him leave, and when he looked out the back door he saw dust, but the car was already around the bend and out of sight. If you can get the investigating officers to put down their comic books long enough, they might be able to get some footprints and tire tracks before it rains or the wind blows them away."

"You want me to dismiss the charges on nothing more than that story?"

"Both sides of the bed had been slept in, but she was on the left side of the bed, where Tip slept. Somebody had moved her there while he was screwing her. I expect her ex-husband will testify to that sleeping habit of hers."

"What else?"

"We don't need anything else. You're postulating that Tip walked into his house, went to the bedroom, took his gun out of the bedside table and shot his wife in the head, then called nine-one-one. That doesn't make any sense."

"It didn't have to happen that way," Martínez said.

"The staff at the FBO at the airport will testify to Tip's arrival time. They log in every aircraft that lands, and his was probably the first of the day. Drive the route from the FBO to his house and walk in. You'll see there was no time for him to make love to her and have an argument before killing her. I think it likely that the medical examiner is going to discover somebody else's DNA inside her."

"We'll see about that."

"Even if the killer used a condom and left no trace, the ME will say that she had sex with somebody, and Tip's DNA won't be inside her."

"Maybe he used a condom."

"He knew she was on the pill. There was no need for him to do that." Eagle was making this up, but he could see Martínez begin to show signs of folding.

Martínez put his feet back on the floor and leaned over his desk. "What evidence do you have that she was having an affair?"

"She has a history, Bob. Tip was screwing her while she was still married to her last husband. I expect that if I send an investigator to Dallas to talk to other members of the tour and their wives and girlfriends, we'll find that she had a reputation among the camp followers. This is an old story, Bob, and it will embarrass everybody concerned when the news desks pick it up from the sports pages. You really want to stir that up?"

"Maybe they've been fighting. Maybe we'll turn that up among their friends."

"So what? Every couple fights, but they rarely murder each other. Now, do you really want to arraign him? If you do, then I'll get him released on his own recognizance and he'll go back to playing golf for a living, and the whole thing will drag on for weeks before I get a dismissal. Do the right thing, here, Bob."

Martínez opened a file on his desk and made a show of reading it, while Eagle sat mute, occasionally crossing and recrossing his legs just to let him know he was still there.

"All right, I'll drop the charges for now," Martínez said, "but if we turn up anything else—anything at all— I'll have him rearrested."

"That's fair, Bob. Now, will you please fax over a

release order to the jail, so I can drive the boy home? He's got some grieving to do."

Martínez buzzed his secretary. "Type up a release order for one Terrence Hanks," he said. "I'll sign it, and you can fax it to the jail."

Eagle stood up and offered his hand. "Thank you, Bob," he said. "You won't regret doing that."

Eagle left the office, got into his car and drove back to the jail, phoning ahead to let them know he was coming and to have his client processed out. He had only a few minutes to wait before Tip Hanks appeared, taking his belongings out of an envelope and stuffing them into his pockets.

"Is it time for the arraignment?" he asked as he shook Eagle's hand.

"You're not going to be arraigned," Eagle said. "I persuaded the DA to drop the charges."

Hanks looked at him incredulously. "How did you do that?"

"He hadn't even read the case file thoroughly," Eagle replied, leading him out the front door. "Once he did, he reconsidered, after I had pointed out how weak his case was."

They got into the car, and Eagle turned toward Las Campanas. "By the way," he said, "I told him that your wife was on the pill; I hope that's true."

"It is," Hanks replied.

"Here's my theory of the case: Your wife was having

an affair, and she didn't expect you home before noon today. Her lover had already shot her, for reasons of his own, when you pulled up, and he ran. Maybe they'll find DNA, maybe not. He could have used a condom. But they won't find your DNA in her, right?"

"Right," Hanks said.

"You're wondering who she was having the affair with?"

"Yes."

"Any ideas?"

"Could have been anybody," Hanks replied. "She liked sex more than any woman I ever met, and she wanted it regularly. Normally, she'd have been in Dallas with me, but she's missed a couple of tournaments lately, saying she wasn't feeling well enough to go. She was a terrible hypochondriac."

"Well, I'm sorry," Eagle said.

"What are the chances that they'll catch the guy?" Hanks asked.

"Fifty-fifty, I'd say. A lot better if there's DNA."

Hanks put his head back against the headrest and sighed. "She didn't deserve this," he said.

"Are you scheduled to play next weekend?"

"No, I passed on the next one. The week after, though."

"That's time enough to get your head together," Eagle said. "Go out and practice as you usually do; look sad, don't laugh at anybody's jokes; keep any conversations about her to an absolute minimum. People are going to be watching your reactions. Same thing when you rejoin the tour." He followed directions to Hanks's front door, and the young man got out.

"I'll send you a check. What do I owe you?" he asked.

"I get ten grand for getting out of bed," Eagle said. "I'll send you a bill."

"Fair enough."

"If the evidence doesn't go your way and Martínez has you rearrested, I'll apply it to my retainer." Eagle reached into his glove compartment and found a card. "This is the number of a service that cleans up crime scenes," he said. "Don't call them until the police let you know they've released the scene. Take care."

Eagle drove away, thinking he'd done a good day's work.

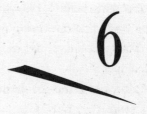

B arbara spent a day shopping in Phoenix and Scottsdale, and found a used, low-mileage Mercedes
station wagon within her budget. By the time she had
finished shopping she still had twenty thousand dollars
of Alvarez's money in her new purse. She employed her
old, legal identity as Eleanor Keeler, which would be all
right as long as Warden Alvarez didn't report her escape.

She found a branch of her San Francisco bank and
arranged a wire transfer of cash from her account, and
they issued her a new checkbook. None of her credit
cards had expired.

After a room-service dinner and a movie in her room
she called Canyon Ranch, in Tucson, a top-notch spa
resort, and booked herself into a suite for a week. Then
the following morning she drove there and checked in.

It was a beautiful place, and her little cottage was near the dining room and classrooms. She didn't need to lose any weight, but she took the opportunity to tone up and pamper herself with facials and massages.

A couple of days after she checked in, as she sat down for dinner in the crowded dining room, an attractive couple asked if they could join her.

"We're Hugh and Charlene Holroyd," the man said, and she shook both their hands. "Eleanor Keeler," Barbara replied. She had no qualms about using the name, because, according to Jimmy, the AP reports of her arrest and trial in Mexico had used the name Barbara Eagle.

Everyone got on together immediately, and they hadn't been sitting at her table more than five minutes before Barbara knew what they had in mind, which was fine with her, because she hadn't had enough voluntary sex for nearly three months, and she missed it.

After dinner they invited her back to their cottage, which was larger than hers, and everybody had a drink. Fifteen minutes later the three of them were in bed together.

Later, when they had exhausted themselves, Hugh asked, "Where do you hail from, Eleanor?"

"San Francisco," Barbara replied, "but I'm thinking of making a change. How about you two?"

"We have a ranch near Los Alamos, in New Mexico," Hugh said. "You should come for a visit. It's nice around there."

"What a kind invitation," Barbara said, kissing Charlene again. "I just might take you up on it."

"You girls play," Hugh said. "I'll just watch, until I, ah, catch my breath."

TIP HANKS SHOWED the cleaners out of the house. They had made his bedroom as new and replaced the bedding and mattress. He was all right, really, except that he was still angry with his wife, and he was glad for the cleaners to take away garbage bags full of her clothes and other belongings. Now there was nothing left of her in the house, and he wanted it that way. He'd kept her jewelry, which was locked in the safe.

The phone rang, and he answered. It was his caddie, Mike Patrick. "Hey buddy," Tip said.

"I heard about it on TV," Mike said. "Are you okay?"

"I'm getting past it," Tip replied. "I'm going to start practicing again tomorrow."

"You want me there?"

"Nah, Mike, I'll meet you in Houston next Tuesday night. You've already booked the hotel, haven't you?"

"Yeah. I just wanted to be sure you felt up to playing."

"I will by next week."

"Okay, I'm just going to lie around the house until then. See you in Houston."

Tip took calls from his agent and sponsors as well;

then things quieted down. He had a call from the medical examiner's office saying that Connie's body had been released. Ed Eagle's office recommended a mortuary, and he ordered the body collected and cremated. Connie had no family, so there was no one to notify.

As he was getting some pocket money from the safe he saw the envelopes holding their wills, and he opened Connie's, which he hadn't seen before. It turned out that she had received a substantial settlement in her last divorce, and she had left everything to him. His net worth had suddenly been increased by some seven hundred thousand dollars. He faxed the will to Eagle's office.

Tip made himself a sandwich for lunch and thought about what had happened. Who the hell could Connie have been fucking? And why would the guy want to kill her? If he'd been five minutes earlier coming home, he might have surprised them. Then it occurred to him that if that had happened, the guy might have killed them both.

He put his dishes into the dishwasher and went back to the safe, where he kept a small nine-millimeter semiautomatic pistol. He threaded the holster onto his belt and pulled out his shirttail to cover it. He would carry it for a while, at least while he was in Santa Fe. He was licensed in the state, and his old Florida license covered him in nearly half the country.

He went into his study and found a stack of bills next

to his computer. Connie had usually paid them online, but he knew how to do it. The one on top was her credit card bill, and there were a lot of lunch charges, and judging from the amounts, they were for two people. That surprised him, because Connie had not made a lot of friends since she had been in Santa Fe. The charges were from half a dozen of Santa Fe's best restaurants.

Tip called Ed Eagle and told him what he had found.

"That's interesting," Eagle said. "I think the police might like to know who she'd been lunching with, but I think we might like to know first. Will you spring for a few hundred dollars for an investigator to visit the restaurants?"

"Sure, Ed. By the way, I faxed you Connie's will. I'd like you to take care of whatever legalities are involved."

"I'll put an associate on it," Eagle said, "and I'll send a messenger out there for the original; we'll need it."

"I'll leave it on the front porch in an envelope," Tip said.

"Good. I'll let you know what our investigator learns, and we can decide if it should go to the police."

"Good, thanks."

"One other thing," Eagle said. "I've spoken to the medical examiner, and there was no DNA present at the scene, not yours or anybody else's."

"So, he would have used a condom?"

"One supposes. Have you thought any more about the killer? Does anyone leap to mind?" Eagle asked.

"No. Connie didn't have many friends in Santa Fe."

"Someone from out of town?"

"Not that I'm aware of."

"Be careful of your behavior, Tip. The police are still thinking about you, and they may even have you followed."

"I thought I was cleared."

"Not necessarily. The charges have been dropped, but the DA could always bring them again, if new and incriminating evidence should emerge. You have to remember that having the charges dropped was a slap in the face to the investigating detectives, so they're not exactly on your side."

"I don't see how they can find anything incriminating," Tip said. "After all, I didn't do it."

"Right. Fax me the credit card bills, and I'll get back to you as soon as our investigator checks them out."

Tip hung up, put the will in an envelope and left it leaning against the front door with Eagle's name on it, then went back to paying bills. He was going to have to hire a secretary, he thought.

7

Teddy Fay's single-engine Cessna 182 RG crossed a range of snowcapped mountains late in the afternoon. It had been a long day against headwinds. He looked to his right at Lauren Cade, who seemed to be dozing. He placed a hand on her knee, and she stirred. "We'll be on the ground at Santa Fe in fifteen minutes," he said.

Lauren looked around. "What are these mountains?"

"The Sangre de Cristos," he said. "They run up to Taos, north of here."

"What about south?"

"They peter out."

"Pretty. Is it going to be cold in Santa Fe?"

"Probably, but it's a dry cold. You won't feel it so much."

"I'm going to have to buy a coat," she said. "I didn't own one in Florida."

"We'll both have to do that," Teddy said.

Albuquerque Center called. "Descend and maintain one zero thousand," the controller said. "Report the airport in sight."

The weather was startlingly clear, and after consulting the GPS map, he thought he could pick out the field. The automated weather recording said that the wind was 190 at 10 knots. Five minutes later he reported the airport in sight.

"Cleared for the visual approach to Santa Fe," the controller said.

Teddy descended to eight thousand, and once at that altitude, he turned left downwind for runway twenty and called Santa Fe tower.

"Cleared to land on twenty," the controller replied.

He touched down smoothly on the runway and taxied to Santa Fe Jetcenter, where a rental car awaited them. He placed a fuel order and arranged hangar space, then he and Lauren drove into the city.

"Teddy," she said, "I know there are some things you haven't told me about yourself."

"Why do you say that?"

"Because you talk so little about your past. I just want you to know that as far as I'm concerned, your life began the day I met you."

Teddy smiled. "I feel exactly the same way," he said.

He had been struggling with how much to tell her, and how to justify his behavior since he had retired from the CIA some years before after a thirty-year career. Teddy had been an assistant deputy director for technical services at the Agency. Tech Services was the innocuous name for the department that supported foreign agents in the field, supplying identities, weapons, disguises, communications and anything else they might need. The work had given him an astonishing range of skills, and he had used them to stay out of prison. He turned to Lauren.

"I'll tell you this much," he said. "I worked for the Central Intelligence Agency for thirty years. I know that sounds like a bad pickup line in a bar, but it's true."

"I believe you," she said. "Is that why you know so much about so many things?"

"Yes, it is."

"Did you have to do bad things?"

"I've done some bad things, and I don't want to talk about them, if that's all right."

"It's fine," she said. "I'd just as soon not know." Lauren had been a sergeant with a special investigative unit of the Florida State Police. She'd left a good career to go with Teddy. He knew it and was grateful.

"I've booked us into the Inn of the Anasazi for a week," he said. "If you like the town, we can look for a house to rent. If not, we can go on to California whenever you like."

They continued into the town, drove through the Plaza and checked into the hotel, which, like just about everything else in the town, was built in Santa Fe style. A fire of piñon logs burned in the lobby, and the piney scent filled the air.

THE FOLLOWING MORNING, eighteen hundred miles east of Santa Fe, Holly Barker arrived at her office a little after seven a.m. Holly was assistant deputy director of operations, reporting directly to the director of operations, Lance Cabot, and she wanted to get to the office before he did. Lance had been on leave when she had returned from a month in Orchid Beach, Florida, where she had once been the chief of police.

She had been in her office for only a moment when Lance rapped on her doorjamb.

"Welcome back," she said.

"Same to you. Anything to report?"

Holly took a deep breath. "Yes. Maybe you'd better sit down."

"Come into my office," he said.

She followed him down the hall and sat on his sofa, next to the chair where Lance liked to sit during meetings.

"So?"

Holly decided to just blurt it out. "Teddy Fay is still alive," she said.

Lance put his face in his hands. "I didn't hear that," he said. "And I'm not going to hear the rest of what you have to tell me."

"I met him in Orchid Beach," she said. "I had no idea who he was."

"He would have planned it that way," Lance said. "Do you think he planned to meet you?"

"No, I'm certain he didn't, but I'm also certain he knew who I was."

"Is he still there?"

"No, he left town shortly before I did. I stopped by the cottage he rented to say good-bye to his girlfriend, a state police officer named Lauren Cade, who I knew in the army. The house had been cleared."

"How do you know it was him?"

"I didn't until the last day. I found him interesting, and a little odd. He was an excellent cook."

"He cooked dinner for you?"

"For my boyfriend, Lauren and me."

"Good God."

"When I stopped by the cottage to see Lauren, there was a big safe in a closet that I didn't know about. He had left a note on the safe for the landlord. The note said the combination was T-E-D-D-Y."

"Any idea where he went when he left Orchid Beach?"

"None," she said. "He could be anywhere."

"He's not anywhere," Lance said. "He's somewhere.

Have you met Todd Bacon, who's the station chief in Panama?"

"No."

"He has a special interest in finding Teddy," Lance said. "Call him and tell him he's done in Panama, to report to me here as soon as he can clear his desk and pack his things."

"Am I going to be involved in this?" she asked.

"Do you want to be?"

"No more than I have to."

"You can brief Todd on your experience with Teddy in Orchid Beach," Lance said. "After that I'll try to keep you out of it. I know you have some sympathy for him."

"I'll do what I can to help," Holly said, but she wasn't looking forward to it.

8

Tip Hanks stood outside the clubhouse at Las Campanas, hitting chip shots to the practice green. About one out of six was going into the cup, but, of course, he was hitting from the same position. Still, he was getting better at sinking chip shots, and that could win tournaments. Tip had had a number of top-ten finishes this season, and one in the top five. He was determined, in the next season, to start winning, instead of just making a good living.

The season playoffs were just ahead—four tournaments—and the winner on points would win the FedEx Cup, and that was a ten-million-dollar check. Tiger Woods was out with a knee injury, so it was anybody's to win.

A member ambled by and stopped for a moment

to convey his condolences. Tip was momentarily surprised. He had been shaken by Connie's death but, he reflected, more shaken when he had been arrested. It had not been much of a relationship beyond sex, and he wondered—not for the first time—if God had somehow shortchanged him in the emotions department.

He walked over to the driving range, teed up a ball and snapped into his brain's swing mode, which obviated any other thought, even of his dead wife. He hit a bucket of balls with his driver and fairway woods and was satisfied with the results. He had improved his driving a lot this season by shaving ten yards off his length and hitting fairways instead of hooks and slices.

He had lunch in the bar, then put away his clubs and went home. When he got out of the car he saw an envelope propped against his front door. Inside was a letter.

Dear Mr. Hanks,

My name is Dolly Parks, and first of all I want to tell you how sad I was to hear of Connie's death. We had met only recently, but I liked and admired her.

We met when I posted a notice on a bulletin board at the farmers market in town, seeking an assistant's position, full- or part-time. She called me, and we had lunch, and she told me that the two of you had discussed hiring someone to deal with the bills, the house maintenance and travel arrangements. I was supposed to start next Monday.

I don't know if you are still interested in hiring someone, but I would appreciate the opportunity to talk with you about it. My number is below.

Her résumé was attached. She had held office and secretarial jobs in New York for a period of ten years or so.

Connie and he had talked about hiring a secretary, Tip remembered. He picked up the phone, called her and asked her to come to the house for a drink in the late afternoon.

He showered and shaved and dressed, then took an hour's nap. By the time he had roused himself and dressed, the doorbell was ringing.

Dolly Parks was unexpectedly attractive—small, blond and shapely. She had dressed in informal but appropriate clothes for her interview. Tip invited her into his study. "Would you like a drink?" he asked.

"No, thanks," she said. "Maybe later."

"I liked your résumé," he said. "Sounds like you're a well-organized person. When did you last see Connie?"

"At the end of last week. She called the day before she . . . died and said that she had checked my references and that I was hired."

"At what salary?" he asked.

"Twenty-five dollars an hour, health insurance, three weeks' vacation after six months. She said that she thought you would need me only half a day, but if the work mounted up, maybe longer. That's why we agreed on an hourly rate. I have one other client in Santa Fe, but I work for him only a couple of hours a day, three days a week."

"That sounds fine to me. I'm leaving on Tuesday to play a tournament. Can you start tomorrow? I'd like to get you familiar with the computer banking I've set up."

"Of course. I'd be glad to."

"Come on, I'll show you some ropes now." He went to his computer and began explaining the banking program.

"I'm already working with that for my other client," she said, "and for the same bank, so I can hit the ground running."

"That's good news," he said. "My caddie, Mike, has been doing the travel arrangements, but he's not very good at it, so I'd like you to take over that. I have an airplane and fly myself, so there won't be much in the way of airline reservations, except for Mike, if he's meeting me at a tournament. He lives in Dallas.

"My checks from the PGA are deposited into a savings account at the bank here, and I make computer transfers to the checking accounts, one for business, one for household and personal. I'll make you a signatory on those two, so you won't need my signature to pay bills, and I'll transfer funds into them as needed. My accountant does regular audits on my accounts, so he'll catch you and send you to prison if you steal." Tip laughed, and she laughed, too.

"I understand," she said. "Do you travel with a laptop?"

"Yes."

"Good. I can scan the bills and e-mail them to you for approval. After a while, I'll learn your spending habits, and you might want to give me a little more freedom."

"Probably."

"I would like you to check every credit card bill, though, to see if the charges are genuine. There's a lot of credit card fraud around, and you don't want to fall victim to that."

"Right. I'll also want you to keep track of my tax-deductible expenses, so you can give them to my accountant at the end of the year. I don't like to deal with taxes any more than I have to."

"I'm very familiar with the IRS schedules and which expenses belong on which schedule," she said, "so that won't be a problem. How much are you gone?"

"I play, on average, about three times a month during the season, which is drawing to a close now. This winter I'll play some in Japan and maybe Australia and the Middle East, to keep the income stream going. I could be gone for six or seven weeks at a time."

"Well, before you leave I'll be familiar with everything, and we'll have e-mail to stay in touch."

"Right." He got up and led her to a door that opened into an empty room next door. "We've used this for storage. Why don't you clean it out and outfit it as an office for you? Get yourself a computer, some file cabinets and bookcases, whatever you need. There's a closet over there for supplies. We have an account with a local office-supply firm."

"I'm good with computers," Dolly said. "If you'll give me a credit card number I'll order a computer online and transfer all the business software to the new computer."

Tip handed her his business credit card. "Call American Express and order a card for you. I'll speak to them when you're on the line with them."

They went back into the study, Dolly made the call and the card was ordered.

"Stop by the bank tomorrow and get new signature cards, and we'll both sign them."

"Certainly."

"I can't think of anything else to tell you, Dolly. Would you like that drink now?"

"Yes, thanks. That would be very nice."

Tip made the drinks from the concealed bar in his study, and they watched the sunset together.

9

Near the end of her stay at Canyon Ranch, Barbara drove to the Tucson Airport and took a plane to Los Angeles. She got a cab to Venice Beach and got out a block from her destination.

She walked slowly to the end of the block, looking at every person she saw, then walked past her destination for another block, then slowly returned, still checking. The man she was visiting was in a potentially dangerous business, and his camera and photography shop might be staked out by the police or, worse, the Feds.

Finally, she went in and asked for the owner. "Name?" the girl behind the counter asked.

"Tell him an old customer," Barbara said.

The girl left, then came back. "You can go in," she said.

Barbara walked to the rear of the store to the office and rapped on the doorjamb.

He looked up and stared for a moment before he placed her. "Ah, hello," he said. "Took me a minute, what with the red hair."

She sat down in the chair next to his desk. "I need the works," she said, "and in two identities." She wrote down the two names, addresses and vital statistics on a pad he handed her.

"How soon?"

"I can give you a week."

"I can do that, but it's going to be expensive; prices have gone up. Sixty grand."

"All right, but everything has to work, has to show up in the relevant databases."

"Always," he said.

She opened her purse and paid him in hundreds, then watched while he checked a sample of the bills on a light box.

"All good," he said. "Let's get a couple of pictures."

Barbara checked her makeup, then posed, once as the redhead she now was, and once with a blond wig.

"You can pick them up a week from today," he said.

"I'd like you to FedEx them, overnight, to this address." She wrote it down for him. "I'm trusting you by paying you before I see the paper," she said.

"I don't fail my best customers," he replied.

She thanked him and left. She walked a couple of

blocks before she found a cab back to the airport. She didn't want to spend any more time in LA than necessary.

CUPIE DALTON SAW the woman coming from a block away. He always spotted beautiful women from a distance; it was a trait learned over the decades. Cupie was ex-LAPD, now a private investigator, and because of his work a lot of faces looked familiar to him. Also, there was something about the way she walked. He ducked behind a palm tree as she approached, then watched her pass and get into a taxi. She was different but still familiar. Images flashed through his mind. "Jesus," he said aloud, "it can't be. I must be getting old."

Cupie was one of two PIs who had been hired by Ed Eagle to find the wife who had stolen his money, and he had been responsible for the ruse that had gotten her to Mexico, where she could be arrested. "It can't be," he said again, but he thought he should call Ed Eagle.

He had already dialed the number, but as he was about to press send, he stopped. No need to make a fool of himself. First, he would check. He looked up a number in his cell phone address book and pressed the call button. A woman answered in Spanish.

"I'd like to speak to the capitán," he said. "Tell him it's Cupie. He'll know."

"Momento," the woman said; then there was a click and the man came online.

"Cupie, my friend," the police captain said. "How are you? Are you in Tijuana?"

"No, Capitán," Cupie said. "I'm in LA, but I just saw a familiar body walk past me, and I thought I was dreaming."

"You always dream of women, Cupie," the capitán said.

"This one is a nightmare," Cupie said. "You took her off a yacht for me a few months ago."

"Oh, La Barbara," the capitán said. "I will never forget her."

"She was convicted, remember?"

"Oh, yes. She will die in prison."

"Are you sure she's still there?"

There was a brief silence. "Do you have some reason to believe she is not?"

"I told you, I could swear I saw her five minutes ago. Can you find out if she's still in prison?"

"Instantly," the capitán said. "Give me your number."

Cupie gave him the number, then went and sat on a bench, looking out over the Pacific.

THE CAPITÁN DIALED the number and listened to it ringing.

"Capitán Alvarez," a voice said.

"Pedro, it's me."

"Good day to you, my friend. Are you in Acapulco?"

"No, I'm in Tijuana. I just wanted to check something with you."

"Of course. How can I help you?"

"Tell me, is the woman, Barbara Eagle, still in your custody?"

Alvarez didn't miss a beat. "Of course she is," he replied. "I fucked her in the ass this morning. She loved it."

"I'm relieved to hear that," the capitán said.

"Why do you ask me this?"

"A friend saw a woman in LA a few minutes ago who looked like her."

"Your friend drinks too early in the day. Next time you're in Acapulco, drive up here, and you can fuck her, too."

"That might be fun, as long as there isn't a straight razor around."

"No worries there, my friend. I would never let her near sharp instruments."

"Thank you, Pedro. I'll call you when I come south and take you up on your offer." He hung up and called Cupie.

"Hello?"

"It's me, Cupie."

"What did you find out?"

"She's still in the prison in Tres Cruces. The warden told me he fucked her in the ass this morning."

"I'm relieved to hear that."

"He says you drink too early in the day."

"Maybe I'm getting old," Cupie said. "Thanks, my friend. I'll buy you a drink the next time I'm in Tijuana."

"You do that." The capitán hung up.

Cupie took a deep breath and let it out slowly. He was glad he'd checked. If he had made that call he might have destroyed his credibility with Ed Eagle, who was one of his better clients.

IN TRES CRUCES, Pedro Alvarez ran into the toilet and vomited. Still this woman haunted him. He wished he'd shot her in the head and buried her in the mountains.

10

Dolly Parks spent the entire day of Tip's departure for the Houston tournament directing the moving in of office furniture. She arranged things efficiently, not forgetting to give herself a nice view of the Jemez Mountains from her seat at her desk.

When everything was arranged as it should be and wiped down for dust she opened the box containing her new computer and set it up, hanging the twenty-one-inch flat monitor on the wall beside her desk. She had only to swivel her chair to the right to have the keyboard at hand and the screen before her. She plugged in all the cables, then tucked the tiny Enano PC away in a corner of her desk.

She took a box of writable CDs into Tip's study and copied all his files, then loaded them into her computer.

A few minutes of testing the bank program and she was up and running. She spent the rest of the day putting away her office supplies on the shelves she had had installed in the closet, and then she was done.

She went into the little powder room off her new office and put her own cosmetics into the medicine chest, then washed the dust from her hands and splashed some water on her face. Exhausted, she went into Tip's study, opened the cabinet containing the bar and poured herself a stiff Scotch; then she stretched out on the leather sofa and watched the sun set behind the mountains as she sipped her drink.

Soon, healed and relaxed by the whiskey, she began thinking about Tip Hanks, his mop of sun-bleached hair and his taut body. She unzipped her jeans and pulled them down to her knees; then, with the Scotch in the other hand, she began to stroke her clitoris. She was already wet, and it took only a couple of minutes of fun to bring her to orgasm.

When she stopped panting she wiped herself with tissues, pulled up her jeans and soon fell asleep on the couch.

TIP LANDED AT HOUSTON'S Hobby Field at dusk and taxied to Atlantic Aviation for refueling and hangaring, then picked up his rental car and drove to the Four Seasons hotel and checked in. He showered and changed, then went down to the bar for a drink before dinner.

Everybody there was properly respectful of his mourning, and he couldn't pay for a drink. There were the usual hanger-on girls, some of whom showed an interest in him, but in spite of his stirrings, he was determined to remain chaste on the tour, at least for a while.

He had dinner with a couple of cronies and got to bed early. He was playing the pro-am the next day with some movie star, and he wanted to be fresh. The golf course had been renovated, and it was his first opportunity to play it since. He took a look at the pin positions in the book before retiring, and he liked what he saw. The course was set up well for his game.

Before he fell asleep he wondered, not for the first time, why he was not more upset about his wife's murder. It was as if he was viewing a film of the event, and he was playing his part badly. All he felt was emptiness.

BARBARA HAD LEFT TUCSON early in the morning, driving east, and she arrived in Santa Fe at dusk and found the FedEx office still open and the package waiting for her. She got back into the car and examined the passports, driver's licenses and credit cards the man in Venice Beach had created for her. They were of his usual excellent quality.

She had another hour and a half of driving to reach

the Holroyds' house beyond Los Alamos, and she was tired, so she checked into the Hotel Santa Fe, at Cerrillos and Paseo de Peralta, a place where she had not been known when she had lived in the town, and called the Holroyds, telling them she'd be there for lunch the following day. She had a quiet dinner in the bar, followed by a good night's sleep.

The following morning she drove up the winding mountain road to Los Alamos, continued through what was visible of the town and followed the directions to the ranch that Hugh Holroyd had given her.

Charlene greeted her with a big kiss as she got out of the car. "You made it! We missed you last night."

"I was whipped when I got into Santa Fe," Barbara said, opening the rear of the station wagon so that a servant could remove her new luggage.

Hugh met her at the door with another big kiss, and she was shown to her room, which, not to her surprise, was connected to the master suite by a door and a short hallway.

She spent the afternoon unpacking, napping and watching a golf tournament from Houston, which featured a player she found very attractive. She was pleased to hear an announcer say he hailed from Santa Fe. Maybe she'd look him up later.

They were served a sumptuous dinner prepared by the Holroyds' chef, then given after-dinner drinks before an open fire in the living room, where they lounged on large cushions. From that moment, Barbara noticed, there were no servants in sight.

Charlene got things started by giving Barbara a playful kiss, and soon they were all naked while Hugh watched the two women make love, and he weighed in from time to time. Then they rested and drank for a while and started in again, this time with Barbara and Hugh. She found them both very comfortable to be with.

AT ED AND SUSANNAH EAGLE'S house up the mountain from the village of Tesuque, they hosted the writer and producer who had arrived in Santa Fe to begin production on Susannah's film project. She had taken the supporting role, on Ed's advice, because the character had a couple of scenes the likes of which would be taken notice of by the Los Angeles film community and members of the Academy of Motion Pictures Arts and Sciences.

Susannah had been nominated twice before, and this seemed the perfect opportunity to seal the deal.

Eagle was interested to talk to Jim Long. Previously, he had seen the producer only on TV, when he had testified at Barbara's trial. Eagle might as well break the ice, he thought.

"Jim, have you heard from Barbara since her incarceration?"

Long shook his head. "From what little I know of Mexican jails, people seem to just disappear into them. She's going to be in for a long, long time."

"I think that's best," Eagle said.

"Maybe you're right," Long agreed. "She was a bad, bad girl."

The group drank, dined and talked on until after midnight; then the visitors excused themselves and drove back to their hotel.

Eagle and Susannah got ready for bed while the cook and her helpers cleaned up after the party.

"What did you think of Jim Long?" Susannah asked.

"Seems like a nice fellow," Eagle replied. "He agreed with me that Barbara will be away for a long, long time."

"I suppose she will," Susannah said. "It's a pity Mexico doesn't have the death penalty."

11

Tip Hanks stood on the eighteenth green and sized up his putt. Not good. He had been at the top of his game for four days, and now he had a one-stroke lead on the last hole. Trouble was, he had a thirty-five-foot putt that was going to go over a little rise in the green, then break on the downhill slope to the hole, while his opponent had a six-foot straight-in putt to tie the match and force a play-off. Tip did not want a play-off. He conferred with Mike, his caddie.

"Play it like the hole is at the top of the rise," Mike advised, "and a foot past. Aim for a line a foot right of the hole. It's going to break left and be very fast downhill."

Tip took another look from ten feet behind the ball and agreed. He took a couple of practice swings, then stepped forward and struck the ball smoothly. It rolled up the rise, slowed nearly to a halt at the top, then curved gracefully down the slope and into the cup. The crowd went nuts.

Tip walked to the edge of the green and leaned on his putter. His opponent had to sink this putt to keep sole possession of second place. He sank it, and it was over. Tip had won it.

He hugged Mike, then shook hands with his opponent and his opponent's caddie. The crowd swarmed around him as he walked to the tent where he would double-check his scorecard and sign it. That done, he walked to the cleared area in front of the clubhouse and was interviewed briefly for television, where he accepted condolences for Connie, then appeared appropriately modest about his win.

All that remained then was to accept the trophy and hit the showers, secure in the knowledge that tomorrow morning there would be a wire transfer to his bank account of one million, one hundred thousand dollars. He was now officially richer than he had ever been, and he had improved his position to fifth in the race for the FedEx Cup.

He was too tired to fly but not too tired to celebrate, so he stayed another night at the Four Seasons and celebrated with the few stragglers who had not immediately flown home. When he returned to his room at bedtime, he found a congratulatory e-mail from Dolly waiting for him. They had exchanged e-mails every day, always with a business reason but always pleasantly. She seemed to be on top of things at home.

The following morning he took off from Hobby Field and flew northwest to Santa Fe. He arrived at the house at noon and saw Dolly's little BMW convertible parked out front. "Anybody home?" he called as he entered the house. He dropped his bag by the door for his housekeeper to unpack and walked into his study.

Dolly came out of her office smiling. "Congratulations," she said, walking forward and offering her hand. When he shook it, she stepped forward and kissed him on the cheek. He seemed surprised. "The transfer is in your savings account," she said, "and I've already sent the check for the taxes to your accountant."

"Thanks, Dolly," he said. "Let's see what you've done with your office." She led him there, and he looked around for a moment. "Very nice," he said, but he was more impressed than that. If she handled his affairs as neatly as she did her office, everything would be fine.

"Have you had lunch?" she asked.

"No. Why don't you join me?"

"I'll tell Carmen," she said, going off to find the housekeeper.

His study was a lot neater than when he had left, and he liked that, too.

BARBARA SLEPT LATE, and when she was dressing she heard a sound she hadn't heard for quite some time: a cell phone ringing. Surprised, she dug it out of her purse. It had to be Jimmy. He was the only person who had the number.

"Hey," she said.

"Where are you?" he asked.

"I'd rather not say," she replied. "Where are you?"

"In Santa Fe."

She was surprised. "Why?"

"I'm producing a film here that's starting production right away."

"Good," she said. "You'll enjoy the town."

"Something else," he said. "It's starring the wife of your nemesis."

"*What?*"

"Relax. It was a good deal for me. You don't mind, do you?"

"Have you seen Ed?"

"Last night. They had me, the writer/director and the star for dinner."

"Isn't Susannah starring?"

"No. She could have, but she took a supporting role. Smart move, too."

"Listen, I've got to run," she said. "I'll call you in a few days."

"Okay. Take care."

She hung up and swore. This was a very big monkey wrench in her works. She had been planning to kill them both, but she couldn't do that to Jimmy; he'd lose a lot of money. She paced around the room. What would she do now? She could stay on briefly with Charlene and Hugh, but only briefly. They'd be sick of her in a few days, and she couldn't blame them.

She picked up the *Santa Fe New Mexican,* which had been left at her door, and sat down with the real estate pages, circling likely-sounding rentals. One sounded particularly nice, and she called the agent and made an appointment to see it.

She sat at the dressing table and inspected herself carefully. Her new hair color and the cosmetic surgery she had had before her incarceration might make it unlikely for people who had known her in Santa Fe to recognize her, but still, she had to be careful.

IN THE EARLY AFTERNOON she drove back to town and, following the directions the agent had given her, drove to the development called Las Campanas, which she knew about from her earlier stay in the town when she had been married to Eagle. The property was a guesthouse, nicely furnished and available at a very reasonable rent, in return for keeping an eye on the house. The couple would not return until next summer.

She signed the lease on the spot and gave the agent a check for a month's rent and a security deposit, then she drove back to the Holroyds' ranch, arriving in time for dinner.

She didn't tell them about her rental. It was best that no one knew where she was. "I've got to go back to the West Coast on business," she said to them.

They expressed suitable regret, and she showed her gratitude for inviting her by making them both very happy in bed that night.

The following morning she packed, then drove back to Las Campanas.

12

Pedro Alvarez sat at his desk, filling out requisition forms for food for his prisoners. He had a very sweet deal with his purveyor: Alvarez checked off good-quality goods on the form, and the purveyor supplied him with cheaper selections for each one, and Alvarez got a very nice cash payment when the food was delivered.

He had accumulated a nice little nest egg—doing this and taking bribes from prisoners for various items he supplied, such as beauty products—and the best part was that his wife knew nothing about his arrangements or his nest egg. He planned to play cards with some friends that evening, and he went to the safe to get some cash. To his astonishment, the money was gone! But how? No one else had the combination to the safe. He opened his wallet, where he kept the combination written on a card: still there. He checked the edge of his desk drawer, where he kept the combination taped: still there.

Barbara! It had to be that bitch. She had taken his wallet or found the combination on the drawer's edge! He couldn't believe it. He felt sick.

The phone rang, and he picked it up. "Alvarez."

"Hello, Pedro," the capitán said. "You don't sound very well."

"Just a little indigestion," Alvarez replied. "Are you well?"

"Yes, and I'm coming to Acapulco tomorrow morning. I thought I might drive up to Tres Cruces and take you up on your offer of fucking the lovely Barbara."

Alvarez was seized with panic. The capitán had many connections in the Ministry of Justice. He had found Alvarez this job. If he discovered that Barbara was no longer in his prison, there would be hell to pay.

He fell back on his earlier invention. "You know, Capitán, the day after you called, two men appeared in my office with a transfer order for the woman, and they took her away."

"Away where?" the capitán asked.

"I don't know. They told me that if I told anyone of her transfer I would lose my job, so I assumed they were from the Ministry."

"That is very peculiar," the capitán replied. "I will make some inquiries."

"Oh, no, please! If you start asking around, whoever is behind this will hear of it and will take it out on me. I beg you, don't mention this to anyone else."

"Pedro, you must know this is highly irregular," the capitán said.

"And I was told to continue to keep her on my roster of prisoners, to make no change."

"Do you know the names of these men?"

"No, but they had a fully executed transfer order with all the proper stamps."

"I see. Then I suppose you had no choice but to surrender the woman to them."

"No choice whatsoever, Capitán. When I questioned them they threatened to call Mexico City and have me disciplined."

"All right, Pedro, don't worry about it. I won't mention it to anyone in the Ministry, or anyone else, for that matter."

"Thank you, Capitán," Alvarez said. "If you'd like to come up, I can give you your choice of other women. None as beautiful as the Eagle woman, of course, but very nice."

"Perhaps another time, Pedro," the capitán said. "I must run now. Good-bye."

Alvarez hung up the phone, and he was bathed in sweat. His money was gone, and he could only hope that the capitán would keep his word.

THE CAPITÁN STARED AT his phone for a moment, then picked it up and dialed a number at the Ministry of Justice in Mexico City. He was greeted warmly by his contact.

"I would like you to do something for me," the capitán said. "Can you check your computer for the El Diablo women's prison in Tres Cruces and see if there is a record of a transfer for a prisoner named Barbara Eagle? She is an Anglo."

"It will take only a moment," the man said. Shortly he returned to the phone. "No, there is no such record. She is carried on the roll of El Diablo as a prisoner there."

"Would the transfer of any inmate be recorded in your computer files?"

"Yes, indeed. The issuance of a transfer order and the execution of the order would both be recorded."

The capitán thanked the man, then hung up. Something smelled of fish, he thought. Then he thought again. No, not of fish—of escape. The woman had somehow got herself out of El Diablo and was now free. Then he remembered something.

He looked up the number for Cupie Dalton, in Los Angeles, and dialed it.

"This is Cupie," a voice said.

"Cupie, it's me."

"Capitán! How the hell are you?"

"All right, I guess. You remember you phoned me a little while back about the woman Barbara Eagle?"

"Yeah, sure, I did."

"You wanted to know if she was still in prison?"

"Yeah, that's right."

"She is not."

Cupie thought about that for a moment. "Barbara is *out*?"

"It would appear so. The day following our conversation two men appeared at the prison with a transfer order, supposedly issued by the Ministry of Justice. The warden told me it was properly executed, and the men took Eagle away, telling him to continue to keep her on his roll of prisoners and warning him to tell no one."

"Good God! Where did they take her?"

"I have no idea. The Ministry has no record of a transfer. I suspect that this was an escape arranged by some friend of hers."

"Is anyone looking for her?"

"No, that would be . . . inconvenient, at this time."

"I can understand how it might be," Cupie said.

"Cupie, it seems possible that your eyes did not deceive you when you thought you saw her."

"It certainly does," Cupie replied.

"My friend, I would be very grateful if you could try and trace her. It is impossible for me to pay you at this time, but if you were able to find her and return her to Mexico, I could arrange a substantial reward for you."

Cupie thought about that. It wasn't as though he had much work at the moment. "Capitán, I would be very happy to try and find her," he said.

"Good, Cupie, very good."

"I can't estimate how much time it might take, but there are leads I can follow."

"Please call and tell me of your progress," the capitán said.

The two men said good-bye and hung up; then Cupie made another call.

"Hello?"

"Vittorio? It's Cupie."

"Hello, Cupie," Vittorio replied. The two men had worked together twice for Ed Eagle, searching for his ex-wife.

"I just heard from our friend, the capitán, in Tijuana," Cupie said. "Barbara is out."

13

Ed Eagle sat in a canvas director's chair on the set of Susannah's film. It was the first day of shooting, and since he had invested in the film, his name was emblazoned on his chair.

Eagle had never watched a movie being filmed, and he found the process painfully slow. Scenes were shot from different angles; there were master shots, two shots and close-ups, and the lighting had to be adjusted for each setup. Grass grew faster, he decided, and he was pleased when his cell phone vibrated. He got up and walked off the soundstage. "Hello?"

"Ed, it's Cupie Dalton."

"Hello, Cupie."

"I'm sorry if I'm disturbing you."

"It's all right. You got me out of watching a movie being made. I've rarely been so bored."

"I have some bad news, I'm afraid."

"Did somebody die, Cupie?"

"Not yet," Cupie replied, "but you'd better watch your ass. Barbara is out of prison."

Eagle froze, and it took him a moment to respond. "How?" he asked.

Cupie told him how two men had appeared at the prison with a transfer order and taken her away. "Turns out the order was a fake."

"When did this happen?"

"I'm not sure, exactly—two, three weeks ago. I think I saw her at Venice Beach about that time."

Eagle took a deep breath. "Why would she be at Venice Beach?"

"There's a guy has a photography business down there, and as a sideline he makes papers for those who can afford him. Or maybe the sideline is the photography."

"So, she has a new identity?"

"That's my guess."

"Any idea where she is?"

"No, but sooner or later she's going to be wherever you are. We both know that."

"Yes, we do," Eagle replied.

"I've been offered a reward, if I can return her to Mexico, but I need expense money for Vittorio and me."

"What do you need?"

"Three hundred a day each," Cupie replied, "and ten grand each if we can take her back."

"Done," Eagle said. "I'll wire you the first week's expenses immediately. Your account information still the same?"

"Yes. I'll be coming to Santa Fe. There's no point in trying to track her, since we know her destination."

"Get on it, then."

"You know, Ed, somebody had to arrange this for her, a friend on the outside."

"Barbara doesn't have any friends," Eagle replied.

"Except for one."

"As it happens, he's here in Santa Fe right now, in the next room, in fact."

"Don't let on that you know she's out," Cupie said. "He's our only link to her."

"All right."

"I'll be there tonight," Cupie said, "and we'll start tomorrow morning."

"Thanks, Cupie. I'll talk to you tomorrow." Eagle called his office and gave his secretary instructions on wiring funds to Cupie; then he waited until the red light went off above the soundstage door and walked back in. They were changing setups.

Jim Long was deep in conversation with the director, and Eagle's first impulse was to collar him, drag him outside and beat the shit out of him. As satisfying as that might be, however, doing so would not help him find Barbara, so he restrained himself.

CUPIE CALLED VITTORIO. "I talked to Eagle. He's wiring expense money, and I'm getting a three-o'clock plane to Albuquerque. Can you meet me?"

"Sure, and you can stay with me. We can save money, not get a hotel." Vittorio lived in a small adobe house in the desert outside Santa Fe.

"See you in Albuquerque," Cupie said. He hung up, packed his bags, got into his car and drove to his bank, where he made a cash withdrawal of four thousand dollars. He left his car in long-term parking and caught the bus to the terminal.

VITTORIO, WHO WAS an Apache, descended from his great-great-grandfather of the same name, stood out in the airport crowd, with his black clothing and black flat-brimmed hat. The inky braided hair to his shoulder blades helped, too.

In the car, Cupie handed him two thousand in cash. Vittorio tucked it into an inside pocket of his vest and started the car. Shortly they were on I-25, headed north toward Santa Fe. "What have we got to go on?" he asked.

"Zip," Cupie said, "except we know she's going to go after Eagle, and Eagle is in Santa Fe. So is James

Long, who is her only friend in the world, as far as I can tell. He's going to be our link."

"Barbara makes friends quickly," Vittorio observed. "Then she fucks them or kills them, or both."

Cupie laughed. "You would know, wouldn't you?" Vittorio had fucked her, and she had pushed him off a ferry in the Sea of Cortez.

"Don't rub it in," Vittorio said ruefully.

"What's the deal with Long?" Cupie asked.

"She fucks him, but she hasn't killed him," Vittorio replied. "I guess she has to leave somebody alive to help her when she's in trouble."

"Yeah, but why does he do it?"

"Some guys will do anything for a good lay, and Barbara is one hell of a lay."

"That's it?"

"What else? Can you think of anything?"

"Not really."

"I didn't think so."

"But how the hell could Jimmy Long engineer this prison break? Who does he know that could forge a transfer order from the Mexican Ministry of Justice?"

"Somebody in the Ministry of Justice, I guess," Vittorio replied. "The guy has made movies in Mexico, you know. He has to deal with government officials and probably bribe them to get the necessary permits."

"Yeah, but the Ministry of Justice doesn't handle that, do they?"

"Beats me," Vittorio said. "You think Barbara could already be in Santa Fe? Or maybe she's just going to hire somebody like last time."

"Last time didn't work," Cupie said, "and the guy's doing life. She's going to want to see to it herself this time; I'll bet on it."

14

Dolly Parks waited until Tip Hanks had come home from his practice session before trying it. She came into his study from her adjoining office. "Tip," she said, "I'm going to need to take a day or two off to find a new place to live. I've had a week-to-week deal at my current apartment, hoping to get a long-term lease, but the landlord wants it back for his granddaughter."

Tip swiveled around in his chair. "Why don't you move into my guesthouse?" he asked. "Connie made me build it for her friends, and I rarely have guests."

"That's very kind of you," Dolly said. "Are you sure it wouldn't be an imposition?"

"Not at all. Come on, I'll show you the place." He led her out of the house by the kitchen door and down a path to the guesthouse. "The house key works in this lock, too," Tip said, unlocking the front door and holding it open for her.

"It's beautiful," Dolly said, looking around the living room, then looking at the two bedrooms and kitchen.

"There's a patio out back, with a path leading to the pool and tennis court," Tip said.

"What sort of rent are we talking about?" she asked, turning to face him.

He looked puzzled. "Rent? No rent, just take it as part of your deal."

She wanted to hug him, but it was too soon. "Oh, Tip, you're wonderful," she said.

"Move in whenever you like," he replied.

Dolly glanced out the living-room window and saw a corner of another house. "Who lives there?"

"Oh, some couple from New York. They're only here in the summer. That's their guesthouse."

Dolly walked to the window and saw a woman taking things from a car and carrying them into the house.

"You've got your own driveway," Tip said. "Right this way." He led her outside and showed her how to drive to her new house. There was also a one-car garage.

"The house has its own linens and washer and dryer, and Carmen will keep it clean and do your laundry."

"It's so wonderful, I can't believe it!" Dolly enthused. This had been easier than she thought.

"I've got to get back to my e-mail," Tip said. "You

stay and look into the nooks and crannies." He left and went back to the main house.

Dolly went into the kitchen and began opening cabinet doors. It was well equipped, and there were even pots and pans and utensils. She liked cooking, and she would enjoy this kitchen.

To her surprise there was a knock at the kitchen door, and she opened it. A very beautiful woman of indeterminate age stood there in tight jeans and a sweater.

"Hi," the woman said. "My name is Ellie Keeler. I'm just moving in next door, and I thought I'd say hello."

"Please come in," Dolly said. "I'm Dolly Parks, and I'm just moving in, too."

"Beautiful place," Barbara said, looking around the living room. "This is the guesthouse, right?"

"Yes. The main house is up the walk."

"Who lives there?"

"His name is Tip Hanks. He's a professional golfer."

"Oh, yes. I watched the end of the tournament in Houston, when he sank that long putt." Barbara went and looked at the bedrooms. "Looks like you haven't moved in yet."

"No, I'll do that tomorrow."

"I'll give you a hand, if you like."

"Thanks, but I don't have a lot of stuff, mostly clothes. I'm moving from a small, furnished apartment in town. Would you like a drink? There's some liquor in a little bar and some beer in the fridge."

"A beer would be great," Barbara replied, settling onto a sofa.

BARBARA WATCHED HER walk away and admired her figure. There was something about this girl, she thought. Something in her is like me. Dolly came back with two beers and took a seat on a chair.

"Where are you from, Dolly?" Barbara asked.

"I grew up in Connecticut—Westport—and I worked in New York for a few years before I came out here earlier this year. How about you?"

"I grew up in La Jolla," Barbara lied. "When I met my husband I moved to San Francisco with him. He was killed a few months ago in a car crash."

"I'm so sorry," Dolly said.

"Well, being a widow requires some adjustment," Barbara said. "You wake up and there's nobody on the other side of the bed. I miss the sex. Have you ever been married?"

"No. I had a couple of close scrapes, but I managed to stay out of trouble."

"Smart girl," Barbara said. "Someone as beautiful as you won't have any trouble attracting men."

"Thank you," Dolly said, "but it isn't always easy. Most of the single men I've met in Santa Fe have been gay. They're good company and good friends, but you know . . ."

"I know," Barbara said.

They talked and laughed for the better part of an hour and got through another beer before Barbara excused herself.

"I've got some unpacking to do," she said. "Maybe we could have dinner sometime?"

"Why don't you come over tomorrow evening, and we'll christen my new kitchen? I enjoy cooking."

"How nice! What time?"

"Say seven?"

"I'll look forward to it."

Dolly showed her to the kitchen door, and Barbara went back to her own guesthouse. This was going to work out well, she thought, if she was right about Dolly.

15

Lauren Cade woke up and found Teddy looking at her. "Hey, there," she said.

"Hey, yourself," he replied. He was sitting up in bed with the morning newspapers.

They had been in Santa Fe for several days now. "I love this town," she said. "Let's look for a house to rent."

"I've got the real estate section right here," he replied. "We'll start looking today, but first there's something we have to talk about."

"What's that?"

"Your new name."

"I noticed that you checked into the hotel as Charles Tatum," she said. "Shall I call you Charlie?"

"That's good," he replied, "when others are around."

He handed her a plastic envelope containing a passport, a driver's license and a credit card.

She took the envelope but didn't open it. "Tell me why we need new names."

"I'm officially dead," Teddy replied, "but there's always the possibility that someone may be looking for me. Holly Barker, whom we met in Orchid Beach, may be the catalyst for that."

"Why Holly?"

"She's an official of the CIA," he said, "and she may have suspicions."

"Why do you think that?"

"I don't necessarily think she does, but I have to prepare for the possibility."

Lauren thought about it for a moment, then nodded. "All right." She opened the envelope, took out the passport and opened it. "Theresa Tatum," she read aloud.

"How about Teri, with an I?"

"I like it," she said. "Who made these IDs?"

"I did. It's one of the skills I acquired when I worked at the Agency. I also learned how to insert these document numbers into the various federal and state databases, so for all practical purposes, they're real."

"What about the credit card?"

"It's from a bank in the Cayman Islands," he said. "It will work the same as any other credit card, but the charges will be deducted from my investment balance at the bank, and the statement is available only online, identified by a number instead of a name."

"That's very clever," she said. "How do you cash a check?"

"I open a local bank account with cash, which I always travel with, then use those funds locally. I can always replenish it from the Cayman account with a wire transfer that's untraceable."

Her brow furrowed. "I read in a newspaper that the U.S. government can now force offshore banks to give them a list of their depositors."

"Doesn't matter. Mine is a numbered account, and the bank doesn't have a name and address for me, not even a false one."

"You're very good, Charlie," she said, kissing him.

"You're not so bad yourself, Teri," he replied.

"One question: I understand why you have to change your name, but why mine?"

"Holly knew you by your real name in Orchid Beach. Her people could trace us through you."

"Sorry. That was a dumb question."

"There's a bio for you in the envelope, too. You have to memorize every detail, like your maiden name, your high school, your college—both of which have very good transcripts for you—your parents' names— they're both dead—and every other detail. You have a credit record under both your maiden and married names, too. If you memorize the bio perfectly, you could withstand a prolonged interrogation. You can make up your own details, as long as they fit. After all, there would be details of your childhood that even your husband wouldn't know about."

"How long have we been married?"

"Three years. Read the bio."

"Teri" started reading while "Charlie" ordered breakfast and began calling Realtors.

AT MIDAFTERNOON THEY STOOD in the living room of the fourth house they had seen, while the agent waited outside to give them some privacy.

"You like it?" Teddy asked.

"I love it. Can we afford it?"

"We can," Teddy replied. The house was in the East Side neighborhood of Santa Fe, on a quiet tree-lined street. It had a living room with a dining area, a kitchen, two bedrooms, two and a half baths and a study where he could work. It was nicely furnished. "Let's do it." He called the Realtor back in and filled out the rental application.

"I'll run this," she said, "and assuming everything is confirmed, I'll have a lease for you by six o'clock, and you can move in tomorrow." Teddy gave her a check on the local account he had opened earlier that day.

They celebrated with a dinner at Geronimo, a restaurant on Canyon Road. The following morning they checked out of the hotel and moved into the house.

"I'm going to need a big safe," Teddy said, looking for one on the Internet.

THAT SAME MORNING, Holly Barker and Todd Bacon sat in Lance Cabot's office at the Central Intelligence Agency.

"Todd," Lance said, "what I have to say to you—indeed, our entire conversation—is limited to the three of us. Do you understand?"

"Certainly," Todd replied.

"We have reason to suspect that Teddy Fay may not be entirely dead."

"I can't say that I'm surprised," Todd replied. "When I pumped those rounds into his airplane's wing it occurred to me that he might be able to make an airport or a field, then disappear."

"He must still have the airplane," Holly said, "because I saw it at the Vero Beach Airport the first time I saw him."

"Did you get the registration number?" Todd asked.

"No," she replied, "because I had no reason to suspect him at that time. In any case, it would have been changed by now."

"It's a Cessna 182 RG, isn't it?"

"I can't remember whether it had fixed or retractable gear," she said.

Holly told him of each encounter she had with

Teddy in Orchid Beach, giving him every detail she could recall.

"Did anybody die while he was there?" Todd asked.

"There was a series of murders of women at the time," Holly replied.

"That's not Teddy's thing," Todd said. "He kills only for very good reasons—or what he believes to be good reasons."

"I agree. There was one death with which he may very well have been involved. The victim was a retired army colonel named James Bruno, and Teddy's girlfriend had once been a victim of rape by Bruno, so he had a very good reason to kill. He was fortunate that the death was declared a suicide."

"He never bothered to make a killing look like a suicide before," Todd pointed out.

"No, but in this case he didn't want to run, so an apparent suicide was the best way to dead-end the investigation."

"Give me the best physical description you can of Teddy," Todd said.

"Six feet, a hundred and sixty pounds; wiry, athletic build; gray hair, probably bald or balding, but he wore a hairpiece when I saw him, and a very good one that I didn't suspect. I don't remember an eye color, and he had no other distinctive features. That's why he's so good at disguises."

"Am I going to have any help?"

"No," Lance said quickly. "Just Holly by phone. We're going to carry you on the Agency's rolls as active but on extended leave. You'll have an Agency laptop and communications equipment and the usual access to our computers here in Langley. If there's anything you can't dig up on your own, Holly will do it for you."

"All right."

Lance handed him a slip of paper. "You can draw this in cash, and you can use your Agency credit cards."

"I want a light airplane," Todd said. "That's how Teddy travels, and I want to travel the same way."

"Holly will arrange that for you. No jets, however."

"I'm not trained for jets," Todd said, "but I'd like something fairly fast."

"I can do that," Holly said.

Lance stood up and offered his hand. "Good luck," he said.

Todd shook the hand. "One thing: You didn't tell me what you want me to do when I find Teddy."

Lance walked him to the door. "I didn't hear the question," he said, closing the door behind them.

16

Cupie Dalton and Vittorio sat in Vittorio's SUV down the street from the Inn of the Anasazi and waited for James Long to show. It was nearly nine a.m. when Long walked out of the hotel and into his car, a silver Lincoln Town Car that the valet had brought around.

"Well, at least he'll be easy to follow," Cupie said. "Let's go, and keep well back."

"Cupie," Vittorio said, "I don't have to be told how to run a tail."

"Right."

"You keep doing that, and I'm going to have to scalp you, as unrewarding as that would be."

Cupie rubbed his bald head. "I like it where it is," he said.

Long drove directly to the soundstage where Susannah Wilde's film was being shot, parked in the parking lot and entered the building.

"He's going to be there all day," Vittorio said.

"Maybe not," Cupie replied.

"So, where's he going to go?"

"Maybe he's going to have lunch with Barbara," Cupie said.

"That would certainly make life easy for us, wouldn't it?"

"Sure would," Cupie agreed. "Vittorio . . . ?"

"What?"

"From my brief conversation with Ed Eagle about Barbara, I got a vibe that wasn't there when we worked for him before."

"What kind of vibe?"

Cupie sighed. "Have you ever killed anybody?"

"Why do you want to know?"

"Because I think that's what Eagle is going to want done."

"Did he say that?"

"No, I told you it was just a vibe."

"You want to kill somebody based on a vibe?"

"Oh, no. When he wants it done he'll say so, or find some other way to make it perfectly clear."

"Have you ever killed anybody, Cupie?"

"Twice, both times when I was on the force, with my service revolver. Both of them were shooting at me."

"Anybody else?"

"No. All right, I answered your question, now you answer mine."

"Yes."

Cupie turned and looked at Vittorio. "Yes, you've killed somebody?"

"I'm not going to tell you again."

"Under what circumstances?" Cupie asked.

"Which time?"

"When you were a cop."

"I was never a cop, Cupie."

"All right, the first time."

"I was fourteen, and a man who lived with us was beating up my mother."

"And?"

"And I took him by the hair, cut his throat with my hunting knife and scalped him."

Cupie blinked. "You actually *scalped* a man? How did you know how to do that?"

"Cupie, I'm an Apache. You might call it cultural memory. Anyway, I'd seen it done a couple of times on the reservation."

"I didn't know that sort of thing was still being done," Cupie said.

"It isn't, much. I said I was fourteen."

"How about other Apaches?"

"When someone wants to make a point, I guess."

Cupie gulped. "How about the second time?"

"I shot a man in the face with a shotgun."

"Why?"

"He was coming at me with a knife."

"Oh."

"Yeah."

"Anybody else?"

"Two others."

"Jesus, Vittorio."

"Jesus had nothing to do with it."

"Who were these people?"

"They were both white men. The first two were Apache."

"Why did you do them?"

"They were both trying to kill me. The first one, I thought I might be a better knife fighter than he was. I was right."

"And the other one?"

"That one was more complicated: I was sleeping with his wife."

"That doesn't sound like you, Vittorio."

"Ex-wife, actually."

"Okay."

"He put out the word that he was going to kill me. I was out behind the house, putting in some fence posts, and I heard his car drive up. He yelled my name and said something uncomplimentary. The back door was open, and I heard him kick the front door open. I was unarmed at the time."

"What did you do?"

"I stood by the back door, pressed against the wall. I figured when he'd had a look around inside he'd see the back door open and come outside. He came out slowly. The first thing I saw was the gun in his hand. I let him take another step, then I hit him in the head with a fence post."

"That's a pretty good-sized piece of wood, isn't it?"

"Bigger than a baseball bat. I caught him across the forehead—he was shorter than I thought—and that did it. I didn't have to hit him again. Then I called the sheriff."

"Why did you do that?"

"You ever tried to get rid of a body?"

"Can't say that I have."

"It's harder than it sounds. If you put it in a river or lake, it comes up, eventually. If you bury it in the ground, the coyotes dig it up. If you put stones on top of the grave to prevent that, then it looks like a grave, and that makes you look guilty. I was defending my life, so I called the sheriff."

"What happened?"

"He'd already heard reports that the guy was looking to kill me, so I didn't have to prove that. And the guy's gun went off when I hit him, so you could say he'd shot at me. And the fence post had his blood and brains all over it, so my story was obviously true."

"So, you walked?"

"He didn't even run me in—he just told me to try to stay out of situations where I might have to do that again. And I've tried to take his advice."

"So, what are you going to do if Eagle asks us to off Barbara?"

"I don't know," Vittorio said, sounding thoughtful. "God knows she needs it."

"Yeah," Cupie replied, "she does."

17

Cupie and Vittorio sat in the car straight through lunchtime, and James Long never showed himself. Around two o'clock they drove to a sandwich shop and came back to the studio with their food. Long's car had disappeared from the parking lot.

"Shit," Cupie said. "We were gone, what, twenty minutes?"

Vittorio put the SUV into gear and drove away from the studio.

"Where are we going?"

"I want to see if he went back to the hotel," Vittorio said, "but . . ."

"Why would he go back to the hotel?"

"I don't know, but where else are we going to look?"

"The airport, maybe?" Cupie offered.

Vittorio took a hard left and gunned it. "All right, the airport. Albuquerque or Santa Fe?"

"Long doesn't seem like the kind of guy who would fly commercial," Cupie said. "Santa Fe."

They drove to Santa Fe Airport, parked the car along the fence and looked around. "Where do they park the rentals?" Vittorio asked.

"I don't know, but guys who fly in private airplanes drive their cars onto the ramp and abandon them."

They walked over to the Santa Fe Jetcenter and peered through the fence and out onto the tarmac. The Lincoln was parked on the ramp, and the trunk was still open. A Citation was taxiing away from the FBO.

"He's going back to LA," Vittorio said.

"Does that mean Barbara is still in LA?" Cupie asked.

"Why would she be in LA?" Vittorio asked.

"I don't know," Cupie said, "but that's the last place I saw her. I told you about seeing her in Venice."

"Yeah, but it doesn't make any sense, not if she wants to kill Ed Eagle."

"Maybe Long's not in touch with her," Cupie said.

"I thought we'd already decided that Long is the only person in the world who would spring her from that prison. After all, he's helped her before."

"Maybe she's staying at his house in LA," Cupie said. "She's done that before, too."

"That might explain why Long is headed back to LA," Vittorio said. "He wants to get laid."

"If he wants to get laid, why did he leave her and come to Santa Fe?"

"I think we should operate on the premise that Barbara is in Santa Fe," Vittorio said. "It's the only thing that makes any sense, given what we know about her, and if she's not here she will be, when she gets around to taking a shot at Ed Eagle."

"Okay, I buy that," Cupie said. "If you were Barbara, and you were lying low in Santa Fe, waiting for an opportunity to kill Ed Eagle, where would you lie low?"

"Not a hotel," Vittorio said. "Too expensive. An apartment maybe, or a house, but something nice. After all, she's been in prison for months. She'll want some comfort."

"If she's in an apartment or a house, she probably found it in the *New Mexican*," Cupie said.

"Why not one of those real estate magazines that are all over town?"

"She wouldn't look there for a rental," Cupie said. "Those are for sales."

They got back into Vittorio's SUV and drove to the newspaper's office. Cupie bought ten days of back issues and took them back to the car. He handed Vittorio half of the papers. "Look for something comfortable, not too big and furnished," he said.

Vittorio began opening the papers to the real estate section. "Here's one," he said, circling an ad.

"Let's go through them all," Cupie said.

They spent most of an hour cutting out and dating ads for possible houses and apartments, then sorted through them, finding seven likely properties.

Cupie went through them again, checking the dates. "There are ads for three houses that stopped running in the past couple of days," he said. "That means they've been rented." He handed the ads to Vittorio.

"Two of them are from the same agent," Vittorio said. He got out his cell phone and called the agent's office and asked for her.

"Hello?"

"This is Sergeant Rivera at the Santa Fe Police Department," Vittorio said.

"How can I help you, Sergeant?"

"You ran ads for two rental houses in the *New Mexican*," he said.

"More than two," she replied. "I specialize in rentals."

"There are two that you stopped advertising: one in Tesuque, one at Las Campanas."

"Yes, both those have been rented."

"Can you give me the renters' names?"

"Let's see," she said. "The Tesuque place went to a Mr. and Mrs. Torrance, and the Las Campanas house—it was a guesthouse—went to a Mrs. Keeler, from San Francisco."

"Can you describe Mrs. Keeler?" Vittorio asked.

"Five-six or -seven, slim, auburn hair, very attractive."

"Thank you so much," Vittorio said and hung up. He turned to Cupie. "What was that guy's name that Barbara married in San Francisco?"

Cupie screwed up his face. "Walter something, electronics zillionaire. I can't think of the last name."

"Could it have been Keeler?" Vittorio asked.

"It could have been, and it was!" Cupie said.

The two men exchanged a high five.

"Let's get out to Las Campanas," Vittorio said.

18

Barbara dressed carefully in casual but elegant clothes: tight silk pants and a tight cashmere sweater that showed off her cleavage.

At dusk she turned out the lights in her guesthouse and walked up to Dolly's place, bearing a good bottle of wine. As she reached the door it occurred to her that she should have left a light on for her return home, but then it didn't really matter, as she kept a small flashlight in her purse. She knocked on the door.

Dolly opened it, smiling. "Hi, there," she said. "Come on in." She was dressed similarly to Barbara but wearing a small apron.

"I don't know what you're cooking, but I brought some wine," Barbara said, offering it.

"Zinfandel," Dolly said, reading the label. "Perfect.

We're having a veal stew. Would you like something to drink?"

"Do you have bourbon?" Barbara asked.

"Bought some this afternoon," Dolly said, going to the little bar and holding up a bottle of Knob Creek. "Tip drinks this, so it must be good." She poured some over ice.

"My favorite," Barbara said, accepting the drink. "Tip seems like quite a fellow," she said. "I was very impressed with that last putt of his. He must do very well."

"Yes, he does. He's won only a few times on the tour, but he's usually in the top ten, sometimes in the top five. I don't think the public understands how much money a pro can make playing that kind of golf regularly and finishing high up consistently."

"How much can he make?"

"A million or two a year, maybe."

Barbara whistled. "I hope he's paying you well."

"He is, and he just added this house to my compensation package."

"Is he single?"

"Yes. He was widowed recently. His wife was either murdered or committed suicide. I'm not sure which."

"In that house next door?" Barbara asked.

"Yes, in their bedroom. Tip came back from playing a tournament in Dallas and found her."

"He must be very shaken up, but he played so well in Houston."

"He seems oddly serene," Dolly said, "but I think he's just a stoic. That's my read on him, anyway."

Dolly sat down beside her on the sofa with her drink. "Dinner'll be ready in half an hour. There's nothing left to do but serve it."

Barbara started to say she was hungry, but she stopped in midsentence. She'd heard a car drive up and stop nearby, and now she heard two car doors close. She got up and peered through the little window in Dolly's front door. "A car," she said. "Two flashlights."

VITTORIO STOPPED THE SUV at the locked gate of the main house, and he and Cupie got out. He handed Cupie a compact flashlight. "These are very good," he said. "Lithium ion batteries: They're bright enough to temporarily blind a man in the dark."

They climbed over the low gate. "Let's have a look at this guesthouse," Vittorio said.

"Pretty dark," Cupie replied. "No lights, and the garage door is closed."

They reached the house and walked around it, shining their lights through windows. "Very neat and clean," Cupie said. "Doesn't look like anybody lives here."

"Not even a toothbrush in the bathroom," Vittorio replied. "Why don't we ask at the house next door? There are lights on there."

Cupie went ahead. "Let me do it," he said. "You're too scary on a dark night."

"I HAVE TO TELL YOU," Barbara said. "One of the reasons I'm in Santa Fe is that I'm being stalked by a man I went out with after my husband died. It would be just like him to show up here or to send a private detective to find me. Looks like two men coming this way."

"Go into the guest room and close the door," Dolly said. "If they come here I'll handle it." She put Barbara's drink in the kitchen sink and her own on the counter. The doorbell rang.

Dolly went to the door, switched on the porch light and opened the door a foot, keeping her boot jammed against it. A plump, baby-faced man in a tweed topcoat and tweed hat stood there. A few feet behind him, in the shadows, stood another man wearing a flat-brimmed hat that partly hid his face.

Cupie swept off his hat and smiled. "Good evening. I'm sorry to disturb you," he said. "I'm looking for the woman who lives next door, a Mrs. Keeler."

"No one lives next door," Dolly said. "The place is owned by some people from New York, but they're only here in the summer."

"I'd heard that this Mrs. Keeler had rented it in the past couple of days, and it's important I get in touch with her on a business matter. Some papers have to be signed."

"I'd know if it had been rented," Dolly said, "and it hasn't. In fact, I spoke to the woman in New York this morning, and she told me they had taken it off the rental market."

"Are you alone here, ma'am?"

"No, the main house is occupied," she said. "Is there anything else?"

"I wonder if I could use your telephone?"

"I haven't had it turned on yet," she said, "and cell phones don't work out here. Good night." She tried to close the door, but he stuck a hand through. "Here's my card," he said. "I'd appreciate it if you would give me a call, if someone turns up in the house."

"Sure," Dolly said. She took the card, closed the door, locked it and turned off the porch light.

Barbara edged into the room. "Everything all right?"

"Shhh," Dolly said, waving her back. "They haven't gone yet. I can still see their flashlights."

A minute passed and she heard car doors slam; then the car's headlights came on and it turned around and went back the way it had come. "Okay," Dolly called out. "The coast is clear."

Barbara came back into the living room. "That was scary," she said.

"The guy at the door wasn't very scary, but he had a friend, and he was."

"Did they give you a name?" Barbara asked.

"They gave me a card," Dolly responded, handing it to her.

"Oh, I know these guys," she said. "My ex had them tailing me in San Francisco."

"They asked for you by name," Dolly said, "but don't worry, I told them the house hadn't been rented to anyone and that the owners had taken it off the rental market."

"Oh, thank you, Dolly," Barbara said, kissing her on the cheek. "Now I won't have to move."

Dolly hugged her. "I know you're going to be happy here, Ellie," she said.

"I think I will be," Barbara replied, returning the hug.

19

Barbara awoke to the sound of her cell phone vibrating on the bedside table. Dolly was still asleep, naked, in the bed beside her, so she took the phone into the living room before she answered.

"Yes?"

"It's Jimmy," he said.

"Hi. It's a little early, isn't it?"

"I'm on Pacific time. Isn't it later there?"

She ignored the probe. "You're back from Santa Fe, then?"

"Yes, I got back last evening, after watching a couple of days' shooting. I just wanted to reassure myself that my writer/director knows what he's doing. He does."

"That's good."

"Something I thought you should know: Yesterday I

was followed by those two private detectives that were watching my house in LA when Eagle was looking for you. I think he must know you're out and probably coming to Santa Fe. I wouldn't go there if I were you."

"That's good advice, Jimmy. Thanks for letting me know about the two men. I'll watch myself."

"You might be better off holing up here with me," Long said. "I'll take good care of you."

"Thanks. I might take you up on that at some point, but I'm okay where I am for the moment."

"Whatever you say," he replied. "Take care of yourself, wherever you are."

"Thanks, baby. I will. Oh, Jimmy . . ."

"Yes?"

"You remember you said that our pilot on the flight back from Mexico did a lot of odd jobs for you?"

"Yes, he has in the past."

"Do you think he might do a little odd job for me?"

"Do I want to know what kind of odd job?" he asked.

"No, but you'd better find out if he's squeamish."

"Ooookay," Long said. "I'll have a chat with him. Can I reach you at the same number?"

"Yes," she said. "Soon, please." She closed the phone.

"Ellie?" Dolly called from the bedroom.

"I'm here," she said, walking back there to get her clothes.

"Come back to bed," Dolly said alluringly.

"Thanks, but I've got things to do today," Barbara replied. "Don't you have to go to work?"

"Eventually. Tip always goes to the practice range early and doesn't get back until midmorning. I'll be at my desk by then. What are you going to do about those two men who came last night?"

"I'm going to keep my lights off in the evening and keep my garage door closed."

"You're welcome to sleep here," Dolly said.

Barbara knelt on the bed and kissed her on a nipple, then on the lips. "That's comforting to know," she said, then got dressed and went back to her own house.

VITTORIO RAPPED SHARPLY on the guest-bedroom door. "Wake up, Cupie! Time to get going. There's coffee on."

"Be there in a couple of minutes," Cupie called back.

Vittorio went back to the kitchen, toasted a muffin and was eating when Cupie wandered in, dressed but still looking sleepy. "Morning. Kind of early, isn't it?"

"We've got things to do," Vittorio said.

"What have we got to do?"

"I want to take another look at that guesthouse in daylight."

"Wouldn't afternoon daylight be as good as dawn daylight?" Cupie asked, pouring himself a cup of coffee.

"If Barbara slept there last night, maybe she's up and around now."

"The house was empty, Vittorio, and the neighbor confirmed it."

"I thought the neighbor was hostile to our inquiry," Vittorio said.

"We were two strange men at her door—one of us very strange—and after dark. What did you expect, to be invited in for a drink?"

"Maybe you're right," Vittorio said, "but then again, maybe not. You ready?"

"Okay, okay," Cupie said, getting to his feet. "You got a to-go cup?"

"Take the one in your hand," Vittorio said.

VITTORIO STOPPED THE SUV at the top of the hill above the house. He could see only a little of the guesthouse, most of it hidden by cottonwood trees. He started down the hill, then put the gearshift in neutral and let it coast down the road, braking to keep his speed from increasing.

BARBARA, SITTING IN HER kitchen over coffee, heard a brake squeal. Quickly, she put her dishes in the sink, then took her coffee mug into the bedroom, first checking that her toothbrush had been put away in the medicine cabinet. She stepped into her bedroom closet and slid the slatted door closed behind her, then stood quietly, sipping her coffee.

Shortly, she heard car doors closing and the rattle of the main gate as someone climbed over it. Then there was the crunch of shoes on gravel. The doorbell rang twice; then she heard them walking around the house. Finally, the footsteps retreated, and she heard the car doors slam. The car started and drove away.

She waited another two minutes before she came out of the closet.

"I THINK she's back in LA," Cupie said.

"Barbara *should* be here," Vittorio responded, "and she fits the description of the woman who rented the guesthouse."

"Just because somebody rented it doesn't mean that she's going to move in right away."

"Possibly."

"You're like a dog with a bone," Cupie said. "If she was here, maybe she flew back to LA with Long. We didn't see him board the airplane. Maybe she was there waiting for him."

"Cupie, have you forgotten what a determined, goal-oriented person Barbara is?"

"No, I haven't forgotten."

"I think you have. She wants Eagle dead, so she has to come to where Eagle is. I think she already has."

"If she has, I think she went back to LA with Long."

"It's not like her to backtrack from her goal," Vittorio said. "Not like her at all."

"I don't disagree with that, Vittorio, but people do unpredictable things sometimes."

"I'm not going to LA," Vittorio said. "You want to go, you go, but here is where the action is going to be, and this is where I'm staying."

"Okay," Cupie said. "We'll stay here, but what are we going to do next?"

"Since we don't know where she is," Vittorio said, "we should stick with Eagle."

"He won't like being tailed," Cupie pointed out.

"Then he shouldn't know," Vittorio said.

20

E d Eagle was back at his law office, having had enough of watching the sausage that was film made ever so slowly. He had some phone calls to return and some correspondence to dictate, and he was at it when his secretary buzzed him.

"Yes?"

"District Attorney Roberto Martínez for you on line one. You in?"

"I'll get it," Eagle said. He pressed the button. "Hello, Bob?"

"Morning, Ed," Martínez said. "I thought you had gone into the film business. You back earning an honest living again?"

"Yep. I discovered that the film business can get along without me. I spent two days at that studio and couldn't think of a single suggestion to make. You wouldn't believe how long it takes them to get a scene in the can."

"No, and I don't want to hear about it," Martínez said, "unless there are some very beautiful women in that movie."

"Only two: One of them is sleeping with the director, and the other is sleeping with me."

"Rats. Listen, can you use some good news?"

"Always."

"The crime lab called me this morning with some new information that casts a new light on the Constance Hanks case."

"You have my undivided attention," Eagle said.

"A technician found two lipstick smears on the pillow on which Mrs. Hanks's head rested when found."

"Did they belong to Mrs. Hanks?"

"One of them did," Martínez said.

"Aaaaah," Eagle said. "And the other?"

"The technician at the scene took samples of all of the lipsticks belonging to Mrs. Hanks—the ones in the medicine cabinet and her dressing table, and the second smear didn't match any of them. A detective interviewed the Hanks's housekeeper on the day of the murder, and she told him she'd changed the bed linens the day before, so the unidentified smear was made within twenty-four hours of Mrs. Hanks's death."

"Any DNA mixed in with the lipstick?"

"You'd think, but I'm afraid not."

"Pity."

"Yes, it is, but I think you can consider your client cleared of this murder."

"That's great news, Bob. I'll pass it on to him. Let me know when you find your female suspect, will you? I'm curious to know who it is."

"Will do. See you around, Ed." Martínez hung up.

Eagle looked up Tip Hanks's phone number and dialed it.

DOLLY WAS IN THE bathroom off Tip's study, peeing, when she heard the phone ring. She decided not to disturb herself, to let the machine get it.

After three rings, the machine answered. "This is Tip Hanks. Please leave your number and the date of your call, and I'll return your call when I get back."

There was a beep, and another, deeper voice spoke. "Tip, it's Ed Eagle. I just had a call from the district attorney, telling me that you have been cleared as a suspect in Connie's murder. This is great news, and I congratulate you. Take care of yourself. Oh, the reason you were cleared is that a crime scene technician found two smears of lipstick on Connie's pillow—one hers, one belonging to another person. It matched none of Connie's, so it appears that the unknown chief suspect is a woman. Go figure." Eagle hung up the phone.

"Shit!" Dolly said aloud. She stood there thinking for a moment, then opened Tip's center desk drawer. There was a handheld recorder there, and she opened it and removed the tape. She took the tape from the telephone answering machine, inserted it into the dictator and turned it on. The message played, but she stopped it after Eagle had said, "Take care of yourself." Then she held down the record button and let the tape run for thirty seconds, recording silence over the last part of Eagle's message. She returned the tape to the answering machine and reinserted the second tape into the recorder and returned it to the desk drawer.

Dolly went back to her desk, where she had left her handbag, and found two lipsticks in it. She took a tissue from a box and wiped all the lipstick from her lips, then picked up a tube, cranked the whole stick out of its holder and broke it off into the tissue. She went back to the bathroom and flushed the tissue and lipstick down the toilet, and watched to see that they cleared the bowl. She then went back to her desk and applied the other lipstick to her lips and returned it to her purse. Finally, she walked through the house and the kitchen and out to where the garbage cans were kept in a small wooden shed. She opened the top and unwound the wire closure from the top of one bag, dropped in the old lipstick case, and reclosed the bag. Finally, she went back into the house.

She was working at her computer when Tip returned to the house a few minutes later.

"Good morning," he said, stopping at her door.

She gave him a broad smile. "Good morning. How did practice go?"

"Really well," Tip replied. "I worked on shaping my drives, and I'm getting really good at it."

"Gonna hit around those doglegs, huh?" she asked.

"You said it. Anything going on here?"

"Nope. Oh, you had a phone message when I was in the powder room. I haven't played it back."

Tip went into his study and pressed the play button, and Ed Eagle's deep voice filled the room, giving him the news: He was no longer a suspect. "Take care of yourself," Eagle said, and the message ended. Tip reset the machine, then went back to Dolly's office.

"The call was from Ed Eagle," he said. "I'm off the hook on Connie's murder, no longer a suspect."

Dolly grabbed his hand and squeezed it. "Oh, Tip, that's wonderful news! I'm so happy for you."

"Thanks, Dolly," he said. "Uh . . . there's something else."

"What is it?" she asked.

"I wonder if . . . I mean, it's pretty soon after Connie's death, but would you like to have dinner sometime?"

"Oh, I'd love to," Dolly replied with enthusiasm. "But I think you're right: We probably shouldn't be seen socializing in Santa Fe so soon. Tell you what: Why don't I cook dinner for you some night soon? I'm a very good cook."

"I'd like that a lot," Tip said, "and I'll look forward to it." He kissed her on top of the head and went back into his study.

Dolly went happily back to her work, thinking of what she would cook for their first dinner together. Something good but not great—she'd want to top it at a later dinner.

21

Todd Bacon landed his Agency-furnished Beech Bonanza at Vero Beach Airport and taxied to parking at Sun Aviation. He left a credit card number for his fuel and asked the woman behind the desk, "A friend of mine named Jack Smithson is in town and he keeps his airplane here. It's a Cessna 182 RG. I wonder if you have a phone number for him?"

The woman checked her computer and gave him a number. "Jack left here a couple of weeks ago and hasn't returned," she said. "I don't know what his intentions are."

"Thanks," Todd said. "I'll call and leave him a message." He rented a car and, using the onboard GPS, drove to the last known address for Teddy Fay. He parked his car next to the cottage and looked inside. It was nicely furnished and clean, but there was no sign of an occupant. Todd looked around, then picked the lock on the front door and let himself in.

He walked through the entire cottage slowly, looking at everything, but he could find nothing that seemed to belong to Teddy, except the large safe in a closet. He remembered that Holly had seen a note left there saying that the combination to the safe was T-E-D-D-Y, and he tapped it in and opened the safe. It was entirely empty. He closed the door and spun the wheel to lock it.

He picked up the phone and found it disconnected, then sat down in the comfortable chair next to it and picked up the local phone book. He turned to the yellow pages, then found a list of moving and storage companies. One of them had a small arrow inked in, pointing to its number. He called the number with his cell phone.

"Beach Moving and Storage," a woman's voice said.

"Hi. This is Jack Smithson. I left some things there to be shipped a couple of weeks ago, and I wondered if they'd gone out yet."

"Let me check." She came back a moment later. "I have nothing in your name, Mr. Smithson," she said. "Could they be in another name?"

Todd had an idea and checked his notebook. "Try Lauren Cade," he said.

She put him on hold for a moment, then came back

on the line. "Yes, those boxes were picked up last Monday and should have been delivered to the storage company in Santa Fe yesterday."

"May I have the name of the storage company, please? I don't know where Lauren is having them sent."

"They were sent to Adobe Moving and Storage on Cerrillos Road," she said.

"To what name?"

"I assume to herself. I have no other name."

"Thanks so much," Todd replied, and hung up, jotting the name in his notebook. He got the number from information and was connected.

"Hi. This is Jack Smithson. I'm calling for Lauren Cade. Was her shipment delivered on time yesterday?"

"What was the name again?" the man asked.

"Lauren Cade." He spelled it.

"No, we received nothing yesterday, the day before or today for a Lauren Cade."

"Is it possible to check your receivables on those days again?"

"I've just done that in the computer. There's nothing for a Lauren Cade."

"Thank you," Todd said, and broke the connection. He looked at his watch. A little late in the day to take off for Santa Fe. He left the cottage and found a motel nearby and checked in. He cranked up his laptop and did a search for fixed-base operators at Santa Fe Airport. There were three, and he called each of them and inquired, first, if a Jack Smithson had arrived there. A no from all three. Then he asked each if they had had a 182 RG arrive. Two of the three had had such arrivals, but only one, Santa Fe Jetcenter, in the time frame that interested Todd. He asked for the tail number.

Todd went to the FAA Web site and accessed the aircraft registration list and entered the tail number. Nothing. He typed in "Jack Smithson" and got nothing.

AS TODD WAS CHECKING the FAA database, Teddy Fay was flying his 182 RG to a small airport in Albuquerque that had a paint shop, flying at low altitude and without filing a flight plan. He landed, taxied up to the shop, got out, found the owner and introduced himself as Ralph Pearson. "I spoke to you on the phone yesterday," he said.

"Oh, yes. You wanted your registration number changed. Have you got your paperwork?"

Teddy gave him the FAA documents he had created.

The man looked over the airplane. "It'll take us two full days of work," he said, "what with drying time and doing the shadowing in the contrasting color. You can pick it up in three days."

Teddy thanked the man, then walked out to the parking lot, where Lauren was waiting for him in the used Jeep Grand Cherokee he had bought. "You can drive me back down here in three days," he said.

They drove back to Santa Fe, to their new rental house, and Teddy went to his computer, where he entered the FAA mainframe and inserted registration for his airplane with the new tail number, giving a false name and an address in Fort Smith, Arkansas.

"I see your boxes arrived," Teddy said. "Did you have them shipped the way I asked you to?"

"I did," she replied. "My name appears nowhere on them."

"Good."

"We're going to have to go out for dinner," Lauren said, "since we don't have any groceries yet. We can pick up breakfast at a convenience store on the way home."

"Fine with me," he said, closing the computer. "Another trip to Geronimo? We haven't been there yet."

"Sure, that's fine. Shall I call?"

"Is the phone working?"

"We didn't get phone service, remember?" she reminded him. "We're using our cells."

"Oh, right."

Lauren called and made the reservations, then brought a drink to him and sat down beside him on the sofa. "What are we going to do with our days, Teddy?" she asked. "I'm used to being busy."

"Then get busy," Teddy replied. "Boredom is a self-inflicted wound. Get to know Santa Fe; learn to appreciate the light and the terrain; read books; TiVo the good stuff at night and watch it in the daytime. Maybe we'll take up golf."

"It all sounds wonderful," Lauren replied, clinking her glass with his. "A whole new world."

22

Todd Bacon landed the B-36TC Bonanza at Santa Fe Airport late in the afternoon and taxied to the Santa Fe Jetcenter, a mock-adobe building with a large ramp. An assortment of aircraft populated the place, from large corporate jets and turboprops to his own turbocharged piston Bonanza.

Todd lost no time in questioning the young woman on the desk. She checked her computer. "No, Paul Janzen, the man who flew the 182 RG, is no longer here. He turned in his rental car yesterday and flew away. He said something about selling his airplane to somebody in Texas," she said.

"And he's not returning?"

"Didn't seem like it," she said.

"Do you know if he was selling the airplane through a broker?"

"No, sir."

"Or what town in Texas? It's a big state."

"Nope. I only saw him twice, the day he arrived and the day he left."

"Was there a woman with him either time?"

She looked thoughtful. "There was a woman in here on the day he arrived, but it didn't look like she was with him. He came in and signed the paperwork for his rental; then he went out to the ramp, got in the car and drove away."

"Without the woman?"

"Yes. Like I said, she didn't appear to be with him. There were several airplanes unloading that afternoon, and she could have been on any of them."

"Can you give me a physical description of the man?"

"I guess he was in his early fifties, dark hair, going a little gray around the ears."

"Anything else you can remember?"

"No. He was just like anybody else."

"Do you remember what kind of car he rented?"

She went to her computer, looked it up and told him.

"Thanks," Todd said, then got into his own rental car, took a good look at the map and drove into Santa Fe. As he got into the city it looked to him like the sort of place he'd like to live himself, and he couldn't blame Teddy if he'd picked it. He drove to the Plaza and found La Fonda, the big old hotel that had served visitors to the town for decades. It had been nicely updated, and he was given a small suite on the top floor. He opened his bags and got out his computer, then logged on to the Agency mainframe and sent an e-mail to Holly Barker.

Checked out Vero Beach and discovered that Lauren Cade had left some boxes in storage there and that they had been shipped to Santa Fe, but the company had nothing under her name. Arrived Santa Fe an hour ago and checked for 182 RG at Santa Fe Jetcenter, but the owner had turned in his rent-a-car and left yesterday. Appeared to be alone on both arrival and departure. Description by woman at the desk vague, could fit hundreds of people. Said he was going to Texas to sell his airplane, no mention of what city.

I'll follow every lead in Santa Fe tomorrow and report on anything I find. I tried to find a photograph of Lauren Cade in the records of the Florida State Police and motor vehicles department, to no avail. I guess you were right about our friend's ability to scrub items on databases.

Todd

HOLLY, WORKING LATE at her desk as usual, read the e-mail, and it was nothing less than she had expected. Teddy was a chameleon with endless bags of tricks, and she wasn't entirely sure that Todd understood who he was up against. Still, he was a resourceful young man who wanted to further impress Lance Cabot, so he was highly motivated.

TODD GREW HUNGRY around dusk, so he showered and changed and stopped at the concierge's desk in the lobby.

"May I help you, sir?" the young woman said.

"Yes. Can you recommend a very good restaurant for dinner outside the hotel? Something with local color?"

"I'd recommend either Santacafé or Geronimo," she said. "I suppose Geronimo has more local color."

"Can you book me a table for one, please?"

She called the restaurant and spoke to them, then turned to Todd. "They have no tables, but you can dine in the bar; you won't need a reservation there."

"All right. Thanks." Todd turned toward the garage, then turned back.

"Can you give me directions?"

"It's very easy. Turn right out of the parking lot, then drive toward the cathedral and take your next right. Go straight at the traffic light, then take your first left onto

Canyon Road. Geronimo is about halfway to the top, and they have valet parking."

TEDDY AND LAUREN were seated at a corner table at Geronimo, Teddy in his preferred gunfighter's seat with his back to the corner. He saw a young man enter the restaurant and walk straight through the dining room toward the bar. Bells went off in Teddy's head. He never forgot a face, but where had he seen this one?

A waitress approached with menus and asked if they'd like drinks. Lauren ordered and waited for Teddy to place his order, but he seemed lost in thought. "Teddy?"

"Oh, sorry. A margarita, please, straight up with salt." The waitress left.

"Give me just a minute," he said to Lauren. "I have to think about something."

"Sure," Lauren said. She watched as he seemed to go almost into a trance: eyes closed, face expressionless.

Teddy reversed the video recorder in his brain and watched the young man enter the restaurant again, then again. Now he had the face fixed in his mind. Panama City. He had been on his motorcycle and he had just shot the Agency station chief on the street outside the American Embassy, when he'd looked up at the windows of their offices. The young man had been standing at a window. Teddy had seen him before in a local bar. He was Agency. Teddy opened his eyes.

"Everything okay, Teddy?" Lauren asked.

"No," Teddy said. "Not entirely. There's someone from the Agency in this restaurant right now."

"Someone you worked with before?"

"No, he's much younger than I. He worked in the Panama station only a couple of months ago, and he turned up on Cumberland Island when I was dealing with a problem. There was something of a chase, but I took off from the beach. He put a couple of holes in the airplane that I had to fix later, before I went to Orchid Beach."

"Is he here looking for us?" she asked.

"Very possibly," Teddy said.

"But there's no way he could have traced us here."

"There's always a way. I could have made a mistake."

"Do you want to leave? Should we run?"

"No," Teddy said. "I have a better idea. Let's just relax and enjoy our dinner." They ordered; then Teddy excused himself to go to the men's room.

TODD BACON SAT at the bar, sipping a margarita. There was a couple at a table near the bar, and it occurred to him that they were a fit for Teddy Fay and Lauren Cade. He was sixtyish and slim and wore an obvious toupee. She was much younger, blond and attractive. He summoned the bartender and lowered his voice. "Do you know the couple to my left?"

"Yes," the man replied. "They're the Hamptons, regular customers."

"For how long?"

"Ever since I've been here, and that's two years."

Todd nodded. Well, that would have been too easy. A man walked past him and into the men's room. A couple of minutes later he walked out and past Todd again. He appeared to be in his early fifties, dark hair, gray at the temples. That matched the description of the man in the 182 RG that was given to him by the young woman at the airport.

Todd shook his head. Now he was getting paranoid. *Everybody* was looking like Teddy Fay.

TEDDY TOOK HIS SEAT in the dining room.

"Everything all right?" Lauren asked.

"Suspicions confirmed," he replied.

Todd Bacon slept later than he had meant to, then ordered breakfast from room service. He still had one lead to follow, and he finished breakfast in a hurry and showered.

Ten minutes later, he was driving out Cerrillos Road, looking for Adobe Moving and Storage. He found it and turned into the parking lot. A middle-aged man was behind the counter.

"Good morning," Todd said to the man. "I wonder if you could help me."

"What can I do for you, sir?"

"A couple of days ago you had some boxes arrive here from Vero Beach, Florida. Can you find that shipment in your records?"

The man turned to his computer. "Vero Beach, Florida," he muttered to himself. "Yes, here it is."

"Can you tell me to whom the shipment was addressed?"

The man peered at the screen. "No name."

"No name? How could you deliver it?"

"The boxes, four of them, were addressed to us, and identified by a number."

"Can you tell me to whom you delivered the boxes?"

"We couldn't deliver them; we had no name and address. I remember they were picked up here at the office by a woman."

"Can you describe her?" Todd asked.

"Fairly tall, wearing jeans and a sweatshirt. Also a baseball cap and dark glasses. I helped her load the boxes into her car."

"What kind of car?"

"A Lincoln Town Car, I think, silver color."

"Can you remember anything else about her?" Todd asked.

"No, just that she was very nice. She might have been pretty without the cap and the sunglasses."

"Thank you," Todd said and left. A silver Town Car—that's what the man with the 182 RG had rented. He drove back to the airport to the FBO. The same young woman was behind the desk.

"Morning," Todd said. "We spoke yesterday."

"I remember," she replied.

"You said that the man with the 182 RG had rented a Lincoln Town Car?"

"Yes, that's right."

"Could I have a look at the car?" he asked.

She turned to her computer. "I'm afraid it was rented again. Left half an hour ago."

"Do you have the credit card information on the man who rented it?"

She looked again. "Paul Janzen, Atlanta, Georgia." She gave him the address and phone number.

"What kind of credit card?" Todd asked.

"I only have the number," she said, and to his surprise, she gave it to him.

"Thank you so much," Todd said, and left, excited now. Back in his own car he dialed the phone number of Paul Janzen. A pizza parlor answered. He called information, but no Paul Janzen had a number in Atlanta.

He drove back to his hotel, sat down at his computer, got into the Agency mainframe and ran the credit card number. To his surprise, it existed but there was no name for it, just the number. Very odd. He got into the FAA database and did a search for Janzen but got nothing.

"This guy is Teddy Fay," Todd said aloud to himself. "But where the hell did he go?"

TEDDY SAT IN HIS new living room, watching Lauren unpack her boxes. He had examined the packages, and they didn't appear to have been opened since he left them in Vero Beach. There was nothing in the boxes that would identify Lauren—no tracking devices, either, just clothes, shoes and makeup. She couldn't be identified from the labels.

"When you picked up the boxes," he said to her, "did anything unusual happen?"

"No," Lauren replied. "They were sitting in the office, and the man behind the desk helped me load them into the Lincoln."

"Did he ask for your name?"

"No. I just gave him the numbers on the boxes, the way you told me to."

Teddy nodded. The young man—Bacon, his name was—had only two nexuses for him in Santa Fe: the FBO and the storage company. If he was any good at all he would have worked both of them to the bitter end, but in both cases, he would have come up empty. Everything he could learn would have pointed to Teddy turning in the rental car and leaving town in his airplane, which he had done, of course.

"We're safe," he said to Lauren. "But we're going to stay in the house for a couple of days." She had already been to the grocery store.

"If you say so," she said. "Why are you so confident?"

"Because *I* could not have found us with the information he had," he replied, "so he couldn't, either. He was sitting in the bar last night when I went to the men's room, and he didn't recognize me, so he doesn't have more than a general description. And we're driving a different car now."

"That makes sense," Lauren said. "He must have come to Santa Fe because we shipped the boxes here, but that's a dead end."

"Let's not ship anything else," Teddy said. "If we need to leave Santa Fe, we'll travel lighter. We can always buy clothes."

"Sure, we can."

"We're going to stay in the house for two more days, until it's time to pick up the airplane; then we're going to take it to Las Vegas, New Mexico, which is a few minutes' flight east of Santa Fe. It's dangerous to backtrack, to take it back to Santa Fe. Bacon could have left word at the FBOs there to call him if I turn up again. If, on the odd chance, we ever need to run, we can drive to Las Vegas in a hurry and take off from there."

"Sounds good," Lauren said. "And we should be safe in Santa Fe, because when Bacon leaves he'll check it off his list and won't come back, having already exhausted his search here."

"I like the way you think," Teddy said. "It's like the reverse of the cop you used to be."

24

Barbara woke up at her usual hour, had some breakfast and prepared for the usual visit from Vittorio and Cupie. She cleaned the kitchen, put away her clothes and stuffed her makeup and toothbrush into the bathroom medicine cabinet.

Promptly at nine o'clock she heard the SUV stop outside on the road, and she took her coffee into the bedroom closet again.

"VITTORIO," CUPIE SAID. "How long are we going to keep making this trip?"

"Until she shows up," Vittorio replied. "The real estate agent has confirmed that she rented the place to Barbara, and that her lease is month-to-month. If she has gone away somewhere, she'll return here, and when she does, she's ours."

They did their usual walk-around of the little house, peering into windows.

"Nothing's changed," Cupie said. "She's not here."

"Until tomorrow," Vittorio said.

THEY WERE CLOSE ENOUGH to the bedroom window that Barbara could hear that exchange. Maybe Jimmy was right; maybe she should go to LA for a while. She called Jimmy.

"Hey, baby," he said.

"I'm taking your advice, sweetheart," she said. "Can you put me up for a while?"

"Yeah, sure."

"I'll get a plane from Albuquerque today and a cab to you. Should be there late afternoon."

"I'll look forward to it," he said.

"Me, too!"

Barbara packed her bag and, being careful to leave the house exactly the way it had been, got the Mercedes station wagon out of the garage and began driving toward I-25, which would take her to Albuquerque. She backtracked a couple of times, driving through residential neighborhoods, to be sure she wasn't being followed, then kept an eye on her tail all the way to the airport. Along the way, she used her cell phone to book a seat on a flight.

VITTORIO AND CUPIE sat in the SUV, parked just off the Plaza, with a view of the entrance to Eagle's office building.

"He's in for the morning," Cupie said. "Let's go to Tia Sophia's and get a good breakfast."

"Cupie," Vittorio said with some exasperation, "you've got to remember that we're not watching for Eagle—we're watching for Barbara."

"Well, she's not likely to come to his office, is she? She's much more likely to wait out near his house and shoot him when he comes home. He's safe in his office."

"All right, all right," Vittorio said, starting the vehicle. "I guess I'm hungry, too." He drove a couple of streets over and found a parking spot near Tia Sophia's, a popular breakfast and lunch spot.

"At least we'll get a table now," Cupie said. "The breakfast crowd has already gone to work."

Cupie was right. Soon they were having huevos rancheros.

BARBARA ARRIVED at Jimmy's house in Beverly Hills a little before six, and he was waiting for her with martinis already mixed. He took her bags upstairs while she relaxed with her drink.

He came back down, poured his own martini and sat down. "So, how's it going?" he asked.

"Not so hot," she said. "Ed knows I'm either in town or on my way. Those two PIs, Vittorio and Cupie Dalton, have figured out that I rented my house, and they're out there every day, trying to catch me there. I'm going to have to get a new place when I get back."

"Sounds like a good idea. They can waste their time looking for you while you're here with me."

"Jimmy, tell me more about this pilot of yours— what's his name?"

"Bart Cross. I've known him since he was a kid, and he's done a lot of work for me on films. I helped him get a union card."

"Is he one of those people who always needs money?"

"I think that's true of most people, babe, but more so of Bart than most. He's a poker player, and no better than so-so. He wins sometimes, but he loses more often. And he has to make the payments on that Beech Baron of his. That's gotta be costing him four or five grand a month, and then there's insurance, hangar and maintenance."

"So, you think he'd be up for making some large cash?"

"How large?"

"I guess I'd go to twenty-five grand," she said. "If I have to."

"Bart would do just about anything for that kind of money," Long said.

"Good. I'd like to meet him tomorrow. Can I have his number?"

"I'll call him for you."

"No, I'd rather do it directly and cut you out of this. We don't ever want him to be able to testify that you put us in touch."

"All right."

"Does Bart know that I escaped from prison in Mexico?"

"Not from me he doesn't, and nothing's been on TV about it here, and he's not the sort to read the papers. I'd say he's ignorant of your Houdini act."

Barbara looked at her watch. It was an hour earlier in Santa Fe, so she called her real estate agent.

"Yes, Mrs. Keeler?"

"I wanted to let you know that I won't be needing the house after the end of the first month."

"I'm sorry you couldn't stay longer," the woman said. "Will you be needing another place?"

"No, I've decided to go back to San Francisco." Barbara gave her a bank account number to wire her security deposit to when her month ended.

"Thank you for all your help," she said, then hung up. She thought about Dolly Parks and whether to call her, then decided not to. Best to cut her trail clean.

"So, you're not going back?"

"Eventually," Barbara said, "but that house is blown for me. I'll find another place, if I need it."

Long went to his desk, opened his address book and wrote down a number. "Here's Bart Cross's cell number," he said, handing her a slip of paper. "He's not working at the moment, so you'll probably catch him at home in the morning."

Barbara tucked the paper into her bra. "Thanks, sweetie," she said. "I'll be sure to tell him you know nothing about my seeing him."

"I've still got your old Toyota," Long said. "It's in the garage, on a trickle charger. It should be okay."

"I think I'll have another martini," Barbara said, holding out her glass.

25

The following morning Barbara called Bart Cross's cell number.

"This is Bart," he drawled.

"We last met in Yuma," Barbara said.

It took him a moment. "Oh, yeah. How are you?"

"Lunch today." She gave him the name and address of a restaurant on the Santa Monica waterfront. "One o'clock sharp," she said.

"Uh, okay."

She hung up. She spent the morning shopping in Santa Monica, especially in a bookshop, where she bought a fairly large-scale map of Santa Fe. Then she went to a RadioShack and bought two prepaid cell phones. Back in the car, she opened the map and marked her rental house and Ed Eagle's house. Then she put on her blond wig and made herself up in an overdone fashion with lots of eye shadow.

AT ONE O'CLOCK, she watched from a distance as Bart arrived at the restaurant and got a table outside. When he was settled she walked over and sat down. "I won't be here long," she said, "so listen carefully." She placed an envelope on the table. "I'll be blunt," she said. "I want two people killed: They'll be together. I'll pay you twenty-five thousand dollars for the job, and another five thousand for expenses. There's ten thousand in this envelope, and the rest will be paid when the work is done. Do you want the job? If not, say so now, and I'll be gone."

Bart lifted the flap of the envelope and peeked inside. "Yes," he said.

"The man is in Santa Fe. His name is Ed Eagle, and he's a lawyer. He cheated me out of a lot of money in the settlement of a lawsuit, and I want him dead by the end of the month. Specifically, I want his throat cut. The other is his wife; I don't care how you kill her."

"That can be done," Bart said.

She pushed the folded map and a key across the table. "There are two houses well marked on this map. Don't open it now. The one on Tano Norte is a guesthouse where you can stay; the other is Eagle's house. Your best chances are going to be morning around nine when he goes to work, or after dinner when he comes home. You'll have to watch him for a while to get the lay of the land."

"All right."

"I want them both dead, together, and you have eighteen days to do it. After that day, you have to vacate the house. If anyone comes to the door looking for me, say that you sublet the house, paid me in advance, and that I may be in San Francisco."

"All right."

"Fly into Double Eagle Airport in Albuquerque, without filing a flight plan, and take a taxi to the big airport." She placed a car key on the table, along with the parking receipt. "This is for a Mercedes station wagon, tan metallic, which is in long-term parking at Albuquerque Airport. The space number is written on the back of the ticket. When the work is done, park the car as nearly as possible to the same spot, and you can give me the key when we meet for your final payment."

She gave him one of the two phones. "Memorize this number," she said, reciting the number of the phone she retained.

"Got it," he said.

"You are to use this phone to contact me and to avoid making calls on your own phone. You will contact me only if absolutely necessary."

"Got it."

"Make no calls from your own cell phone after you leave LA Clear?"

"Clear."

"When you are back in LA, call me and I'll arrange to pay you the remainder of your money. After you have it, destroy the cell phone and scatter the pieces. Any questions?"

"No."

"Call me if you need more information. I'm leaving now. If anyone sees you here with me, tell them I'm a hooker who tried to pick you up. One more thing," she said. "If they're both not dead by the eighteenth day, you're dead." She got up and walked away.

BART PUT THE MONEY and the map into his inside coat pockets. His heart was beating rapidly. This was a gift from heaven, he thought. He put the prepaid phone in his pocket and got out his own cell phone and dialed a number.

"Yes?"

"It's Cross."

"You better have my money."

"That's why I'm calling. I can give you the cash whenever you like."

"Where are you?"

"I'm at a restaurant in Santa Monica." He gave the man the address.

"I'm five minutes away," the man said.

Shortly, a car pulled up in front of the restaurant, and a large man got out. He came to the table.

"Sit down," Bart said.

"I don't have time."

"If you want to get paid, sit down."

The man sat down. "You're a pain in the ass," he said.

Bart slid the menu across the table. "The money is under it," he said. "Put it in your pocket."

The man did so. "Nice doing business with you," he said.

"We won't be doing any more business," Bart said.

"Fine by me." The man got up, got in his car and drove away.

The waitress appeared. "Is anyone joining you?" she asked.

"No. I shooed away a hooker, and some guy mistook me for somebody else." He ordered lunch and sat, basking in the sunshine, feeling great.

BARBARA DROVE BACK to Bel Air, to Jimmy's house, thinking hard all the way. She had to have a backup plan. There was simply no way she was going to put all her eggs in a basket named Bart Cross.

She was still thinking about it when she walked into the house.

"Hey," Jimmy called from his study.

She walked into the room and fell into a chair. "I know how early it is, but I need a drink."

Jimmy got up and made a martini for her. "Here you go."

"I met with Bart," she said.

"Everything go all right?" he asked.

"Seemed to. Do you think he has any guts?"

"Guts is something Bart has never been short of," Jimmy replied. "I saw him take a bigger guy in a bar fight in Long Beach once. Bart was smaller, but he was meaner, too."

"I hope you're right," Barbara replied.

Jimmy shrugged. "Worse comes to worst," he said, "if you want something done right, you have to do it yourself."

And like that, she had her backup plan.

26

Todd Bacon sat at his computer, composing a report to Holly Barker. He was embarrassed to have so little to tell her. He pressed the send button and sat, staring at his computer screen, wondering what to do next. As he watched, an e-mail notice appeared in the lower right-hand corner. He checked his inbox.

Call me at this number, the unsigned message read.

Todd called the number.

"Sounds like you're coming up dry," Holly Barker said, without preamble.

"So far," Todd admitted. "I believe he was here, but now I think he may have left town."

"I understand why you believe that," Holly said, "but don't believe it. If he was in town he'd want you to think he'd left."

"Well, then, he's pretty convincing," Todd replied. "I don't know what to do next."

"Stop looking for him," Holly said. "Find Lauren Cade. After all, she's what got you where you are."

"I don't even have a photograph," he complained. "All I've got is the description you gave me."

"That has already changed," Holly said. "She's no longer a blonde, I can promise you that, but she can't change her body. She's a slim girl with impressive breasts and a skinny ass. I know the tits can be bought off the shelf, but not the ass. Look for the combination. Go where people go—restaurants, grocery stores, shops. She's in a new town, and she's going to want new clothes. Everybody in Santa Fe goes to the Plaza sooner or later. Go there and look. You're a good-looking guy. When you see someone with that combination who's not a blonde, try and pick her up. You might get lucky."

"They didn't train me for this at the Farm," he said, referring to the Agency's training facility in the Virginia countryside.

"Then you'll have to train yourself," Holly said. "When you find her, you'll have found a new skill."

"If I were an older guy with a younger girl, like him," Todd said, "I'd stick close to her."

"Maybe he will," Holly said, "but don't expect him to look his age. He's good at changing his appearance, and he's not going to make himself look like an old man while he's with someone as great-looking as Lauren. If he's sixtyish, look for a man who looks fifty or younger."

"Are you sure I can spend the Agency's time on something as ephemeral as this?"

"The boss has already made that decision," she said. "He has, in effect, cut you loose. You're just going to have to get out there and give yourself a chance to get lucky. Gotta run." Holly hung up.

Todd hung up and sat there, thinking. Holly's suggestion seemed crazy, too random. He was convinced he had a better chance of finding Teddy's airplane than he did of finding Teddy himself.

He brought up his flight-planning program on the computer and looked at the Santa Fe area. Maybe Teddy had just moved his airplane to a less conspicuous spot. Todd thought about what he himself would look for if he were deciding at which airport to land. He'd want fuel, certainly, so that would eliminate some little backcountry dirt strip. He'd want maintenance services, too. Small aircraft needed taking care of, and he'd want a mechanic, maybe an avionics shop as well. The field should be within easy driving distance of Santa Fe, say fifty to sixty miles.

He looked at all the surrounding airports. There was Albuquerque International, but that was too big, and fuel and services would be too expensive. There were a dozen or so small airports, mostly shown on the map as red circles, but many of those wouldn't have the necessary services. There were two general aviation airports marked in blue: Double Eagle, outside Albuquerque, which was fifty miles or so away, and Las Vegas, to the east, about the same distance.

He checked his airport guide: Las Vegas had no services, except a restaurant, but Double Eagle had a full-service FBO, with both mechanical and avionics shops.

Todd thought about flying down there, but it was only fifty miles; it would be almost as fast to drive. He got his car from the garage and drove south through town to I-25. He set his cruise control at five miles an hour under the speed limit and tried to stay awake.

TEDDY AND LAUREN LEFT their rented house and drove out Old Pecos Trail.

"How long a drive is it?" Lauren asked.

"An hour or so. Then it will take you at least two hours to drive to Las Vegas and pick me up."

"I'm sleepy," Lauren said, moving her seat back to a reclining position. "I'm going to take a nap."

Teddy set his cruise control at five miles an hour over the speed limit and let the SUV take care of itself. There wasn't a lot of traffic, and soon he began overtaking a red Taurus ahead of him, driven by a man alone. He moved to the left lane and let his car overtake the other. As he passed it, he caught a glimpse of the driver's profile. It was the young Agency man, Todd Bacon, whom

Teddy had seen at Geronimo a couple of nights before. He put on a baseball cap and increased his speed.

TODD WATCHED the Jeep Grand Cherokee sail past him and thought nothing of it. If there'd been a couple inside he would have been more interested.

TEDDY KEPT HIS speed up all the way to his exit from the interstate, and by that time Bacon's car was out of sight. It was unlikely that they'd be heading to the same destination. He drove to the airport and, in the parking lot, woke up Lauren. "We're here," he said. "Do you want some coffee before you start for Las Vegas?"

"No," she replied, stretching. "I'm fine." He got out, and she moved to the driver's seat. "See you there," she said, then pulled out of the parking lot and headed back toward the interstate.

TODD REACHED HIS EXIT and turned toward Double Eagle Airport. Halfway there he passed the Grand Cherokee he'd seen earlier, but this time it was driven by a woman. The two cars passed too quickly for him to get a good look at her.

AT DOUBLE EAGLE, Teddy went to the paint shop and found his airplane sitting on the ramp. He inspected the paint job on the new tail number, then went into the office and paid his bill, getting a five percent discount for cash. He went back to the airplane, did a quick preflight, checking the tanks to be sure the fuel he'd ordered was aboard; then Teddy got into the Cessna, started the engine and began running through his checklist.

TODD PARKED HIS CAR and walked past the FBO and onto the ramp, to check the place out. A Beech Baron was landing, and he watched it touch down; then he turned and began walking to the FBO. Then he saw something that interested him. There was a paint shop on the field, something that hadn't been mentioned in his airport guide.

He walked into the hangar and saw a small glassed-in office to one side, where a man worked at a desk. He rapped on the door. "Good morning," he said.

"Morning," the man replied. "Can I help you?"

"I was just wondering, have you had a Cessna 182 RG in recently for some paint work?"

"Yeah, I had a customer who wanted his tail number changed."

Todd tried to control his excitement. "When was that?"

"He paid his bill less than half an hour ago," the man replied. "He might still be on the line."

Todd ran out of the hangar and looked at the parked airplanes, running along the line. There were plenty of Cessnas, as usual, but he didn't see a 182 RG. Then he turned and looked toward the runway, where a Cessna was beginning its takeoff roll. He watched it lift off and then saw the landing gear come up. He squinted, but it was too far away to read the registration number on the side. He kept watching it as it climbed, until it began making a turn to the east and disappeared.

Todd ran back to the paint-shop office. "Can you tell me what tail number you painted on that airplane?" he asked.

"Sure," the man replied, and gave him the number.

"Do you have a name and address for the owner?" Todd asked. "I'm looking to buy a nice 182 RG."

The man looked through some papers stacked on his desk. "Yeah, here's the FAA form. I'm afraid he's from Arkansas, though, and he told me he was headed home."

"Let me make a note of this, and I'll call him," Todd said, scribbling down the information. He thanked the man, then ran for his car.

BART CROSS TAXIED HIS Beech Baron to the ramp at Double Eagle Airport, then ran through his shutdown checklist and cut the engines. He got his luggage out of the rear compartment, then went into the FBO to arrange for parking and fuel. Shortly after that he was on his way to Albuquerque International Airport to pick up the Mercedes station wagon.

27

Todd gunned his red Taurus and headed for the interstate. Teddy, if he wasn't really going to Arkansas, would likely be headed for Las Vegas, the second of his airport guesses, and Lauren would be driving there to meet him. She had at least a half-hour head start—more like three-quarters of an hour. He turned onto the I-25 and set his cruise control at seventy-five. This was no time to get stopped by the state patrol.

TEDDY LANDED at Las Vegas after a forty-minute flight and taxied up to the little municipal terminal. He gave his fuel order to a lineman, then went inside to the front desk, where a man sat behind the counter. "Good afternoon," he said.

"Hey," the man replied. "You just refueling? Anything else we can do for you?"

"I'd like to hangar my airplane," Teddy said. "Do you have any space?"

"I've got a T-hangar that might work for you," the man said. "Let's go take a look." He led the way to an old Jeep, and they drove along a line of hangars and stopped at the last one. The man unlocked a padlock and pulled up the bifold door. "You've got power, but if you want heat, you'll have to furnish your own heater."

Teddy looked around. The hangar was ideal—clean and conveniently located.

"The price includes pull-out service when you need the airplane, or I'll give you a key and you can pull it out yourself, if you feel like it."

Teddy asked the price, negotiated and took the hangar for a three-month period. "I'd be grateful if you'd keep this confidential," he said to the man. "The tax man might be around."

"Sure thing," the man replied, grinning.

They drove back to the terminal, and Teddy paid in cash for the rental and the fuel and collected his hangar key, then went over to the little airport restaurant to have a cheeseburger and to wait for Lauren to catch up. He looked at his watch and figured he had an hour to wait. When he had been there for forty-five minutes, he ordered a burger for her and had it put into a bag.

She arrived on time, and he drove back so that she could eat her burger on the way to Santa Fe.

TODD HAD PASSED Santa Fe and had been on the road for an hour and a half when he saw the tan Grand Cherokee approaching in the opposite lane, with a man driving and a woman in the passenger seat. He had just passed the exit for Serafina, and he didn't know how far it was to the next exit. He was about to drive across the meridian of the four-lane highway when he checked his mirror and saw a car approaching from behind him with something on the roof. He switched off the cruise control and let his speed drop, while cursing his bad luck. It was a state patrol car, and it stayed behind him all the way to the Los Montoyas exit, where he was able to make a U-turn and head back toward Santa Fe. He put his foot down, then turned the cruise control on again at ninety. He hoped the police car was the only one in the sector.

TEDDY SAW THE TAURUS carrying Todd Bacon coming and watched him pass, then disappear in his rearview mirror. He got off the interstate at the next exit, opened the glove compartment and handed Lauren a map. "Navigate me to Santa Fe on the surface roads," he said. "We just passed Bacon going the other way, and he saw me."

She opened the map and told him to take the next right. When they got to Santa Fe, Teddy drove to the dealer where he had bought the Grand Cherokee, found the same salesman and made a deal to trade for a very nice, low-mileage Volvo station wagon with four-wheel drive and winter tires.

"I'm not going to let this guy run me out of Santa Fe," he said to Lauren as they drove toward home. When they arrived there he went immediately to his computer and went through the Agency mainframe to access the New Mexico Department of Motor Vehicles and started making changes.

TODD GOT OFF the interstate at the Santa Fe exit, surprised that he had not caught up with Teddy's Grand Cherokee. He drove into town on Old Pecos Trail, checking every parking lot for the SUV but not seeing it. He drove back to La Fonda, parked the car, went upstairs and got on his computer. He logged in to the Agency mainframe and accessed the New Mexico DMV. He did a search for tan Grand Cherokees and found four registered in Santa Fe. He looked away for a moment to find a pad to write on, and when he returned his attention to the computer screen there were only three Grand Cherokees. He could have sworn there had been four a moment before, but he wasn't positive. He jotted down the names and addresses of the owners and went back to his car. He was going to start running them down now.

TEDDY HAD CHANGED the owner's name and address to one in Albuquerque. Now he changed the name and address of the Volvo to a Taos owner, then exited the Agency mainframe.

Lauren, who had been watching over his shoulder, said, "That was very slick." She kissed him on the neck.

28

Bart Cross found the Mercedes station wagon, transferred his luggage from the taxi and drove out of the airport area to I-25 and headed north to Santa Fe.

He had flown Jim Long to the city a couple of times when he was shooting films here and had once stayed for three weeks, when he and a stuntman had driven a stagecoach in a Western, so he knew the town pretty well. He drove through downtown and around the Plaza, just to get a look at it again, then picked up some food for dinner and headed north on the road to Taos and turned off at the sign for Las Campanas. He followed the road map Barbara had given him and found the house and guesthouse with no problem. He put the station wagon in the garage as instructed, put his clothes away and heated up the roast chicken he had bought for dinner. While it was warming, he found the liquor and poured himself a bourbon over ice. He had just turned on the TV for the news and sat down with his drink when he heard car doors slamming outside.

"THERE'S A LIGHT ON," Vittorio said as they pulled up at dusk.

"She's finally come home," Cupie replied. He got out of the car, pulled his Smith & Wesson snub-nosed .38 from the holster, checked that it was loaded and snapped the cylinder shut. He did not return it to the holster.

"Stand beside the front door and cover me," Vittorio said, then stepped up to the front door and used the knocker.

BART ALREADY HAD a gun in his hand. He looked through the little window in the door and saw an Indian in a flat-brimmed black hat. He leaned on the wall next to the door, the gun in his fist, and opened the door a foot or so with his left. "Yeah?"

"I'm sorry to bother you," Vittorio said, "but I'm looking for Mrs. Keeler, who rents this house."

"I'm a subletter," Bart said. "There's no one else here."

"May I ask how you came to sublet the place?" Vittorio asked pleasantly.

"There was an ad on a bulletin board where I work, at a film studio in LA. We did the deal over the phone. She was in San Francisco."

"How long will you be subletting?" Vittorio asked.

"Till the end of the month—longer if my work here calls for it. Will you excuse me? My dinner's getting cold."

"Of course. I'm sorry to have troubled you," Vittorio said. He turned to go back to the car.

Bart watched through the window in the door as another man fell in behind the Indian, and saw him returning a pistol to its holster. He locked the door, found the cell phone Eleanor Keeler had given him and called the number he had memorized.

BACK IN THE CAR, Cupie slammed his door. "Now can we stop coming out to this place all the time, please?"

"All right, all right. Sounds like Barbara doesn't need her house anymore. You think she's really in San Francisco?"

"That's what I heard the guy say," Cupie replied. "If he did the sublet deal on the phone, he would have been calling a San Francisco number, if that's where she was. And by the way, he had a gun in his right hand, out of sight."

"Did you see it?"

"No," Cupie said. "I smelled the oil."

BARBARA GOT TO the cell phone in her purse on the fifth ring. "Yes?"

"It's me. I'm at the house. There were two men just here looking for you: an Indian and a fat guy, like you said."

"That's Vittorio and Cupie Dalton," she said. "What did you tell them?"

"That I saw an ad on a bulletin board at the studio and called you in San Francisco and sublet the place. They asked how long I would be here, and I said until the end of the month, maybe longer, if work required. They left peaceably, and I saw Dalton putting away a gun as he went."

"If they come back again, kill them, and I'll pay you another ten grand," she said.

"Hey, wait," Bart replied. "Let's not litter the landscape out here with corpses before I get the main job done."

"They've seen you now. It would be in your interests to kill them as quickly as possible."

"We'll see. I'm not ready to commit to that right now."

"They work for Eagle," she said. "When it's done, they'll come looking for you, and I don't want them to find you."

"Look, lady, I don't want this job to spin out of control. Jim will cover my alibi that I'm working for him here."

"We'll see. I'll mention it to him. He's coming back there in a few days to see how his shooting is going."

"Tell him to find me some work here when he comes," Bart said. "That'll help with my alibi."

"All right." She hung up.

VITTORIO AND CUPIE SAT in the Blue Corn Café on Water Street and ate dinner.

"I think he's a hit man she hired," Vittorio said.

"Why do you think that?" Cupie asked.

"That's just how it smells," Vittorio said. "It doesn't make any sense for Barbara to be in San Francisco, or to sublet the house before she's done with Eagle. We need to keep an eye out for this guy."

"I didn't see him," Cupie said. "What does he look like?"

"Six-two, dark hair, thirty-five to forty, athletic; wearing jeans, cowboy boots and a Western-style shirt."

"I didn't see a car."

"In the garage," Vittorio said. "We don't know what kind. That's a disadvantage for us."

"Jesus, this food is hot," Cupie said, wiping his sweaty face with his napkin.

"It's the peppers," Vittorio replied. "Better get used to it while you're in Santa Fe."

"I'll never get used to peppers," Cupie said.

"We need to be at Eagle's house early tomorrow, before he leaves for work. That's a vulnerable time for him."

"You think this guy has already got him staked out? Looks like he just got here."

"No way to know," Vittorio said.

TODD BACON GOT BACK to his hotel room hot and tired. He had chased down three Grand Cherokees, owned, respectively, by an old lady, a local doctor and a couple in their seventies. He had been to the Las Vegas Airport and talked with the man who ran the place, who told him he hadn't seen any Cessnas that day and that he hadn't had any hangar space for rent.

That didn't make any sense at all. There was no other airport where Teddy Fay could have taken his airplane except Las Vegas, given the direction he had flown in and the fact that Lauren Cade had obviously picked him up there. He still hadn't gotten a decent look at either of them, and the Grand Cherokee had just melted away in Santa Fe.

This was driving Todd nuts.

29

Shortly before dawn Vittorio had scrambled up the hill above Eagle's house and placed himself in a nest of good-sized rocks. He had a hunting rifle with a big scope by his side, already sighted for the distance. Cupie was down the road below the house, in some other rocks, positioned to fire into an automobile racing down the hill from Eagle's place.

They were using handheld radios the size of a Snickers bar, and Cupie pressed the push-to-talk button. "Are you sure this is the best place for me?" he asked. "I can't see a goddamned thing."

"You can see the road in both directions, can't you?" Vittorio replied.

"Well, yeah."

"Then you can warn me when a car is coming up the

hill, so I can be ready, and I can warn you when one's on the way down the hill, having made an attempt on our client."

"Yeah to that, too," Cupie admitted. "I just won't see any of the action."

"I've got the action covered," Vittorio said. "You just keep your eye on the road, and don't get seen by anybody."

"You expect me to hit the driver of a car, first shot, with a revolver with a two-inch barrel?"

"Okay, we'll get you a better piece for the job. You'd have a shot anyway, if you extend your arm, brace against a rock, then cock and squeeze. Don't try it double-action."

"Yeah, yeah, yeah," Cupie muttered. "I'm going to bring some kind of folding chair, too. This fucking rock is incompatible with my ass."

"You've got your own built-in cushion, Cupie." Vittorio chuckled. "Quit your bitching."

"Have you got the coffee Thermos?"

"Yes, I have."

"I want one of my own tomorrow."

"You had your coffee before we left," Vittorio pointed out.

"I can't have a second cup?"

"Tomorrow you can have all you can choke down."

"It's your fault if I fall asleep."

The sun crested the mountain above the house, and

the light from it worked its way across the parking area in front and eventually illuminated the front door. It was close to eight before the door opened and Eagle stepped onto the front porch, followed by Susannah. He turned, gave her a kiss and walked toward his black Mercedes, while Susannah, with a wave, went back inside.

Vittorio pressed the button. "He's outside. Anybody coming?"

"Nobody either way," Cupie replied.

"He's in the car, and it's moving. It's a black Mercedes. Don't shoot him."

"No? I was looking forward to it," Cupie growled. "Okay, he's driving past."

"Can he see you? He won't like it if he knows we're staking out his house."

"He won't see me. There, he's gone, down the mountain toward Tesuque. Can we get out of here now?"

"Let me get the car, and I'll pick you up in three minutes."

"Bring coffee," Cupie said.

TEDDY FAY LAY IN BED, Lauren's head on his shoulder. They had made love—Lauren liked it best in the morning—and she had gone back to sleep.

Teddy reviewed his day. It was his practice when settling in a place, however temporarily, to immediately start work on new identity documents, so as to be prepared to run if he found himself being pursued. He'd start that this morning.

He was being pursued, sort of, but his pursuer wasn't certain he was still in Santa Fe. He'd had a call from the man at Las Vegas Airport: Bacon had been there inquiring about him, but the man had told him no Cessnas had landed there and that there was no hangar space available. That would have confused Bacon.

Teddy had put himself in the younger man's shoes: He was looking for two people, neither of which he had ever had a good look at, nor did he have photographs of them. He didn't know where they were living or what car they were driving, and their trail had gone cold. How long would Bacon hang on before giving up?

Teddy felt some sympathy for the boy. He had outfitted hundreds of young agents over his decades with the Agency, sending them out to God knew where, to die or to return, often disillusioned with the work they were doing. A few came back excited, still wanting more. Bacon would be one of those, given Teddy's experience of him.

Teddy had given a lot of thought as to whether to kill Todd. He would, if he had to, if the boy got too close, but if he had to, if Bacon simply disappeared, as Teddy was capable of making him do, then they might send out another agent, maybe more than one, and he would certainly have to move.

Teddy liked Santa Fe, and so did Lauren, and he didn't want to move. If he could convince Todd Bacon they were gone, then maybe they could stay; maybe they could make a real home here. Teddy missed having a home. He was a nest builder, and he always assembled the twigs necessary to make that nest. His new safe would arrive today, so he could pack away his equipment and hunker down. He was looking forward to that. He wished he had some pictures to hang. They would have to look in on the galleries on Canyon Road.

TODD BACON ENDED HIS phone call to Holly Barker, his face red and hot. She was starting to think of him as an amateur; he could tell by the sound of her voice. He could hear the exasperation as she made more suggestions.

Now he was going to have to start cruising grocery stores and ladies' shops, looking for Lauren Cade. It was the least effective thing he could do, he thought, but he couldn't think of anything better.

He'd thought of checking out new hookups of electricity and telephones, but if Teddy had sublet a house, those things would already exist, so that was a time waster. What else did new people in town have to do for themselves besides utilities? He couldn't think of anything.

Maybe Holly was right; maybe Lauren would want

new clothes in a new town, and maybe she would go shopping for them. Maybe the Plaza was where he should waste his time looking for her.

Or maybe he should just spend the day in bed with the newspapers and half a bottle of bourbon. He would be just as effective that way, and he wouldn't strain himself.

"Oh, what the fuck," he said aloud, getting out of bed and heading for the shower.

30

Tip Hanks finished an afternoon of hitting with his driver and fairway woods on the practice range. He had a drink at the clubhouse bar, then drove home. He showered and put on a robe, then went into his study to check his e-mail.

He stuck his head into Dolly's office. "Anything going on?"

"A couple of phone messages," she replied. "They're next to your computer. How was your practice session?"

"Just great. My swing is right where it should be. I'm looking forward to this weekend." He had a tournament in San Diego.

"Good news. You must be tired. Can I get you a drink?"

"Sure," he said. "I'm just going to check my e-mail."

She got up and went to the bar while he went to his computer. Nothing pressing: just one e-mail from his agent and one from his clothing sponsor, and he dealt with those.

She walked up behind him, set his drink near his computer mouse and began massaging his shoulders.

"God, that's good," he said, relaxing to her touch. "Where did you learn to do that?"

"From having it done to me, I guess," she replied. She pulled his head back to nestle between her breasts and continued to rub his neck and shoulders.

"Mmmm, nice cushion," he said, feeling for his drink and taking a pull at it. "You're a woman of many talents." He had enjoyed her cooking a while back, but he had kept his hands off her.

She spun him around and pulled his head back to her breasts, still rubbing his neck.

He was becoming aroused now. He kissed her on a breast, and she made a welcoming noise. He pushed her sweater up and unhooked her bra. Her nipples answered the call.

"You're bad," she breathed.

"You make me want to be bad," he said.

She pushed him back in his chair and knelt in front of him. She was tall enough for him to reach her lips, and they kissed repeatedly.

His robe fell open, and she took him in her hand and stroked him. He was already fully erect, and she bent down and kissed his penis a few times. He pulled her head down, and she took him into her mouth. He was making all the right noises; then suddenly he came.

She continued what she was doing until he fell back, spent, then took him by the hand, picked up his drink and led him to his bed, pulling back the covers. "You need a nap," she said, setting his drink on the bedside table.

"Take a nap with me," he said.

"No, you need the rest," she replied. "I'll be here when you wake up."

She was lying on the sofa in the study a couple of hours later, when he came and knelt beside her. "Your turn," he said, undoing her jeans and pulling them off.

She lay back and enjoyed herself. He was really good at this, she thought—not quite as good as Ellie, but very good. Where had Ellie gone? Why hadn't she said good-bye?

VITTORIO AND CUPIE had assumed their positions near Eagle's house, waiting for him to arrive home from work, when Cupie came on the radio. "Mercedes station wagon heading up the hill. You read?"

"I read you," Vittorio said. "I'm watching for it."

The station wagon appeared, driving slowly up the road; then it slowed to a crawl in front of Eagle's house, as if the driver wanted to get a good look at it, then continued up the road and out of sight.

"Whoever that was took a good look at the house," Vittorio said into the radio. "I couldn't see who was driving; the car's roof was in the way."

"That's not the sort of car a hit man would drive," Cupie said. "He'd be in a rental if he was from out of town."

"Agreed," Vittorio said. He sat for a few minutes, thinking that it was good to have Cupie around. He spent too many of his days alone, and it was nice to have somebody to bitch at.

He jerked back to reality as the station wagon reappeared, headed down the hill. Vittorio still couldn't see the driver. He picked up the radio. "The Mercedes is headed back down the hill. See if you can get a look at the driver."

"Here it comes," Cupie said. "Naw, the setting sun is reflecting in the windshield; can't see past that. He's gone. Did he check out the house again?"

"He didn't seem to slow down, but he was driving slowly," Vittorio replied.

"Hey, here comes Eagle," Cupie said.

"I've got him," Vittorio replied as Eagle's car appeared down the road. The black Mercedes pulled into the driveway, and Eagle got out, looked around, then went into the house. He didn't seem to use the garage much. "Okay," Vittorio said into the radio, "he's in the house. I'll pick you up shortly."

He got the car and drove down to where Cupie waited.

"Let's stop at the Tesuque Market and get a drink and some dinner," Cupie said.

"Good idea," Vittorio replied. The Tesuque Market was a grocery, restaurant and bar that did a good business from the local residents and some tourists, too. "Look," Vittorio said, pointing at the cars parked outside. The Mercedes station wagon was among them.

Vittorio found a parking place, and they found a table on the front porch and ordered a drink. As they were looking at the menu a man walked past their table, a newspaper under his arm and a bag of food in his other hand. He got into the station wagon, backed out and drove away.

"You know who that is?" Vittorio asked.

"Never saw him before," Cupie replied, sipping his drink.

"That's the guy who's staying in Barbara's house."

"You think he's driving her car?"

"That's my guess," Vittorio replied. "If she went to San Francisco or LA she wouldn't drive, would she? She'd fly."

"Yep," Cupie replied. "We need that guy's name."

"The car won't be registered to him. How will we get that?"

Cupie thought about it. "We could hit him over the head and take a look at his wallet."

"There's gotta be a lazier way," Vittorio said. He got up, walked into the market and over to the checkout counter, where a young girl was sitting at the register, looking bored. "Excuse me," Vittorio said to her. "That guy who just walked out: Do you know his name? He looked familiar."

"The tall guy?" she asked.

"Yeah, with the Western shirt."

She looked down at an electronic credit card reader and pushed a couple of buttons. "Barton Cross, it says here," she said.

"Nah, he's not who I thought he was. Thanks." Vittorio returned to the table. "His name is Barton Cross," he said to Cupie.

"Mean anything to you?"

"He said he worked at a movie studio and he was doing some work here. That would probably be on James Long's movie, wouldn't it?"

"Yeah, probably. I think that's the only production in town at the moment."

"What's that studio in LA that Long works out of?"

"Centurion," Cupie replied.

Vittorio got out his cell phone and dialed information, and they connected him.

"Centurion Studios," an operator said.

"Mr. Barton Cross, please."

"Just a moment." There was a click followed by ringing.

"Long Productions," a man's voice said.

"May I speak with Barton Cross," Vittorio asked.

"Bart is on vacation," the man replied. "Can I take a message?"

"Do you know when he'll be back?"

"End of the month, I think."

"I'll call back then." Vittorio hung up. "Bart Cross is on vacation for a couple of weeks."

"Not working in Santa Fe?"

"Nope. On vacation."

"I like him for a hit man," Cupie said.

"So do I," Vittorio replied.

31

Barbara dialed the throwaway cell phone she had given Bart Cross and got no answer. "Damn him!" she said aloud. "I told him to keep that phone handy!"

Her own throwaway suddenly rang. "Yes?"

"It's me," he said. "I was in the shower and didn't get there in time."

"All right," she said. "Are you making progress?"

"I had a good look at the property today," he replied. "I know you want me to use a knife, but I think the better plan is to use a rifle from up the road. There's a good view of the front of the house, and I can get a clean shot when he leaves for work."

"I want you to use the knife," she said. "I want him to have time to think about why he's dying before he does. That won't work with a rifle; you'll just put his lights out. I want her to find him bleeding, too, before you do her. You can shoot her if you want to, after she's seen him."

"You're one angry lady," Bart said.

"Yes, and you don't want me angry at you. Are you doing the things I told you?"

"Yeah, I'm using only this phone, not my own."

"What about credit cards?"

There was a brief silence. "Well . . ."

"You used your own credit card?"

"Just once, at the Tesuque Market."

"Don't you know that can let the police place you in Santa Fe?"

"It won't happen again, and there'll be no reason for them to look at me."

"I want you to take the station wagon back to Albuquerque tomorrow, put it in the same spot in the parking lot, then steal a car."

"That's a bad idea," Bart said. "I'd have to use a credit card. They won't let you pay cash up front."

"Don't you have any false ID?"

"I have one, but it's not a driver's license."

"Then after you leave the wagon in the parking lot, buy a used car and abandon it in the parking lot when you're done. It'll be there for weeks, maybe months, before anyone notices it."

"You paying for a new car?"

"No, that's part of your expenses. You wouldn't have to do this if you hadn't so stupidly used your credit card. I'm just trying to keep you from getting arrested."

"All right, I'll do it your way," he said.

"Take the car back to Albuquerque first thing in the morning."

"All right."

"Call me tomorrow and tell me what you've done."

"I was going to kill him tomorrow morning."

"You're not ready until you fix the car problem," she said, then hung up.

BART WOKE UP LATER than he had planned: It was after nine. He got himself together, got out the car and headed for Albuquerque. As he got onto I-25 he remembered that he hadn't closed the garage door. He thought about going back and doing it, but he would be gone for only a few hours, so what the hell?

He drove to Albuquerque International and re-turned the station wagon to the parking lot, left the ticket under the sun visor and got a cab into town. "Is there a street with a lot of car dealerships?" he asked the driver.

"Yeah, sure."

"Take me there."

The driver dropped him off in front of a Toyota dealer, and Bart strolled around the used lot. He was looking for something old, anonymous, but with fairly low mileage. Instead, he stopped in front of a shiny pickup truck.

A salesman approached. "Nice one, isn't it?"

"Not bad," Bart said, checking the mileage.

"Driven by a woman who had a landscaping business, so it never carried anything heavier than a bag of fertilizer and a few plants. It's not like it was used for construction."

The key was in the ignition, and Bart started the truck. "Let's go for a ride." He returned after driving it three or four miles. It was perfect. "Can you ship it to LA?" he asked.

"Sure. Probably cost you five hundred."

"What are you asking?"

"Ten thousand; that's a wholesale price."

"I'll give you seventy-five hundred, cash."

The man got out his cell phone. "Let me call my boss." He got out of the truck and made the call while Bart walked around the vehicle, looking for flaws. There weren't any, and it had new tires on it.

The salesman closed his phone. "Eight thousand is as low as he'll go," he said to Bart.

Bart thought about it; he had about fourteen thousand on him. "Deal," he said.

"Let's go into the office."

"I'll bring it back end of the month, and you can ship it," he said.

"No problem. I'll make the arrangements today, and if you pay now, all you'll need to do is phone me and I'll pick up the truck at the airport. You'll be flying out, I guess."

"That's right," Bart said. "You can keep a key."

VITTORIO SLOWED AS HE neared Barbara's little guesthouse. "The garage door is open," he said, "and there's no car inside."

"Why don't we see if we can get into the house through there?" Cupie offered.

They pulled into the driveway and got out. Vittorio led the way into the garage. "Inside door," he said, pointing. He tried it, but it was locked.

"I can handle that," Cupie said, taking out his wallet and removing a set of lock picks he'd made from a filed-down hacksaw blade. He had the door open in less than a minute.

Both men wiped their feet carefully, then stepped inside. It was a mess.

"The guy's a pig," Cupie said. "He's only been here a couple of days, and look at it."

They poked around the living room, where dirty plates and chicken bones had been abandoned, then went into the bedroom.

Vittorio opened a bureau drawer. "Looka here," he said, pulling a sock onto his hand and holding up a Beretta nine-millimeter pistol. "And a silencer, too," he said, holding up the tube. "Nice work," he said, inspecting it. He replaced the two items and looked further. "And this," he said, holding up a large bowie knife and removing it from its holster.

"It's practically a sword," Cupie said. "What is it, a foot long?"

"About a ten-inch blade," Vittorio said. "And you could shave with it. Why would a guy travel with an ax like that?"

"Maybe he plans to use it," Cupie said.

They made sure the place was as they'd found it, then got out.

"Where do you suppose Cross is?" Cupie asked.

"He won't find Eagle coming or going," Vittorio said. "He's safe in his office at this hour."

BART PULLED INTO his garage early in the afternoon, went inside and called Barbara.

"Yes?"

"I'm all set," he said. "I bought a vehicle."

"What kind?"

"An old pickup truck. I'll ditch it when I leave."

"When, then?"

"Tomorrow morning," Bart replied.

"Call me when you're done."

32

Todd Bacon left La Fonda and stepped into the Plaza, the main square of Santa Fe. Two sides of the area contained shops and art galleries, while a third side was taken up by the old Palace of the Governors, the seventeenth-century seat of power in the city's early days. The fourth side was of less interest to him, since it was mostly taken up by restaurants and a bank.

He began working his way through the shops on the opposite side from the Palace of the Governors. They specialized mostly in women's clothing and art. He wandered through each shop, looking cursorily at its wares and paying particular attention to the female shoppers. They came in all shapes and sizes except one—fairly tall, slender, with noticeable breasts: Those seemed to be in short supply.

He tried the west side of the Plaza, which had more art and less clothing, but came up dry. Finally he turned his attention to the Palace of the Governors.

An Indian street market featuring silver jewelry and some pottery took up most of the broad sidewalk under a portico, and the crowd was thick around the sellers, who had spread their wares on blankets. Todd drifted through the crowd, glancing at the displays but paying more attention to the shoppers.

They seemed to be mostly tourists, sloppily dressed and carrying shopping bags. Then one woman stopped him in his tracks: She fit the physical description of Lauren Cade—five-seven, made taller by Western boots that looked new; chestnut-colored hair; and a tight sweater, secured at the waist with a broad belt and a silver buckle that accentuated her breasts, which were more than ample.

She would have attracted his attention at any time, but since she was the first woman he had seen who matched what he was looking for, he had trouble keeping his eyes off her.

She locked eyes with him for a moment, then went back to looking at jewelry. He noticed that she was wearing a gold wedding band. That would have been disappointing on a personal level, but it fit a woman who was traveling with a man.

Todd had a creepy feeling that he was being watched from behind, and it occurred to him that if he was right about the woman, her companion might be nearby, and if it was Teddy Fay, he was dangerous, even in a public place.

He turned around and scanned the faces of the men present: Two of them could be Teddy, he thought, but they were both with women, so he turned back to watch the putative Lauren. She was nowhere to be seen.

Todd began searching the crowd for her, trying not to show the panic he felt at losing her. Then his eyes swept the Plaza and he saw her, already on the other side of the square, disappearing down a side street. He broke out of the crowd and began to run.

LAUREN MADE IT AROUND the corner, but as she hazarded a glance back, she saw the man break from the crowd and start across the Plaza. *Damn*, she thought, another two seconds and he wouldn't have seen her.

She hurried across the street and into a building that had a restaurant on the ground floor and a stairway up to galleries on a mezzanine. She ran up the stairs and looked for a way out of the rear of the building. An exit sign over a door drew her, and she opened it to find fire stairs descending to an exterior door. In a moment she was out the rear of the building and into a parking lot that faced the street behind. She ran to the sidewalk and turned up the street in the general direction of where she had parked the car, near the cathedral.

TODD REACHED THE CORNER and surveyed the street, which was not crowded. He couldn't see her anywhere. He started down the street, looking through the windows of each shop, then crossed and worked his way up the other side, toward the Plaza. She was nowhere to be found.

LAUREN CROSSED THE STREET in front of the cathedral and hurried to where she had parked the green Volvo station wagon. Before she approached the car she checked carefully to be sure the man was not behind her; then she jumped into the car, got it started and pulled into traffic, which was moving slowly because of a stop sign at the end of the block.

She kept checking the rearview mirror, looking for the man, but she didn't see him. Then it was her turn at the stop sign, and a moment before she was able to turn, she checked the mirror again and saw him come running around the corner into her block.

TODD STOOD ON the bumper of a pickup truck parked on the block, to give himself some more height, and looked up and down the street. The slow-moving traffic was being held up by a stop sign. He got down from the truck's bumper and began walking down the middle of the street, checking the driver of each car.

LAUREN TURNED RIGHT AT the stop sign, because that would put her on the opposite side of the car from her pursuer. She forced herself not to do it quickly, because that might attract his attention. Ahead of her was a long, straight stretch of roadway, leading to and crossing a main artery, so she took the first left, then another, then a right, then another right, which she hoped would keep her out of his line of sight.

TODD REACHED THE CORNER just after a green Volvo station wagon made a turn to the right, then drove away. A woman was at the wheel, but all he could see was the back of her head. He began running, but before he could close the distance between them she turned left, and he lost sight of her again. By the time he reached the next corner she had disappeared. The big problem was, he had no idea if the woman in the car was the woman at the Indian market.

LAUREN MADE IT BACK to Canyon Road, then turned onto Garcia Street and pointed the car toward home, constantly checking her mirror. Once home, she pulled into the garage and closed the door behind her. She jumped out of the car and ran into the kitchen, where Teddy was sipping a cup of tea.

"I think I got made," she said.

"Where?"

"At the jewelry market in front of the Palace of the Governors," she said. "When he turned his back for a moment I got out of there, but I think he spotted me. Then I lost him for about ten minutes, but he nearly caught up to me in traffic, though he couldn't have had any idea which car I was in."

"Do you think the Volvo is blown?" Teddy asked.

"No, I don't think so."

"Describe the man."

"Six feet, a hundred and eighty, short, sandy hair, sort of muscular, like he works out a lot."

"Did you make eye contact?"

"Once, just for a second. Then he turned around and looked at the people behind him. He may have been looking for you."

Teddy put his arms around her and kissed her on the cheek. "He's lucky I wasn't there," he said.

33

Bart Cross woke up at four a.m., shaved, showered and began cleaning up the house. It took him the better part of an hour to make it presentable, then he wiped all the surfaces down with Windex to remove his fingerprints, packed his gear and threw it into the bed of the pickup.

On the front seat were three empty FedEx boxes. Using his super-sharp bowie knife he cut apart two of them and pasted them to the doors of the pickup with two-sided tape. The third box he closed and sealed, and put it back onto the front seat with a clipboard he had bought.

He locked up the place and closed and locked the garage, and by five thirty he was making his way toward Tesuque on dark roads.

He drove up the hill past Ed Eagle's house and found a perch where he could keep an eye on the place through binoculars, then sat down among the rocks and ate a breakfast he had prepared the night before. At about six thirty he heard a car come up the road, but when he looked down the hill in the dim light he saw nothing.

VITTORIO DROPPED OFF CUPIE at his usual rock, then drove past Eagle's house and into the rocks, where he normally parked. He was in place by the time the sun began its climb, and he knew that Eagle would appear around a quarter to eight. He pressed the button on the radio. "You okay, Cupie?"

"Yeah," Cupie responded. "I've got my coffee."

BART KNEW THAT EAGLE arrived at his offices at eight, so he figured him to leave the house fifteen minutes before that. He watched the time carefully. At twenty before eight, he got into the truck, slipped into a navy blue Windbreaker and matching baseball cap, checked his gun and knife, and started down the hill, coasting, so they wouldn't hear any engine noise. At precisely a quarter to eight, Bart pulled into the Eagle driveway at the exact moment when Eagle left the house. As Bart got out of the truck, carrying the empty FedEx box and the clipboard, Eagle stopped on his porch to kiss his wife good-bye.

VITTORIO'S ATTENTION was diverted for a moment as he watched a hawk circling in the sky, hunting. When he looked back at the house he was astonished to see a dark pickup truck parked in Eagle's driveway, and a man in a Windbreaker and baseball cap getting out, as Eagle stood on his front porch, talking with Susannah. Then he saw the FedEx logo on the side of the truck and the box and clipboard the man was carrying, and he relaxed. Just an early FedEx delivery.

BART SMILED to put the two people at ease and walked toward them. "Good morning, Mr. Eagle," he said. "FedEx delivery for you."

Eagle turned and faced him, while his wife went back into the house and closed the door. "You're kind of early, aren't you?"

"Gotta get the day started," Bart replied, handing him the clipboard. "Sign on line one, please; first delivery of the day." He patted his pockets. "Left my pen in the truck."

"That's all right," Eagle said, reaching into an inside pocket. "I've got one."

Now both of Eagle's hands were occupied, and Bart saw his chance. He whipped the bowie knife out of its scabbard stuck down his pants and swung it in a wide arc at Eagle's throat, feeling it hit the mark and seeing the blood spurt. Eagle went down on one knee, clutching at his throat, and Bart backhanded him and knocked him to the ground, then ran for the front door.

VITTORIO COULDN'T BELIEVE what he had seen. He drew his gun and his cell phone simultaneously and dialed 911 as he made his way, running, through the rocks and down the hill.

"Nine-one-one. What is your emergency?" the operator asked.

"I need an ambulance and the police. A man has been knifed in the throat and the assailant is in his house, where his wife is." He gave the address, closed the phone and grabbed his radio. "Cupie, Eagle is down, ambulance on the way. Get up here and be careful; single assailant in the house now!"

BART DREW HIS PISTOL and entered the house, leaving the door open behind him. He saw no one inside. "Mrs. Eagle?" he called. "I have a package for you, too. I need a signature." He got no response. Holding the gun at his side, he made his way toward where he believed the kitchen would be. Then he heard running footsteps from the driveway outside.

"Ed," a voice shouted. "Hold this on the wound and apply pressure."

BART FOUND THE KITCHEN and went out the rear door as fast as he could. He made his way around the corner of the house and peeked at the front porch. Eagle was lying on his back, and whoever had been there must have gone inside. He sprinted for the pickup truck, got it started, backed out and started up the hill, away from Tesuque. In his rearview mirror he saw a fat man huffing and puffing his way up the hill; then he was around a bend and gone.

VITTORIO WENT into the house carefully, his gun drawn. He checked the kitchen, then crept into the living room, which was empty. He was headed toward where he thought the bedrooms would be when he heard the truck start outside and the crunch of tires on gravel. Shit, the guy was gone. "Mrs. Eagle?" he yelled. "Are you all right?"

Susannah Wilde Eagle stepped from a doorway, a pistol held out in front of her, and fired two rounds.

Vittorio was spun around and went down.

———

CUPIE STOPPED TO CHECK on Eagle, who was breathing and pressing a bloody cloth to his throat. "Hang on, Ed, an ambulance is on the way." He walked into the house just in time to hear two gunshots. "Oh, shit," Cupie said aloud. "I hope he hasn't shot Susannah."

BART DROVE AS QUICKLY as he safely could over the hill, then turned toward the north side of Santa Fe and made his way on back roads until he crossed under I-25. He traveled south, toward Albuquerque, keeping parallel with but avoiding I-25, where he knew the state patrol might already be looking for the truck. At one point, nearly to Double Eagle Airport, he stopped and pulled the FedEx signs off the truck, called the dealer from whom he had bought the truck and told him he could pick it up from the parking lot at Double Eagle and ship it to LA, as planned. Then he called Barbara.

"Yes?"

"It's done."

"You're sure he's dead?"

"I cut his throat and left him bleeding out on his front porch."

"What about the woman?"

"Problem there. She went back into the house. I followed her in, but turns out Eagle had two men, those PIs, watching the house. I got out just in time, but I heard shooting from inside. I don't know who fired or got shot."

"Do the PIs know who you are?"

"They don't know my name, and only one of them, the Indian, has seen me."

"Where are you now?"

"I'm nearly to Double Eagle. I'll ditch the car and be in the air in twenty minutes."

"Call me when you're back in town." She hung up, and so did he.

He drove the last mile to Double Eagle, got his gear out of the truck and wiped the vehicle down with Windex, then hurried to the ramp where his airplane was parked. He'd already paid for his fuel and parking, and he wasn't going to file a flight plan.

He got the engines started and began working through his checklist as he taxied. At the end of the runway he did a quick run-up of the engines, then announced his intentions over the airport frequency, checked for landing traffic, then taxied onto the runway and shoved the throttles forward.

Half an hour later he was at sixteen thousand five hundred feet, sucking oxygen, on his way to Burbank Airport, in the San Fernando Valley, near where he lived. He felt elated.

34

Vittorio held out a hand and yelled, "Don't shoot, Susannah!"

"Vittorio?" she asked. "My God, have I shot you?"

"Call nine-one-one and tell them we need two ambulances instead of one," Vittorio replied, struggling to sit up and check his wounds. He found he had taken a bullet high and to the left in his chest, and after checking his breathing and the blood flow, he figured it had missed the lung and the artery. "You have any bandages?" he asked Susannah. "Just a clean dishcloth will do."

She ran to the kitchen and returned with a dishcloth, and he pressed it to his chest. "Where's Ed?" she asked.

"He's on the front porch. Cupie is with him."

She ran for the front door.

Vittorio changed his position for comfort and heard

something hit the tile floor. He looked behind him and saw a bloody, intact bullet on the floor. Thank God she had been using hardball ammunition instead of hollow-points. He calculated that unless they found internal injuries he hadn't figured on, he would need only stitches, a dressing and a shot of ampicillin.

He felt exhausted now, having used up all his available adrenaline. "Cupie!" he yelled.

Cupie came running through the doorway. "Vittorio, you okay?"

"Not exactly," he said. "Did she call for another ambulance?"

"I did," Cupie said, kneeling beside him and pulling away the dishcloth so that he could check Vittorio's wound. "Not bleeding too bad," he said. "Just enough to keep it clean." He checked Vittorio's back. "Same here," he said. "I think you got lucky. Hang on, I'll get another dishcloth."

Vittorio waited patiently for him to return with the cloth, which Cupie pressed to his back. Then Cupie leaned him against the wall. "Did you get a look at the guy?" he asked.

"Nah," Cupie said. "He was already in the truck when I saw it, and I had the light-reflection problem on the window. How about you?"

"He was wearing a baseball cap, and I was looking down on him."

"Was it Bart Cross?"

"I don't know. He was tall enough, but that wasn't Cross's vehicle."

"He could have stolen it," Cupie said. "I hear sirens."

"About time," Vittorio said. "Don't let them give me morphine. I want a clear head."

"Whatever you say," Cupie replied.

"How's Eagle?"

"I don't know," Cupie said. "Ed is still bleeding, but holding pressure on the wound may be slowing it down. The cut looks long but shallow to me. Susannah is on the case."

The sirens got louder, and there was the sound of tires crunching on gravel and doors slamming.

"I'll get somebody in here," Cupie said.

Vittorio started to speak, but a wave of nausea overcame him. He took a deep breath, then sagged to the floor and passed out.

VITTORIO WOKE UP in a hospital room with Cupie asleep in a chair next to him. He fumbled around, found the control unit for the bed and sat himself up and elevated his feet.

Cupie stirred. "You're awake?"

"Yeah. How's Eagle?"

"In surgery. They have a vascular specialist here, so Ed's got some sort of shot. I'm type O, so I gave some blood. Eagle is A-positive."

"I'm A-positive," Vittorio said.

"You can't spare any," Cupie said.

"When can I get out of here?"

"What? You haven't even talked to a doctor yet. You got some place to be?"

"I want to know if Bart Cross is still out at that guesthouse in Las Campanas."

"I can check on that without your help," Cupie said drily.

"Well, stop fluttering around here like an old woman and do it," Vittorio said.

"I'm not fluttering, and you need some morphine," Cupie said, pressing the call button.

A nurse appeared. "Can I help you?"

"This man needs morphine," Cupie said.

"I don't want morphine!" Vittorio said. "I told you!"

"Ignore him," Cupie said to the nurse, and she disappeared. "You're way too cranky," Cupie said, "and that will get your blood pressure up and slow your recovery."

"I thought you were going to go check on Bart Cross," Vittorio said.

"Just as soon as I hold you down for the nurse," Cupie replied.

WITH VITTORIO SETTLED INTO a morphine haze and Eagle still in surgery, Cupie drove out to Las Campanas, to the guesthouse where Cross had been staying. He drew his gun and hammered on the door. "Police!" he yelled. "Open up!"

That got him nowhere. He walked around the house, looking into windows. "Neat as a pin," he said aloud to himself. "The rooster has flown the coop."

He got into Vittorio's car and drove back to the hospital. Vittorio was sitting up in bed, dozing lightly. He opened his eyes when Cupie walked in. "Eagle's still alive," he said. "That's all I know. He's in the ICU, and Susannah is with him."

There was a knock on the door, and two men in suits walked in, flashing badges.

"I'm Romera; this is Reed," the taller of the two said. "You feel up to answering some questions, Mr."—he read a card in his hand—"Victoria?"

"It's Vittorio," Cupie corrected him. "No last name."

"And who might you be?"

"Cupie Dalton. I work with him." He jerked a thumb toward Vittorio.

"How's Eagle?" Vittorio asked.

"Still out," the detective replied. "Lots of tubes in him. You want to tell me what happened?"

Vittorio recited the chain of events as economically as possible.

"The guy shoot you?" Romera asked.

"No, Mrs. Eagle shot me, mistook me for the guy."

"Jesus Christos, what a mess!" Romera said. Reed wrote it down. "Where were you, Mr. Dalton?"

"I was staked out down the hill sixty or seventy yards. The pickup didn't pass me, must have come down the hill from up the mountain. He escaped that way, too."

"And neither of you got a look at the guy's face?" Romera asked.

"No," Vittorio said quickly. "And I didn't know him."

"I didn't even see him," Cupie said. "Just the truck."

"What kind of truck?"

"Pickup, maybe a Chevy," Cupie replied. "I'm not good with trucks."

"I am," Vittorio said. "It was a Toyota. It had a FedEx logo on the door and a New Mexico plate."

"Was he wearing a FedEx uniform?"

Vittorio shrugged, causing him pain. "Maybe. A dark Windbreaker and matching baseball cap."

"You want to bring any charges against Mrs. Eagle for shooting you?" Romera asked.

"Of course not," Vittorio said. "She just mistook me for the guy who cut her husband."

"Whatever you say," Romera replied. "She's shot a couple of other people in the past, you know—her ex-husband in LA and a woman delivering flowers to Eagle's house here last year."

"Yeah, and the woman was trying to kill them both."

"You figure the ex-wife is behind this, then?"

"I do."

"But she's in prison in Mexico," Romera said. "I checked."

"If you say so," Vittorio replied.

B art Cross landed at Burbank and taxied to his
T-hangar, on a quiet part of the field. He
opened the hangar door with a remote control, then
swung the airplane around facing away from the hangar, ran through his checklist and cut the engines.
He sat for a moment in the airplane, thinking, then
picked up his logbook and wrote in the flight to Albuquerque and a return the day before. That would
check with the parking lot's electronic records and
give him an alibi.

He got out of the airplane, hooked up the towbar
and pushed it backward into the hangar. As he was
about to leave, someone he knew taxied past him to
two hangars down, cut his engine and got out.

"Hey, Bart," the man said. "How's it hanging?"

"Not bad," Bart replied. "Spent a few days in Santa Fe at a friend's house."

"That's not bad, either."

"Hey, Tom, if anybody should ask, you saw me put away my airplane yesterday, okay?"

"Sure, kiddo. You can do the same for me sometime."

"Thanks, Tom." Cross walked to the parking lot, got his car and drove home. He'd be back at work tomorrow. As he pulled into his driveway his cell phone went off. "Hello?"

"Where are you?" she asked.

"Just got home from Santa Fe. The car is back where I picked it up."

"Will you be there tonight? I want to pay you."

"Sure thing. I'm too tired to go out."

"Where do you live?"

He gave her the address and directions from Coldwater Canyon.

"I'll be there late, maybe very late. I've got to make a stop on the way."

"I'll be here," he said.

She hung up.

Bart picked up the papers on the doorstep on his way into the house but tossed them aside without reading them. He needed a nap.

CUPIE GOT BACK TO the hospital and found Vittorio sound asleep in his bed. He walked back to the nurses' station.

"Hi," he said to the nurse. "Anything new on Mr. Eagle's condition?"

"Still in the ICU," she said. "He's awake, though, and the prognosis is good."

"Can I see him for a minute?" Cupie knew this was a favor, but he had been chatting her up for such an occasion.

The nurse looked both ways, up and down the hall. "Okay, just for a minute, Cupie. His wife just went down to the cafeteria. Third door on your left. If he's asleep, don't wake him."

Cupie went down to the door marked "Intensive Care" and let himself in. There was only one patient, and he was awake. Cupie pulled up a chair. "Ed, how you doing?" he asked.

Eagle took a deep breath. "Tired," he said.

"Don't talk, just listen. The guy got past us. Our fault, but we know who he is. We'll take care of it, no charge."

Eagle nodded. "What about Barbara?"

"She's not in town, on purpose, but we have an idea where to find her."

Eagle nodded again.

"You want us to take care of that, too?"

Eagle closed his eyes and seemed to go to sleep.

Cupie tiptoed out of the unit and walked back to Vittorio's room. He pulled up a comfortable chair close to the bed and turned on the TV, keeping the volume low. He surfed through the channels, looking for a local news program, finally settling on an Albuquerque broadcast. He sat through a weather forecast; then the anchor came back on-screen.

"This just in from Santa Fe," he said. "A spokesman for Saint Michael's Hospital has announced that local attorney Ed Eagle, a trial lawyer known throughout the West, is in what doctors describe as a normal recovery after surgery for a knife wound in an assassination attempt early this morning. His prognosis is favorable. Police are still searching for the unknown assassin."

"And they're not going to find him," Cupie said aloud to himself. "But we are."

"That's right," Vittorio said.

Cupie turned to find Vittorio awake and looking at him. "Hey. You feeling better?"

"Much, thanks. The morphine was the right thing to do."

"Bart Cross has cleared out of Barbara's place and is probably back in LA by now."

"I want out of here," Vittorio said.

"Yeah, I know, pal, but you're going to stay right where you are until your doctors pronounce you fit to walk around like a person."

"We have a call to make. I didn't mention Cross to the cops."

"I noticed. Don't worry, he'll keep, and we know where to find him."

"He's not the only one we need to find."

"I'm with you, buddy. You just relax for a few days and get strong, okay?"

But Vittorio had dozed off again.

BARBARA WENT WITH Jimmy Long to a dinner party in Beverly Hills. Before she left, she did a Google search for Ed Eagle and found a report on the AP that he was recovering in a Santa Fe hospital. When she left for the dinner party, she didn't take any cash with her.

She enjoyed the party, and Jimmy enjoyed himself a little too much, so she drove him home in his black BMW and put him to bed. He would sleep late tomorrow, she thought.

She went to her luggage and got what she needed, then got back into the Beamer and drove up Coldwater Canyon, then down into the Valley. She followed Cross's directions carefully and found his street. It was past one o'clock now, and she drove around the block twice to be sure there was no activity in the neighborhood. Every house on Cross's block was dark, except his. She stopped at the top of a little hill and called his cell number.

"Hello."

"I'll be there in five minutes," she said. "We'll make this quick."

"I'll be here."

"Right," she said. "Turn off the porch light." She hung up, switched off the engine, put the car in neutral and coasted slowly downhill with her lights off, stopping in front of the house. She got out and closed the door quietly, and with a brown envelope in one hand and her other hand in her large purse, she walked to the house. The porch light was off.

She rang the doorbell and waited. Shortly, he came to the door and opened it.

"Hey, I didn't hear you drive up. Come on in," he said, and turned to lead her into the living room.

Barbara took the silenced pistol from her purse and shot him once in the back of the head. He crumpled and fell forward onto the floor, striking his head on the coffee table on his way down. She backed away a couple of feet to avoid splatter and shot him again in the head, then looked around.

The cell phone she had given him was on the coffee table, and she put that into her purse. She went through his pockets and took his wallet, which contained a dozen hundreds, then found his bedroom and searched it. She found a lot of other cash, her cash, in a bureau drawer and took that, then left the house, opened the car door and pushed until it started rolling, then got inside and waited until she was at the bottom of the hill before starting the car.

She stopped at a quiet place, took the batteries out of the two cell phones, wiped everything clean and dropped it all into the brown envelope. She removed the credit cards from the wallet and put that into the envelope, too. On the way home, she found a house being remodeled with a Dumpster outside and tossed the phones and the wallet into it. A few blocks later, she dropped the credit cards into a sewer, then drove to Jimmy's, undressed and got into bed with him.

Barbara slept like a lamb.

36

Cupie went to the hospital the following morning and found Vittorio's bed empty. He looked up and down the hall and spotted him at the nurses' station.

He walked down to where Vittorio stood, filling out a form. He was fully dressed, and his left arm was in a sling. "What are you doing out of bed?"

"I'm checking myself out of here," Vittorio said. "I'm fine."

"He really shouldn't leave here," the nurse said, "but he's stubborn."

"I've got a pocketful of pills to take," Vittorio said, signing the document and handing it to the nurse. "Now the hospital has zero liability."

"The doctor isn't going to like this."

"I don't like it, either," Cupie said, "but there's no stopping this guy."

"Let's get out of here," Vittorio said, starting down the hallway. They looked in on Ed Eagle, who had been moved to a room, and found him asleep. "Just as well. I don't want to talk to him until this is over. Let's go," he said to Cupie, and they walked out into the parking lot. "We need to be in Los Angeles."

"No, we don't," Cupie said. "We're going to your place, and we'll talk about LA tomorrow."

"Cupie—"

"Shut up and get in the car, Vittorio."

Vittorio got in, and Cupie drove him home.

As soon as they were there, Cupie called Centurion Studios and asked for Bart Cross.

"Long Productions," a woman said.

"May I speak to Bart Cross, please?"

"Who is this?"

"A friend of his. He asked me to call him when I came to LA, and I'm here."

"I'm afraid I've got some bad news for you," the woman said. "Bart has died."

"Died? How?"

"He was murdered last night."

"Murdered?" Cupie asked. "Who murdered him?"

"The police don't know yet. His cleaning lady found him this morning in his living room. He had been shot."

"I'm shocked to hear that," Cupie said. "Can you give me his address? I'd like to send some flowers."

The woman gave him the address. "It's just west of Burbank Airport," she said, "off Coldwater Canyon."

"Thank you very much," Cupie said.

"May I have your name, please?"

But Cupie had already hung up.

"Barbara killed him," Vittorio said. "She must have found out that Eagle is still alive. This means she's in LA."

"And probably at James Long's house," Cupie said. "I know a cop in Burbank. Let me make a call." He put the phone on speaker and dialed the number.

"Burbank police," a male voice said.

"Detective Dave Santiago," Cupie said.

"Hang on." The phone rang.

"Detective Santiago."

"Dave, it's Cupie Dalton."

"Hey, Cupie, how are you?"

"Not bad. You working the Bart Cross murder?"

"I'm not the lead, but I was out there early this morning. Did you know the guy?"

"Friend of a friend. What did you see out there?"

"He took two in the head from behind," Santiago replied. "Looked like a pro to me."

"When did it happen?"

"TOD was between midnight and two a.m., the ME says."

"Any leads?"

"None. We're just getting started. What's your interest in this, Cupie?"

"Just idle curiosity," Cupie said. "I heard the name on the news and thought I knew him."

"Should we talk to your friend?"

"Nah, he knows nothing. He doesn't even live in LA. Thanks for the info, Dave. I'll pass it on."

"Buy me lunch one of these days."

"Sure thing," Cupie said, and hung up. He turned to Vittorio. "There you go."

"It's Barbara. She went there to pay him off—or at least Bart thought that. I bet they didn't find any money in the house."

"I didn't ask."

"She found out Eagle is alive and burned Cross to cut the trail to her."

"Yeah, but she knows that won't do it for us," Cupie said. "She knows we know. That means she'll run. She won't be in LA when we get there."

"She'll be coming to Santa Fe," Vittorio said.

"Maybe, but not right away. Once Eagle talks to the cops, she'll be too hot here. Maybe she'll just hire somebody else."

"She'll be very pissed off that Eagle is still alive," Vittorio said. "I think she'll come here pretty quick."

"She won't go back to the same house," Cupie said. "She knows we know about that place."

"What was that detective's name who talked to us?"

"Uh, Romeo? No, Romera, or Romero."

"I'm going to call him," Vittorio said, picking up the phone.

"What for?"

"Eagle's going to need a police guard while he's in the hospital, and maybe when he gets out, too."

"What's wrong with us?"

"We didn't do so hot before," Vittorio pointed out.

"But if we call in the police, we're not going to get a shot at Barbara."

"If they've got any brains, they'll be guarding him anyway," Vittorio said.

"They weren't guarding him as recently as an hour ago," Cupie said.

Vittorio punched the speakerphone button on the phone, called the Santa Fe Police Department and asked for Detective Romera.

"Romera," the man said.

"Detective, this is Vittorio. You talked to me yesterday at the hospital."

"Yeah, I remember."

"I got out this morning, and there was no police guard on Ed Eagle."

"I think the guy with the knife is long gone," Romera said.

"You're right about that, Detective, but the woman who hired him could still be around."

"The ex-wife?"

"It's gotta be."

"You think she'll hire another man?"

"Maybe, or maybe she'll want to do it herself. I know her. She's very determined."

"You may have a point," Romera said. "I'll put a couple of uniforms on Eagle's hospital room."

"Twenty-four hours a day?"

"Yeah, I guess so."

"They should get a list of nurses authorized to be in there and check everybody against the list who goes into the room."

"Yeah, okay. Thanks for calling." Romera hung up.

"He didn't sound too enthusiastic to me," Cupie said.

"Maybe not, but he's got enough street smarts to know that if Eagle gets killed in the hospital he, personally, will be left holding the bag. He'll put the guards on."

"I guess you're right," Cupie said. "So, what are we going to do?"

"Maybe we can stop her from getting as far as the hospital," Vittorio said. "If we can find her."

37

Todd Bacon sat in his hotel room, staring at his computer screen. He had reported in, told Holly Barker that her idea had worked but that he had lost Lauren Cade. She had not been pleased, and he wasn't pleased with himself, either.

Now he was faced with new difficulties. Lauren, knowing that she had been spotted, would go to ground, and what's more, she now knew what he looked like. He didn't even know if it had been she in the Volvo station wagon; that was just a guess.

Nevertheless, he logged on to the Agency mainframe, accessed the New Mexico DMV records and did a search for green Volvo station wagons. They were apparently popular in the state, because the search turned up fourteen of the cars in green, none of them in Santa

Fe. There was, however, one in Taos that had been registered the day he had spotted Teddy in the Grand Cherokee. That would have been the day he would have traded cars, and Teddy certainly knew enough about the Agency's computers to hide the trade.

This was a lead so slim that it hardly qualified as a lead, but it was all he had. The Taos car was registered to a Walt Gooden. A quick call to 411 confirmed that no one by that name had a phone in Taos, nor did he, after another check, have one in Santa Fe. Well, Teddy wouldn't have registered the car in the alias he was using, would he?

Todd continued to deduce. If Lauren had gone to ground after being spotted, would Teddy have done the same? And if so, what might cause one of them to leave wherever they were living? They weren't going to run—they had already demonstrated that. But they could just wait him out. After all, Todd wasn't going to spend the rest of his career on this job, no matter how important it was to Lance Cabot.

Food. They had to eat. Maybe one of them would leave to buy supplies—not only a meal but groceries. Todd reasoned that they would not go just to a convenience store, where choices would be limited, but to a proper supermarket, where they could find a large enough variety to keep them in good meals for an extended time, maybe a week or ten days.

In his travels around Santa Fe Todd had seen only

one large supermarket, though certainly there must be more. He had seen a large Albertsons in a shopping center with a big parking lot. It was as good a place to start as any. He went down to the garage and started to get into his rented red Taurus, then stopped. Teddy had already seen that car. He went into the hotel, to the rental car desk, and exchanged the Taurus for a silver Toyota, then drove to where he had seen the Albertsons store.

A sea of cars greeted him. He figured if they were going to shop for groceries, they would park as close to Albertsons as possible, so he started at the front door and began driving slowly up and down the rows of parked cars, checking for Volvo station wagons. He found a silver one and a white one but no green one. He continued to look.

Finally, he had covered the entire parking lot without finding the car he was looking for. He'd come back tomorrow and start again. Then, as he was driving back toward the supermarket, he saw a green Volvo station wagon, empty. He checked the plates: New Mexico, Santa Fe County. He double-parked, got out of his car and tried a door on the Volvo. Locked. He walked slowly around the car, looking inside. He saw a map of the state and nothing else.

Todd returned to his car, opened the trunk and opened a case he traveled with. He chose two items, closed the case and the trunk, and returned to the

Volvo. He looked around for cops or someone paying attention to him, found no one, then dropped to the ground, crawled halfway under the car, far enough that no one could reach unless they crawled as far as he had, and attached the little box magnetically to the frame. He pressed a button on the side and watched a red light start to flash. It would continue for two minutes.

He got up from under the station wagon, went back to his car, drove a hundred yards away and stopped. He switched the GPS device on and pressed the button for current location. The device took a moment to locate itself, and then a map of Santa Fe appeared. He pressed another button, and a red light on the map began to flash. It had nailed the location of the green Volvo station wagon. Now he didn't have to closely tail the car; when it moved, he could follow at an unseen distance.

He found a parking space and sat in the car, waiting.

BARBARA WAS WATCHING television in Jimmy's study when he came home from the studio. "Hi," she said.

He didn't reply but went to the bar, poured himself a stiff drink, then flopped down in his easy chair.

"Something wrong, sweetie?" she asked. He hadn't even offered her a drink.

"Yeah, something's wrong," he replied, without looking at her.

"What is it?"

"You remember the pilot who flew us back from Mexico?"

"Of course. What was his name?"

"Bart Cross."

"Oh, sure. What about him?"

"I gave you his name, remember?"

"I had forgotten," she said.

"Did you ever speak with him?"

"No. I decided he might not be the right man for the job."

"Well, Bart is dead," Jimmy said. "He was shot at his home last night. It's all over the papers."

"I haven't read a paper today," she said.

"There was something else in the paper," he replied. "Somebody attacked Ed Eagle with a knife in Santa Fe yesterday but failed to kill him."

"Oh?"

"Yeah. Sounds like somebody was doing you a favor."

"Well, trying, maybe."

"Barbara, did you hire Bart to kill Eagle? I mean, I knew you were going to do something like that, and I didn't really care."

"I think you know the answer to that," she said.

"Did you hire Bart Cross?"

She said nothing, just went to the bar and poured herself a drink, then came back and sat down.

"Yes," she said.

"And did you kill him for failing?"

"Jimmy, he made mistakes. The police would have been onto him before the week was out. He'd have given me up in a plea bargain."

"Well, I can't argue with that," he said, "but I don't like you killing a man who worked for me, somebody I liked."

"I'm sorry. It was necessary."

Jimmy took a deep breath and sighed. "Barbara, you're going to have to leave here and not come back for a long time."

"All right, if that's what you wish."

"I mean right now. I'll drive you to the airport. I don't want there to be a record of a taxi pickup here."

Barbara stood up. "I'll go and pack now and be ready in half an hour."

"Thank you," he said.

TEDDY CAME OUT OF Albertsons and saw that it had begun to snow, and he figured that if it kept up like this there would be at least six inches on the ground by morning. He put his groceries in the luggage compartment and returned his cart. Then, as he approached the Volvo, something occurred to him. He squatted and read the side of one of the tires: It was rated for mud and snow. The salesman had told him the vehicle was equipped with snow tires, and he knew that was a whole different thing. The driveway at the house was pretty steep, and in a couple of inches of snow, and with these tires, the car wouldn't make it up.

He got into the car and headed for Cerrillos Road.

THREE HUNDRED YARDS AWAY, Todd Bacon was parked across the road from the National Cemetery, reading the local paper, when the GPS unit beeped. The Volvo was on the move.

He started the car.

TEDDY FOUND A DISCOUNT tire dealer on Cerrillos and asked if they had Pirelli 210s in stock. They did and could install them immediately and give him a small trade-in on his current tires. He was directed to drive the car into a service bay. He got out and watched as the hydraulic lift raised the car until the tires were at a working level.

He thought he'd have a look at the chassis to check for rust, so he stooped and walked under the car. He inspected everything carefully, then stopped. Something had been placed under the car; he knew it instantly, because he had designed it himself. He reached up and detached it from the frame. Good thing it had snowed, he thought. In a day or two the device would have been covered with road grime and difficult to spot.

He walked out of the service bay and looked around: no Volvos, but there was a dark green Ford wagon parked outside. He bent down and attached the device under the rear bumper, then went back into the service bay, where his car was waiting. He lowered the hydraulic lift, and when the technician came toward him, he told the man he had changed his mind.

He got back on Cerrillos Road and drove to the dealer where he had bought the Volvo, remembering that he had seen a sign offering a ten-day car exchange with no questions asked.

TODD WAS STOPPED AT a traffic light when he checked the GPS unit again. The Volvo was moving again, this time headed north. He checked his fuel and found that he had been given the car with only a quarter of a tank, so he pulled into a gas station and topped off the tank. He could catch up at his leisure.

When he got back into the car he discovered that the Volvo had departed Santa Fe to the north and was headed toward Tesuque. He followed.

38

Dolly lay in bed with Tip Hanks, her head on his shoulder and her hand cupping his balls. She had just given him the blow job of his life, judging from his reaction, and for all practical purposes he was now hers. All she had to do was keep it that way.

Dolly had made a very nice career for herself. Born Helga Swenson in Milwaukee, Wisconsin, she had been a bookkeeper in a small factory for four years, and during that time she had taught herself to steal while covering her tracks. She had made only one mistake, one made by many embezzlers: She had taken a vacation.

An embezzler, she had learned, couldn't do that, because someone else would do the bookkeeping in her absence and discover her crime. By that time, however, Helga had stolen nearly a million dollars, and she still had seven hundred thousand of it in a safe-deposit box.

She had returned from her two weeks in the islands to find several messages from her boss on her phone machine, and one from a police officer. She had immediately packed a bag and booked into a motel for the night. The following morning, she was at the bank at opening time and cleaned out her box. She drove to Chicago, sold her car, bought another from another dealer and headed west.

She was a smart girl, and she had taken the precaution of obtaining a genuine passport and a driver's license under a new name, using a stolen birth certificate, so she made a clean getaway.

She repeated her crime at two other companies, in Kansas City, Missouri, and Tulsa, Oklahoma; then she had had a bit of luck. Departing Tulsa, she had met a man in the bar of a fine hotel in Dallas, and before the week was out she was his mistress in a nice apartment and his personal assistant. He was a consultant in the oil business and traveled almost constantly, leaving her in charge of his bank accounts, which she had looted while charging a new wardrobe to his credit cards. Since she paid the bills, he never noticed.

She had moved on to Santa Fe and met Tip's wife in a bar, too, and after years of switch-hitting had no trouble in endearing herself. Constance Hanks had been smarter than her earlier bosses, though, and had caught her stealing cash from Tip's desk drawer. Then she had found herself in the position of sex slave instead of sex partner, and she had not enjoyed it. She found a way out when she discovered a gun in the bedside drawer while looking for a sex toy. She planned the event carefully and surprised herself with her own coolness and lack of guilt. She had no plans to repeat the experience, because it was too dangerous, but it was nice to know she had the guts to do it if she had to.

Tip Hanks, unbeknownst to him, was now on the brink of a major hit to his financial status. His inheritance of his wife's estate would soon result in a very large cash deposit being made into his bank account, to which Dolly was now a signatory, and she was tracking the progress on the settling of the estate.

Dolly had become more sophisticated in her techniques over the years. On a vacation in the Cayman Islands she had had a conversation with a banker and, as a result, had learned how, through a series of wire transfers to accounts established around the world, to make cash virtually untraceable, especially in the relatively modest amounts she stole. Less than a million dollars, she had learned, would not interest a Treasury or FBI agent, who would certainly have bigger fish to reel in. Still, she had managed, through thrift and daring, to amass a small fortune of nearly two million dollars, and she meant to see that it grew.

Soon she would arrange a convergence of the

settling of Connie Hanks's estate with one of Tip's five-day trips to a golf tournament, and when he returned home he would discover that his checks were bouncing. By that time, of course, she would be establishing herself in another city, perhaps Los Angeles, in an area not frequented by golf pros.

Dolly gently left the bed of the snoring Tip and got into the shower. She had already, at his invitation, moved from the guesthouse into the master suite, and Tip was talking marriage, when a suitable period of mourning had been served. She liked Tip, but she liked his money more.

ED EAGLE WAS SITTING up in bed when Susannah arrived with flowers and magazines.

"How are you feeling?" she asked, kissing him fondly.

"Stronger," Eagle replied. "Not so tired. I'm going to bust out of here in a day or two."

"Maybe, sport, but you're not going back to work just yet. I get to pamper you a little more before you do that."

"You think we really need the cop on the door?" he asked.

"You bet your sweet ass I do," Susannah replied. "You don't think Barbara is done, do you?"

Eagle sighed. "I guess I don't, and the thought depresses me."

"Then don't think it," she said. "Let me do that."

"You know, don't you, that if you keep on shooting people we're going to end up in court."

"You have a point," she agreed. "Vittorio has been a prince about it, though. He says my mistake was perfectly understandable, and I cannot bring myself to disagree with him."

"I paid his hospital bill," Eagle said.

"And I've been sending him his meals while he recuperates," Susannah said. "Turns out he loves Mexican, and you know what a good Mexican cook I am."

"I do indeed," Eagle said, squeezing her hand.

"Listen, Ed, I was going to bring this up, even if you hadn't nearly died, but do you think you're in a position to ease up on the practice of law? I don't mean sell the firm, just take, say, half as many cases, personally."

"Well," he replied, "there's nothing like a near-death experience to make you reevaluate your existence. I don't want to make any rash promises. Let me think about it."

"That's all I ask," she said, "for the moment."

AT THAT SAME MOMENT Barbara was getting off an airliner in Albuquerque. She collected her bags and took a taxi to the long-term parking lot and found her car there, with the ticket tucked under the driver's sun visor. She found a decent restaurant in Albuquerque and had some dinner, then checked into a motel.

The following morning she looked for a medical supply store in the yellow pages and purchased some hospital scrubs, a white lab coat, a stethoscope and some of those awful white sneakers that nurses wear.

While in the store, she saw a woman with beautiful hair and asked who her hairdresser was. She spent the afternoon there getting a facial, a manicure and pedicure, and becoming a brunette.

It was time to get this thing done, once and for all.

39

Cupie came back from town to Vittorio's house with some groceries and liquor, and found his host watching a soap opera on television.

Vittorio quickly turned off the TV. Cupie settled into a chair and passed him the *Los Angeles Times* he had bought in Santa Fe. "Read the article."

Vittorio read.

"Barbara was burning her bridges," Cupie said. "Smart girl."

"Isn't she something?" Vittorio tossed back the newspaper. "So, she's headed here, right?"

"Right. And we don't have to worry about Eagle as long as he's under guard in the hospital."

"You forget that he was under guard when he got

his throat cut," Vittorio pointed out. "And you and I were the guard."

"Just a slipup," Cupie said. "Anybody can make a mistake."

"A mistake that got Eagle cut and me shot. You think that the SFPD is smarter than we are?"

"Look, as long as he's in a hospital room with a guard on the door, he's fine," Cupie said. "There's only one way into the room, remember? Watch your soap opera." Cupie turned on the TV.

"What soap opera?"

"Has Craig found out yet that Jonathan is the father of Alexandra's baby?" Cupie asked.

"Not yet," Vittorio replied.

BARBARA SPENT THE DAY reading magazines in her room; then at dusk she drove up to Santa Fe. She remembered a suite hotel that catered to traveling salesmen, and it was not far from the hospital. She phoned ahead and booked a suite.

Once in the city she went first to the hospital and had a good look at it. There were two entrances, one for the emergency room and a main entrance. She parked outside and soaked it all in. As she sat there a uniformed policeman came through the door to the main entrance, buttoning his coat against the cold. He stood outside the door and lit a cigarette. He was no more than thirty yards from her, and she got a good, long look at him: maybe fifty, once muscular and athletic, now with a gut and jowls and a complexion that indicated a large and regular use of alcohol. She couldn't read his name tag from where she sat, but she would remember that face and build.

She drove to her hotel, checked in and began going over things in her mind. She called the hospital on her cell phone.

"How may I direct your call?"

"This is Crystal Florists," Barbara said. "We have a delivery. Is Mr. Ed Eagle still in room 304?"

"No, he's in 106," the operator said. "Shall I connect you?"

"No, thanks. I don't need to speak to him."

"Just deliver your flowers to the ground-floor nurses' station," the operator said. "One of the nurses will see that the patient gets them."

"Thanks. Good night," Barbara said. She hung up. A good first step.

TIP HANKS LEFT FOR his golf tournament and would be gone for five days, and Dolly, having become accustomed to regular sex, got out of the house. She drove up Canyon Road to Geronimo, where she had met with Ellie Keeler, and took a seat at the bar. "A margarita, please, straight up with salt," she said to the bartender. Half a minute later the drink materialized, and she closed her eyes and took her first, very welcome, sip. "Aaaaah," she breathed.

"I'm going to feel exactly the same way in just a minute," a male voice said beside her. "One for me, too," he said to the bartender, and it was done.

Dolly turned her head and got a first look at her companion in tequila: tall, athletic-looking, sandy hair, a little on the short side, early thirties.

"Aaaaah," he said, having taken his first sip.

Dolly laughed. "What did your day hold that made you need a drink?"

"Sunset," Todd responded. "I'm on vacation. I don't need a better excuse."

"What are you on vacation from?" she asked.

"Would you believe me if I told you I'm a CIA agent?" he asked.

She shook her head. "Nope."

"Then don't ask." He smiled and stuck out a hand. "I'm Todd Bacon."

She took the hand, which was large and warm. "I'm Dolly Parks. *Where* are you on vacation from?"

He thought about that. "I'm afraid I don't know."

"You don't know where you're from?"

"Well, until very recently I lived in Panama, but I was recalled, and as yet, I'm unassigned."

"Where would you like to be reassigned?"

"Here, I think. Santa Fe is a wonderful place."

"Then why don't you get your company to transfer you here?"

"I'm afraid my company doesn't do business here."

"Then change jobs."

"I'm afraid there is very little demand for ex-CIA agents in Santa Fe."

"That's your story, and you're sticking to it, huh?"

"That's my story. Where do you hail from?"

"Oh, I'm a midwesterner, but I've lived in Santa Fe for a few months now."

"Think you'll make it permanent?"

"As wonderful as it is, I doubt it. I'm not very good at putting down roots."

"That's funny," he said. "Neither am I."

"Think you'll ever improve?" she asked.

"Probably not," he replied. "It wouldn't do my career any good."

"How's your career going?"

"Extremely well," he said. "Even better than I'd hoped. What do you do?"

"Oh, I'm a sort of general, all-around factotum for a golf pro."

"Which one?"

"Tip Hanks."

"Oh, sure. I see him play on TV now and then. He lives in Santa Fe?"

"He does, but he left today to play this weekend in California."

"And left you all alone?"

"Sad, isn't it?"

"Then I think you should have dinner with me," Todd said.

A woman's voice came from behind him. "Well, hello, Dolly, to coin a phrase."

Todd and Dolly both turned to look. Todd saw a very attractive woman, older, maybe early forties.

"Ellie!" Dolly said. "Where have you been?"

"I had to go back to San Francisco to take care of some business," Barbara replied. "Can I buy you two a drink?"

"Hi, I'm Todd," he said, extending a hand. "I had just asked Dolly to join me for dinner. Why don't you join us both?"

"Love to," Barbara replied. "If that's okay with you, Dolly."

"Of course it is," Dolly replied.

"Bartender," Todd said, "do you think you could find us a table for three?"

Dolly thought the odds of a very good evening had improved by a factor of three.

40

Todd woke up sometime in the middle of the night. There was a woman asleep on his shoulder and another asleep with her head on his crotch. He wasn't sure, in the dark, which was which. The two of them had exhausted him during the first hour of their visit to his room at the Inn of the Anasazi, and his last memory before drifting off was of the two of them occupied with each other. This was a first for Todd, but he hoped it wouldn't be the last.

His frustration with his work in Santa Fe had reached a new high when he had followed the red light on his GPS unit north from Santa Fe, then through a turn toward Taos. Baffled, he had pulled closer to the Volvo until he saw the green shape, and when the car ahead had stopped at a gas station he continued past it, only to find that it was a Ford, not a Volvo.

He made a U-turn and pulled into the station, just in time to see an elderly woman pumping gas. When she went into the station to pay, he did a quick search under her car and, swearing aloud, found the little box under her rear bumper.

He returned to his car and drove back to Santa Fe. How the hell could Lauren Cade—or, for that matter, Teddy Fay—have found the thing? It was uncanny, and he could not come up with a plausible explanation for how the switch of the device to the Ford had happened.

Now his frustration had melted into a warm pool of carnal gratification, and he didn't feel so bad about losing the Volvo. Fortunately, he had not lost the little box, which would live to spy again.

The woman whose head was on his crotch stirred, and he stirred, too, when he found himself in her mouth.

"Oh, good," she said, "you're back." Then she returned to work. It was Dolly.

TEDDY WAS FINISHING his breakfast when Lauren came in from taking out the garbage. "I'm confused," she said. "Why do we have a Tahoe in the garage?"

"It was the only thing the dealer had that was in good shape and had four-wheel drive and snow tires."

"Why do we need it?" she asked.

"Did you look around when you went outside? There's six inches of snow on the ground. Happens every year about this time."

"Oh, come on, Teddy. What happened?"

He explained about his discovery of the little black box under the Volvo.

"Good God. How long had it been there?"

"Not long," Teddy replied, "or young Mr. Bacon would have been all over us. My guess is he saw the Volvo in the grocery-store parking lot and recognized it from when he chased you. Don't worry, I transferred the device to another car, so he's out there somewhere following a Ford around."

She kissed him on the cheek. "You are so smart."

"Well, I'm a little smarter than Todd Bacon," Teddy said. "And I'll try to keep it that way."

THE THREE OF THEM had breakfast at the table in Todd's room, notwithstanding the look on the room-service waiter's face. Nobody was embarrassed, but everybody was pretty much wrung out, Todd thought.

"You were wonderful last night," Dolly said to him.

"We were all wonderful," Barbara said.

"We must do it again sometime," Todd offered.

"I'm going to be tied up for a few days," Barbara said, "but you kids enjoy yourselves."

251

"What's in that?" Dolly asked, pointing to a sturdy-looking aluminum case on the bench at the end of the bed.

"Spy stuff," Todd replied, popping a piece of sausage into his mouth.

"Todd," Dolly said to Barbara, "is sticking with the old pickup line about being a CIA agent."

"Why do you think it's a line?" Barbara asked. "I mean, there are people who are CIA agents, and some of them must get to Santa Fe from time to time. Wouldn't it amuse you to believe him?"

Todd laughed. "What do you do, Ellie, and what brings you to Santa Fe?"

"I'm a rich widow for a living, and I go where I please. At the moment, I'm pleased to be in Santa Fe."

"Where were you most recently?" he asked.

"In San Francisco," she replied. "And before that, in a Mexican prison."

Todd laughed. "You see, Dolly, Ellie has an even better story than mine."

"Perhaps we all have noncredible backgrounds," Dolly said. "I'm an embezzler on the run!"

"Then let's all stick with our stories," Barbara said.

41

Susannah arrived at the hospital with a cake tin filled with Ed's favorite cookies, only to have a nurse stop her on the way to his room.

"I'm sorry, Mrs. Eagle," the woman said, "but your husband has picked up an infection. We've got him on IV antibiotics, but he's going to have to stay a few more days, until his temperature is normal and he's strong enough to walk by himself."

"Is there anything that can be done that isn't already being done?" Susannah asked.

"No, ma'am," the woman replied. "He's getting everything he needs except, maybe, a cookie."

Susannah smiled wanly and continued to Ed's room. She greeted the cop at the door, then went into the room. "Good morning!" she said brightly.

Ed's bed was in the sitting-up position, and he turned to greet her with a wan smile of his own. "Hey, baby," he said wearily. "Seems I've got an infection and a fever. You're going to have to wait awhile to take me home."

She sat on the bed and brushed the hair from his forehead. "That's all right, sweetie," she said. "You just rest." She set the cake tin down on his belly. "I brought you some cookies," she said.

Eagle lifted the tin. "Pretty weighty for just cookies," he replied.

"Well, there's a little pre-Christmas gift in there, too."

"I hope it's bourbon," he said.

"Let's just say it's good for what ails you."

"Yesterday this time I thought I'd be going home this morning."

She kissed him high on the cheek, a place he liked. "Don't you worry about a thing," she said. "Every little thing is under control."

DOWN THE ROAD a couple of hundred yards, one of the little things that was not under control was taking the cellophane wrapping off a box of very expensive chocolates. Barbara checked herself in the mirror. She had spent the earlier part of the morning at a copy and computer shop, making herself an ID that said she worked for the state Department of Health. She had copied a state seal off the department's Web site, photographed herself in scrubs, printed the photo, added her typeset name and printed the badge, then laminated it. It wasn't perfect, but it would pass. She also made a state sticker for her windshield and downloaded a full-size copy of a New Mexico State employee license plate, which she printed out on a plastic material with a sticky side. She tucked the box of candy under an arm and left the hotel for the hospital. She applied the phony license plate over the real one and stuck the state sticker on the inside of her windshield, on the driver's side.

She parked in the employees' lot and walked past the fat cop, who was outside, smoking again. "Morning," she said with a wave. He hardly noticed her. She walked down the hallway and saw the relief cop at Eagle's door, marking it very nicely.

"Good morning," she said cheerfully to the man. "Have one of these delicious chocolates. They were a gift, but if I eat them all I'll gain twenty pounds." She thrust the box at him.

He picked out one and popped it into his mouth. "Thanks," he mumbled.

Now both the cops knew her by sight. She walked on down the hallway to the nurses' station, where three women were at work. "Good morning, ladies," she said. "I'm Ruth Barrow from the state. I'll be here for a few days, doing safety checks."

"What kind of safety checks?" one of the nurses asked.

"Oh, it's nothing to worry you ladies about. You obviously run a very tight ship here." She opened the chocolate box. "Help me out here, will you? This was a gift, and if I eat them all I'll explode," she said, laughing at her own joke.

The women gathered around and fished candy out of the box. "Take two," Barbara said, "and save me from myself. I see you've got a prisoner down the hall. Is that a common thing here? Isn't there a lockup ward?"

"Oh, no, it's not a prisoner. That's Ed Eagle's room. He's a local lawyer who got attacked by a madman last week."

"My God," Barbara said. "I hope they caught the guy."

"Not yet," the nurse replied. "That's why the cop is on the door. There are two of them; they take turns."

"That's good," Barbara replied. "I mean, everybody's got to pee sometime."

"Smoke is more like it," the nurse said. "They're both junkies, have to light up every few minutes."

"I've heard of Ed Eagle," Barbara said. "How's he doing?"

The nurse shook her head. "Not well. He was doing all right until last night, when he contracted an infection. It's going to take a few more days before he'll be strong enough to go home."

"Well, I certainly hope he recovers quickly," Barbara said. She was going to be able to take her time and get this right.

VITTORIO GOT INTO the passenger seat of his SUV, and Cupie got behind the wheel.

"You sure you're up to this?" he asked Vittorio.

"I'm feeling just great. Now get this crate moving."

"Where are we going?"

"I think the best thing we can do, given our lack of information, is to look for that Mercedes station wagon," Vittorio said. "She doesn't know we know about it, and if we find it, all we have to do is sit on it until she shows up."

"Where do you want to start?"

"Well, right now the hospital is ground zero, because Eagle's there. I want to visit him anyway and see how he's doing, so let's start there."

Cupie put the car into gear and drove off toward Santa Fe. They passed through some beautiful high desert before reaching the urbanized outskirts.

"You know," Cupie said, "I wouldn't mind retiring here one of these days. I love the climate."

"You'd enjoy it," Vittorio replied, "but I can't ever see you either retiring or leaving LA. You've still got a daughter there in the DA's office, haven't you?"

"Yeah, she's trying a lot of cases now, getting some

good experience, but between her job and her boy-friend, I'm lucky if I have lunch with her every other Sunday."

Vittorio directed him to the hospital. "Let's take a look around the parking lot before we go in," Vittorio said.

Cupie moved slowly up and down the rows of cars, then pointed. "Over there," he said, "in the employees' lot."

"I see it," Vittorio said. "Let's get over there and take a closer look."

Cupie drove into the lot and pulled up behind the Mercedes station wagon, and Vittorio got out and walked around it, then came back and got into the car. "Nah," he said. "It's got a New Mexico government tag and a health-department sticker on the windshield."

"Why would a state employee be driving a Mer-cedes?" Cupie asked.

"Must be a personal car. It's got an employee's tag."

Cupie found a space in the visitors' lot, and they walked into the hospital and down the hall toward where a cop sat outside Eagle's room. As they ap-proached the nurses' station, a woman in scrubs with a chocolate box under her arm walked away, down the other end of the hall, toward the elevators.

"Nice ass," Cupie muttered.

"Morning, gentlemen," the nurse behind the desk said. "Sorry. Mr. Eagle isn't having any visitors today."

"Something wrong?" Cupie asked.

"He's contracted an infection. We're dealing with it, but he's not up to seeing anybody but his wife."

"We'll come back tomorrow," Cupie said, and he and Vittorio left the hospital.

"Let's go check the hotel lots," Vittorio said, getting into the car.

42

Barbara left the hospital and drove back to the computer shop where she had made her state ID and license plate. She had an idea about how to improve them.

The man at the desk directed her to a vacant computer, and on a whim, she decided to check her old e-mail address. There were hundreds of spam messages, but as she scrolled down she found an e-mail from a law firm she had paid a retainer to when consulting them about overturning her late husband's will. On the morning he was killed in the car crash he had signed a new will that severely limited what she would get in the event of his death. The lawyer had advised her that the will was impenetrable, and there was nothing she could do about it. In addition, the will contained a clause that would reduce the sum paid to any beneficiary to one dollar if the beneficiary contested the will.

There had been one thing she could do, though, and she had done it. She had hired someone to murder her husband's attorney.

"Mrs. Keeler," it read, "there has been an interesting development concerning your late husband's will. It could be greatly to your benefit if you would telephone me as soon as you receive this e-mail." It was signed by Ralph Waters, and the e-mail was dated the day she had escaped from prison in Mexico.

This was interesting, Barbara thought. She forgot why she had come to the computer store and immediately returned to her hotel, where she sat down and called the attorney on her cell phone. He came on the line immediately.

"Mrs. Keeler? This is Ralph Waters. Thank you for returning my call."

"I'm sorry I didn't call sooner, Mr. Waters," she said, "but I've been traveling. What is your news?"

"I know I don't have to remind you about the terms of the will your late husband signed on the day of his death."

"They are etched in my memory," she replied.

"I expect so, but a couple of weeks ago I was playing golf with a lawyer friend of mine who serves on the ethics committee of the California Bar Association, and he told me a very interesting story. A woman named

Margaret Jepson, known as Margie, who was the secretary of Joseph Wilen, your husband's attorney, has made a report to the bar association that may change everything."

"Tell me," Barbara said.

"I'm not sure yet what her motives are, but she says that the will that was probated was not the will that Walter Keeler signed that morning, that Joe Wilen made some crucial changes to it *after* he heard of Mr. Keeler's death in the accident. According to Ms. Jepson, Wilen harbored some ill feelings toward you, so he made certain changes to the will in the word processor, reducing your share to a stipend of fifty thousand dollars a month and the use of, but not the ownership of, Mr. Keeler's San Francisco apartment; then he initialed the pages with the same pen Keeler had used and substituted them for two pages that he removed and destroyed. He told Margie Jepson and an associate in his firm, Ms. Lee Hight, of his actions, since both of them had witnessed the will, and they agreed to join him in a conspiracy to reduce your inheritance."

"The son of a bitch!" Barbara said. "I knew there was something wrong. Walter would have never done that to me. Do we know what the original pages said?"

"Ms. Jepson reportedly has a copy of the will that Mr. Keeler signed, so that would bolster our position. Worst case, if her testimony holds up we could get the will thrown out and then the previous will would apply, and even though you had been married only a short time and might not be mentioned in the earlier will, California law would entitle you to a large share of the estate."

Barbara's heart was pounding. "As I recall, Walter had more than a billion dollars in liquid assets, plus real estate, and others, like a jet airplane."

"That is correct," Waters said. "And there are more good tidings: The will has not yet cleared probate, so none of the assets have been dispersed. Only your stipend has been paid out."

"That's wonderful!" Barbara said. "What should our next move be?"

"I'll need to depose Ms. Jepson and get her to sign an affidavit confirming her story; then I can take it to a judge with a petition to invalidate the will and reinstate the original version. If he signs off on it, then we can submit the original will for probate. Our fallback position would be to get the will declared invalid and reinstate the earlier version."

"Mr. Waters, I direct you to do just that," Barbara said, "and along the way I'd like to see that bitch Lee Hight disbarred for her part in the conspiracy."

"That won't be necessary, Mrs. Keeler, because Ms. Hight died of breast cancer last month. I suspect that is one reason that Ms. Jepson has come forward, since telling her story relieves her conscience and doesn't punish anyone."

"One other thing, Mr. Waters," Barbara said. "I want you to hold this in absolute confidence. I do not want the press to get wind of it. Is that clear?"

"I'll do everything I can, Mrs. Keeler, but at some point this will become a matter of public record, and given the prominence of Mr. Keeler, someone is going to notice."

"I'm going to give you my cell phone number," Barbara said, "and you are not to share it with anyone else." She gave him the number. "I do not wish to be contacted by anyone but you, and should the press contact you, you are to make no comment without my authorization. Is that clear?"

"Perfectly clear, Mrs. Keeler. I'll be in touch." They both hung up.

Barbara leapt from her chair and did a little dance around the room, then fell back into the chair, laughing and crying. She was going to get, at least, hundreds of millions out of this! Then she stopped and began to think.

As far as she knew, her absence from the Mexican prison was not known north of the border. If she now murdered Ed Eagle, the whole story of her divorce from him and her arrest and imprisonment in Mexico might very well come out in the news reports of his death, and she might be either charged with his murder or extradited to Mexico and prison.

"Shit!" she screamed. She was going to have to lie

low until the will was probated, and probably for some time after that. She picked up the phone and called her new friends, Hugh and Charlene Holroyd.

"Ellie, how are you?" Charlene asked. "Hugh, pick up the extension."

"Hey there, Ellie," he said. "We've missed you."

"I'm very well, thanks," Barbara replied. "Do you suppose you could put me up for a little while?"

"Of course. You can have your old room back," Hugh said.

"Or if you'd like more space, take our guesthouse. You can visit us whenever you like," Charlene added.

"The guesthouse sounds wonderful," Barbara said.

"Where are you now?"

"In Santa Fe."

"Well, come on over here," Hugh said. "May we expect you for cocktails?"

"You certainly may," Barbara said. "I'll see you then." She hung up, lay back in her chair and sighed.

It would be fun to see the Holroyds, but she had been so looking forward to killing Ed Eagle.

43

Teddy Fay sat down at his computer and logged in to the Agency mainframe, first establishing his own computer's position in Elmira, New York. He went to the personnel files and pulled up Todd Bacon's service record.

Young Bacon, he learned, had been born in Charleston, West Virginia, to a single mother, had been a star athlete and valedictorian of his high school class, and had attended Columbia University on a full academic scholarship, majoring in languages while playing football and rowing for his school. He had been recruited for the CIA by a professor there and had graduated summa cum laude. He was perfect for the Agency.

He had excelled in every area of his training at the Farm and had had three foreign postings since. In Panama, after Teddy had assassinated the station chief, who had recognized him in a bar, Bacon had been made acting station chief.

It was shortly after Bacon's promotion that he had crossed Teddy's trail on Cumberland Island, in south Georgia, and had managed to put some bullet holes in his airplane's wing. Teddy was uncertain how or why Bacon had made the leap from Panama to Georgia, but he had to believe that the young agent was pursuing him.

Teddy thought he could see the fine hand of Lance Cabot in all this, and that meant Holly Barker as well. This was irritating, since Teddy, after faking his death, had enjoyed being dead. He could not believe that it was in the Agency's interests to pursue and kill him. The media had bought the story of his death, and it would be embarrassing if it was learned that he was still alive. Probably Cabot was just tidying up a messy corner of his realm as deputy director of operations, and if so, Holly Barker would be involved too, since she was his assistant deputy director.

He went to the interoffice e-mail program and addressed a message to her.

My Dear Holly,

It was so very good to encounter you in Florida recently. I had thought that since we were not at loggerheads there, you and your superior were prepared to let sleeping dogs lie, as it were. However, the presence of your representative in my last city of residence, and his ingenious but ineffectual attempts to locate me, has told me that someone at Langley wishes to put me permanently to sleep. That is regrettable, and not just for me.

You may tell your superior(s) that I am now reestablished in another part of the world, and should your young protégé, or anyone else, pursue me, I will be forced to put him out of his misery and to do so in a very public manner, requiring distasteful explanations to be made.

I should think that your young man could be more useful to the Agency alive and that he might better be employed elsewhere. If your superior(s) can see the way clear to preserve your agent's good health and not to send others after him, I will promise to henceforth live very quietly. If not, things could get very, very messy.

You may respond to this missive at your internal box number 100001.

Hugs and kisses,
T.

Teddy gave his e-mail a high-priority rating and inserted a sender's line not his own.

———

HOLLY BARKER SAT at her desk, making notes for a report she had to write on a recent Agency operation, when her computer made a chiming noise and a box appeared on her screen, reporting that she had received a high-priority internal message from the director. She opened and read it with growing consternation, then printed it, saved the message and went next door to Lance Cabot's office.

"A moment?" she asked from his open door.

"Come in," Lance replied, not looking up from his desk.

Holly closed the door behind her, which got his attention, then sat down and passed the message across his desk.

Lance began to read it, and she saw a tiny flicker of something on his usually impassive face. When he finished, he put the message down. "I don't believe it," he said.

"You'll notice that the e-mail appears to have been sent from the director's computer," Holly said.

"The gall!" Lance said, with more emotion than she had ever seen him display. "He broke into our mainframe and into the director's mailbox!"

"Looks that way," Holly said. She leaned forward. "Lance, what is your response going to be?"

"Response? You think I'm going to respond to this?"

"It's addressed to me. I'll respond, if you like. He's apparently created an internal mailbox for himself."

"When did you last hear from Todd Bacon?" he asked.

"This morning. I'm afraid Teddy is running rings around him."

"Should we send someone to help him?"

"Lance, read the message again."

"I've read it twice."

"Then you understand that he is going to start killing again. Do you want that?"

"Of course not."

"Please remember," Holly said, "that Teddy is professionally and personally very well equipped—perhaps as much as anyone in the Agency—to eliminate anybody who tries to get to him, and he's right: If he starts to do that, then explanations are going to have to be made."

"Are you telling me that Todd can't handle this?"

"I have a high opinion of Todd," Holly said. "He is certainly a rising star here and could succeed at any number of assignments. He could also get dead on this one. In fact, I'm surprised that since Teddy so obviously knows about him, he isn't dead already."

"Do you believe, as he implies in his message, that Teddy has moved on from Santa Fe?"

"That's what he does when he thinks he might be discovered: He moves on. I have no reason to doubt him."

"Todd found him once. He could find him again."

"That could very well be the worst possible thing that could happen, both to Todd and to you and, by extension, to me."

"So, Holly, you're worried about your hide?"

"In dangerous situations, Lance, I always worry about my hide."

"Not the mission?"

"This isn't a mission, it's a vendetta, and vendettas can always turn around and bite you on the ass."

"I'll give it some thought."

"Do you want me to respond to the e-mail?" Holly asked.

"Yes. Say, 'Message received and understood.'"

"Is that a threat or are you agreeing to his terms? We'd better be clear."

"I don't want to be clear," Lance said. "I want him to worry."

"Then respond to the message yourself," Holly said, standing up and walking out.

44

Vittorio and Cupie spent their entire day touring Santa Fe's hotel parking lots, motel parking lots, shopping malls and the Plaza. They had spotted two tan Mercedes wagons, both driven by people who were not Barbara.

They returned, dejected, in the late afternoon, and Cupie poured them both a drink. "Maybe we can't protect Ed Eagle," he said as he sank into the recliner next to Vittorio's.

"You going to fink out on me?" Vittorio asked.

"No. We both have an obligation to Eagle, because we let him nearly get killed while we were on the job." He sat silently for a moment, then picked up the phone on the table between the two chairs and called a number.

"Detective Santiago," a voice said.

"Dave, it's Cupie Dalton."

272

"Hey, Cupie. Twice in one week. That's something."

"Dave, you remember the Bart Cross killing."

"Sure."

"Did you find anything interesting at his residence?"

"In the way of evidence? Not much. His killer was a pro—I'd bet on that."

"Did you take any personal stuff from his house, like a diary?"

"Nah, there was no diary. Come to think of it, there was an airplane logbook."

"Now, that's interesting," Cupie said.

"Why?"

"Well, I'm trying to put together a picture of his last few days, in connection with a protection job I'm working on. I think he might be the guy who tried to kill a client of mine, put him in the hospital."

"I see."

"Could you copy the last, say, four pages of the logbook and fax or e-mail them to me?"

"Sure, I guess so. Which do you prefer?"

"E-mail, if you can scan them."

"Give me a few minutes," Santiago said. "You're buying lunch, right?"

"Wherever you like, Dave. I'll take you to the Brown Derby, if you like."

"Cupie, you know very well the Brown Derby closed twenty-five years ago."

"Okay, you can name the place."

"Spago Beverly Hills."

"Done."

"What time?"

"Not today, Dave. I'm in Santa Fe on a case. As soon as I get back. I promise."

"Okay. You'll have the pages shortly."

Cupie gave him his e-mail address and hung up.

"What are you looking for?" Vittorio asked.

"I've no idea," Cupie replied. "Anything. I'm desperate."

They drank their drinks; then Cupie's laptop made the little chiming noise that signaled a new e-mail.

"Incoming," Cupie said, getting out of his chair and setting his drink down on the desk, next to his laptop. He pulled up Dave Santiago's e-mail and opened the attachment, then connected his laptop to Vittorio's computer and printed it.

"So," Vittorio said, "what have you got?"

Cupie went slowly through the pages. "Seems Bart Cross kept a very meticulous logbook," he said, "including dates and names of his passengers." Cupie got to the last page. "Here we go: Bart flew Jim Long to Acapulco and came back the next day with Long and—bingo!—Barbara! Cleared customs at Yuma."

"Yuma? Why Yuma?"

"Well," Cupie said, "if you had just escaped from jail in Mexico, you might want to land at some out-of-the-way place, right?"

"Yeah, I guess," Vittorio said.

"Then he went back to LA and landed at Burbank."

"What about after that?" Vittorio asked.

"A few days later he flew to Albuquerque! Shortly after that we saw him at Barbara's house. Then the day of the attempt on Eagle, he flew back to Burbank. That was the day he got killed."

"I guess Barbara didn't take the news of Eagle's survival too well," Vittorio said.

"Hey, look," Cupie said. "In the notes section he wrote down the color and tag number of Barbara's Mercedes wagon! Arizona plate." Cupie wrote down the plate number in his notebook. "Now we know exactly what to look for."

"I'm getting tired of looking for tan Mercedes wagons," Vittorio said. "Too many of them out there. We saw three today."

"Always good to get the correct plate number, though," Cupie replied. "We got more than that, though."

"What else we got?"

"We know that Jim Long busted Barbara out of the Mexican jail—or at least got her out of the country after she got out."

"That *is* interesting," Vittorio said. "It's the sort of information that might make Long willing to talk to us."

"Tell you what," Cupie said. "Eagle's going to be in the hospital for a few more days. Why don't we go to

LA tomorrow and pay a little visit on our famous film producer?"

"We got nothing else to do," Vittorio said.

Cupie called Long's office at Centurion Studios.

"Long Productions," a woman said.

"Hi. Can you tell me if and when there's going to be a funeral for Bart Cross?"

"Why, yes," the woman replied. "Are you a friend of his?"

"Yes, indeed," Cupie said.

"Well, there'll be a graveside service at Forest Lawn tomorrow afternoon at three. Got a pencil? I'll give you instructions."

"Shoot," Cupie said, then wrote down everything. "Will Jim Long be there?" he asked.

"Yes, he will," she said. "Can I tell him you're coming?"

"Thank you, yes," Cupie said, then hung up before she could ask his name.

"Okay, we know where Long is going to be at three tomorrow afternoon."

"We'll ambush him, then," Vittorio replied.

"If anybody knows where Barbara is, it's Jim Long," Cupie said.

"Maybe she'll be at the funeral."

"Hey, I hadn't thought of that. Maybe we can shoot her and throw her into Cross's grave."

The thought made Vittorio smile.

45

Cupie and Vittorio got off the airplane at LAX and took the bus to the long-term parking lot, where Cupie had left his car. He tossed their bags into the trunk, then opened an aluminum case. "I can offer you a small nine-millimeter or a snub-nosed Smith and Wesson .38. What is your pleasure?"

"I'll take the nine-millimeter," Vittorio replied. "I know you ex-cops like the S and W."

"It's compact, and it doesn't jam," Cupie said, handing Vittorio the semiautomatic in its holster.

Vittorio threaded the holster onto his belt and looked at his watch. "We'd better go directly to the cemetery," he said. "I'd like to look at the setup before people arrive."

Cupie knew the way to Glendale and Forest Lawn.

They stopped at the gate for a map, and the guard showed them where the grave site was.

"This is one hell of a big cemetery," Vittorio said, looking at the map while Cupie drove. "Three hundred acres, a quarter of a million graves, it says here."

"Yeah, anybody who's anybody is buried here," Cupie replied.

"How do you suppose a guy like Bart Cross gets buried here?"

"Long probably paid for the plot."

They drove for ten minutes, following the map, to a corner of the cemetery where there were, mostly, lines of graves marked by flush bronze plaques.

"Over there," Vittorio said, pointing to where a backhoe was at work.

Cupie found a parking spot, and they looked around the area. He pointed to a marble bench with a view of the grave site. "Let's have a seat and wait." He took a newspaper from his jacket pocket and opened it to the crossword puzzle, while Vittorio seemed to zone out, closing his eyes and looking like a statue of himself.

CUPIE POKED VITTORIO on the knee. "Here they come," he said. A hearse leading a short procession of half a dozen cars appeared and drove up a service road near the grave site. Attendants removed the casket from the rear and placed it on a trolley, which they rolled to the graveside. They positioned the casket over the grave, while a few other cars appeared and parked. Soon there was a group of fifteen or twenty people gathered around the grave, and a minister in a dark suit began to read from a Bible.

"Not a bad turnout," Cupie said. "I doubt if I'll do as well."

"There's James Long," Vittorio said, nodding toward the foot of the casket.

"Got 'im," Cupie said.

They watched as the service concluded and the casket was lowered into the grave. People began walking back to their cars.

"Long is in the BMW," Cupie said, "and he appears to be alone. Let's follow and look for an opportunity to brace him. I don't think this is the place for it."

"Whatever you say," Vittorio replied.

They got back into Cupie's car and waited for Long's BMW to pass them; then they fell in behind at a reasonable distance. Long headed in the general direction of Centurion Studios, then, after a mile or so, pulled into a gas station, got out and began to refuel his car.

"Now," Cupie said, pulling into the station and parking to one side. He and Vittorio got out and approached Long, who was leaning against his car and talking on his cell phone while the pump did the work.

"Good morning, Mr. Long," Cupie said. "Remember us?"

"I'll call you back," Long said, and closed his phone. "How could I forget?"

"We won't take much of your time," Cupie said. "We just want to inform you of some of the evidence against you that the police will soon be pursuing."

"What are you talking about?" Long said, looking nervous.

"We can demonstrate to the police that you abetted the escape of Barbara Eagle from a Mexican prison, then flew her to Yuma in Bart Cross's airplane," Cupie said.

"I abetted no one in anything," Long replied, but he didn't move.

"We've got the pages from Bart's airplane logbook, mentioning both your names and your destinations," Vittorio said. "That, of course, led to an attempt on Ed Eagle's life by Bart. You introduced Barbara to him, remember? Then, there's the matter of Barbara's murder of Bart. You're up to your neck in all this, Mr. Long."

"You guys are not cops," Long said.

"I used to be," Cupie said, "and I know lots of guys who still are, even one in Burbank who's investigating Bart's murder."

"What do you want from me?" Long asked.

"We want Barbara," Vittorio said. "And if we can't find her ourselves, then we'll just have to go to the police with our evidence, and they'll start talking to everybody involved, including you. So, it's down to you or

Barbara. What's it going to be? You can do yourself a favor by telling us now where she is."

"I don't know where she is," Long said. "I threw her out of my house after I learned of Bart's death. I don't know where she went."

"But you know where she's going to end up, don't you?" Cupie asked. "You're her only friend in the world; you've helped her at every turn. You know what she's up to."

"She's obsessed with Ed Eagle," Long said. "I don't have to tell you that. I drove her to LAX, so I assume she took a plane somewhere, probably to Santa Fe."

"And once she gets to Santa Fe, where will she go?"

"I don't know."

"Looks like our next call is to the Burbank police," Cupie said.

"She told me she met a couple at a spa in Tucson who live near Los Alamos," Long said. "Name of Holroyd. That's all I know. Maybe she's there, but I can't tell you for sure."

"And how do you get in touch with Barbara?" Cupie asked.

"She uses throwaway cell phones," Long said.

"Give me the number," Cupie said.

Long recited a number while Cupie wrote it in his notebook. "This better be correct," he said.

"It was working as recently as a few days ago," Long said. "You'll keep me out of this?"

"That's not up to us, Mr. Long," Vittorio said, "but if the information you've given us is correct, we won't bring the police into it. The Burbank department has Bart's logbook; they'll be calling on you eventually. You'd better get your story straight and call your lawyer. Or take a prolonged vacation in Mexico."

The gas pump stopped.

"Your tank is full, Mr. Long," Cupie said. "Good luck." Vittorio and Cupie walked back to Cupie's car and got in.

"Well," Vittorio said, "we've got more to go on now than we've had so far."

"Too fucking right," Cupie said, looking at his watch. "We can still make the six thirty flight to Albuquerque."

46

Teddy Fay logged on to the Agency mainframe, apparently from Billings, Montana, and checked the mail for box 10001.

Message received and understood.

The e-mail was unsigned, but it was from Lance Cabot's mailbox. Still, it was inconclusive: Was he off Teddy's back? Or did he understand but not give a shit? This wasn't good enough.

"Any news?" Lauren asked as she came from the kitchen.

Teddy showed her the message.

"That's great!" she said.

"It could mean anything," Teddy responded. "Lance

Cabot, Holly's boss, is a very tenacious young man, and at times, he can be reckless."

"What's your next move?" she asked.

"Well, it's clear I'm going to have to make one. I can't just sit back and wait to see what happens."

"That sounds ominous," she said.

"Not necessarily. I'm going to give Lance until tomorrow to communicate with his agent; then I'm going to go looking for young Todd Bacon."

"What will you do when you find him?" Lauren asked.

"I haven't decided yet," Teddy replied. He went to the command level of the e-mail program and checked Holly Barker's trash box. There were four discarded messages from Todd Bacon, and Teddy read them, chuckling at the report about the GPS tag he had placed on Teddy's Volvo. The first message mentioned La Fonda.

Teddy then hacked into the central computer of the company that supplied rental cars to the Santa Fe Jetcenter and found that Todd had rented a red Taurus there, but Teddy hadn't seen that car on the day when Todd was following him. He went further and found that La Fonda used the same company, and that Todd had exchanged the Taurus for a silver Toyota. He made a note of the license plate.

LATE THAT NIGHT, Teddy put a few things into a case, then drove to La Fonda, only five minutes away. He entered the hotel parking garage and began looking for a silver Toyota. He found two, and the second one had the correct plate number.

Teddy opened his case and removed a later version of the same tracking unit that Todd had placed on the Toyota. He fastened it in place under the car, then closed his case and left the garage. Back in his car, he turned on the handheld GPS unit and got a response from the Toyota.

Good, he thought. Now he could choose the time and place of his meeting with Todd.

TODD WAS, at that moment, in bed with Dolly in his hotel room, doing one of the things that she clearly loved most. After he had brought her and himself to a screaming climax, he lay back in bed with her head on his chest and ran his fingers through her thick hair.

"What's become of your friend Ellie Keeler?" he asked.

"I don't know," Dolly replied. "I haven't heard from her."

"That name is familiar. Is her first name Eleanor?"

"Yes."

"How did you meet her?"

"She rented the guesthouse next door to Tip's place

when I was living in his guesthouse. She knocked on the door, and I gave her a drink."

"I'll bet that's not all you gave her." Todd chuckled.

She reached up and slapped him lightly across the face. "Behave yourself," she said.

"I was thinking, why don't we get together again? She was quite something."

"Yes, she is, isn't she? I'd like that."

"Do you know how to get in touch with her?"

"I have her cell phone number," Dolly replied. "I'll call her in the morning, if you like."

"Tomorrow night is good for me," Todd said. "I'll take the two of you to dinner, if you can get hold of her."

"I'm sure she'd like to get hold of you," Dolly laughed.

"And you as well," Todd said.

VITTORIO AND CUPIE got back to Vittorio's house late, after stopping for dinner on the way from Albuquerque Airport.

Vittorio found the Los Alamos section of the phone book and looked for the name "Holroyd." There was only one listing.

"It's on Big Bowl Road," he said.

"Do you know it?"

"Yeah. A zillion years ago the mountain where Los

Alamos is was an active volcano. One day the thing exploded, blowing the top off the mountain and sending pieces of it as far away as Kansas. The result was that a big, shallow bowl of a valley was formed where the top of the mountain used to be, and that's where Big Bowl Road is. It's very beautiful up there."

"Well, tomorrow, why don't we do some sightseeing?" Cupie suggested.

"I think that's a good idea."

"Is there a house number?"

"Yes, 1228. That's part of the new federal plan to give every house in the U.S. a street address, for the emergency services, in case they have to find it. It means that the Holroyd house is twelve-point-twenty-eight miles from the nearest intersection with a main road, so it shouldn't be hard to find."

"Now," Cupie said, "we have to talk about what we do if we find her."

"Yeah," Vittorio replied. "I guess we do."

BARBARA HAD REACHED the Holroyds' house in time for dinner, and their cook had done some of her best work. They feasted on venison that Hugh had shot near his house.

"There's plenty of it up here," he said. "All you have to do is conceal yourself, make sure you have a clear field of fire and wait. One will come along soon."

"Hugh, how long have you two lived up here?"

"Seven years," Holroyd said, "though we travel a lot. We also kept our place in San Francisco."

"That's where I live, too," Barbara said.

"Wait a minute: Keeler. Were you married to Walter Keeler?"

"Yes, I was," Barbara replied.

"I read about his death in that awful accident," Hugh said. "I'm very sorry."

"Thank you. Did you know Walter?"

"Yes. I did some business with him, supplied aluminum avionics trays for the units he manufactured. I liked him."

"So did I," Barbara said.

"I knew his lawyer, too—Joe Wilen?"

"Oh, yes," Barbara said. "I knew him, too."

"I didn't like him as much as Walter, though. He tried to screw me on a deal once."

"He did the same for me," Barbara said. She told them about how Wilen and his associate had changed her husband's will.

"Well, I hope you finally get everything that's coming to you," Hugh said.

"I usually do," Barbara replied.

47

E d Eagle was pushed in a wheelchair to the door of the hospital, and a cop held the car door open for him. Susannah got behind the wheel; then the cop got into the unmarked car behind them and followed them home.

Ed walked into the house and looked around. "God, but I've missed this place," he said.

Susannah helped him off with his coat. "And you've been missed here, too." The first couple of nights after he was hospitalized, she had slept on a cot near him, but when he was better she had gone home nights.

"Do you want to lie down?" she asked.

"No," he replied. "I want to call the office and tell them I'm still alive." He went into his study, called his secretary, got a few phone messages and told her he'd be back at work the following Monday.

Susannah made them lunch and sent sandwiches out to the two cops, who sat in their car, the motor running, the heater turned up.

"Do you feel safe?" Susannah asked.

"No."

"Neither do I."

"She's still out there somewhere," Eagle said. "I wonder where Vittorio and Cupie are."

"I had a call from Cupie yesterday. He said they were making a quick trip to LA. He didn't say why."

CUPIE AND VITTORIO DROVE up the winding mountain road to Los Alamos, drove through the town and out the other side.

"Next right," Vittorio said, looking at the map. After Cupie had turned, Vittorio said, "Check the odometer for the mileage. We want to drive twelve-point-twenty-eight miles."

They wound down the road into the broad valley, Big Bowl, and as they came up on the house number, Vittorio pointed to a large stone with the name "Holroyd" etched into it.

"Now what?" Cupie asked. "We can't just drive down the driveway."

"There was a dirt road forty or fifty yards up the hill," Vittorio said. "Turn around and let's take a look in there."

Cupie did as he was instructed, then stopped. "I think we ought to go on foot from here," he said. "If Barbara is at the end of this track we don't want her to see the car."

The two men got out of the car and began walking down the road. After a hundred yards they passed a copse of piñon trees and the view down the hill opened up. They could see the Holroyd house and what appeared to be a guesthouse.

Vittorio stopped and took a small pair of binoculars from his coat pocket. He scanned the house carefully, then handed the lenses to Cupie. "Look at the corner of the guesthouse," he said.

Cupie got the binoculars focused, then panned from the main house to the guesthouse and stopped.

"What does that look like behind the corner of the guesthouse?" Vittorio asked.

Cupie grinned. "The rear of a tan station wagon," he said.

"Okay," Vittorio said. "Now we have to go talk to Ed Eagle."

LATE IN THE DAY the phone rang, and Eagle picked it up. "Hello?"

"Mr. Eagle," a cop said, "I've got Vittorio and Cupie out here, and they want to see you."

"Send them in," Eagle said. He hung up and walked to the front door to meet them.

"Good to see you looking well, Ed," Cupie said.

"It's good to feel well," Eagle replied.

"We want to apologize again for letting that guy get at you," Vittorio said.

"Apology unnecessary," Eagle said. "You probably saved my life by getting an ambulance here so fast." He took them into his study and sat them down.

"Here's what we know so far, Ed," Cupie said. "When Barbara got away from the jail—and we still don't know how she did that—she was met by James Long in Acapulco and flown back to the States by a pilot who worked for Long named Bart Cross. They dropped Barbara off in Yuma. Somewhere between Yuma and Santa Fe she met some people called Holroyd, from Los Alamos.

"Barbara rented a guesthouse at Las Campanas and was apparently in Santa Fe for a few days, at least. Then she went back to LA and hired the pilot, Cross, to kill you. After he attacked you he went back to LA, probably thinking you were dead. Then Barbara, having heard that you were still alive, went to his house in Burbank and shot him. We were able to get hold of some pages from his aircraft logbook that confirms some of this.

"Yesterday, we went to LA and watched Cross's funeral at Forest Lawn, from a distance, and after that we followed James Long to a gas station and questioned him. He talked to us, because he's afraid he'll be implicated both in the attack on you and the murder of Cross."

"The son of a bitch," Eagle said. "And we're actually in business with him on this film Susannah is making."

"Right. Long gave it up that he drove Barbara to LAX, and that Barbara might look up the Holroyds in Los Alamos, and this morning we drove up there and confirmed that a car like hers is parked at their guesthouse."

"So, she's in Los Alamos?"

"A few miles the other side," Vittorio said. "What we need to know now is what you want to do about her. We can call the police, but the problem is, she's not currently wanted for anything in this country. We could tell the Burbank cops that she killed Bart Cross, but there's only the aircraft logbook to tie her to him at all, and we have no evidence that she hired Cross to kill you."

"I see the problem," Eagle said. "She'll be wanted in Mexico for breaking prison, I assume."

"There's a problem there, too," Cupie said, "because nobody seems to know she's out of prison except the warden and a cop I know in Tijuana, who got the warden to tell him."

"How could nobody know about a prison break?" Eagle asked.

"We believe that the warden had been screwing Barbara, or vice versa, and that she probably found an opportunity to get out through his office or his attached apartment, and that when he found her gone, he simply didn't tell anybody. When you think about it, the only way she could be proved missing would be for the government to send some people down there and count noses. But that hasn't happened."

"So, getting her arrested in Mexico, the way we did before, isn't an option?"

"Not really. And she entered the country legally, at Yuma, so right now nobody can lay a hand on her."

"So, I'm supposed to sit around and wait for her to try to kill me again?"

Cupie and Vittorio exchanged a meaningful glance.

"What?" Eagle asked.

"The next step is entirely up to you, Ed," Cupie said.

Eagle looked at them both. "You have a recommendation?"

"No," Cupie said. "We don't, and I think we should be careful what we discuss."

Eagle gazed out the window at the landscape for a long moment. "I'm going to have to think about this and talk with Susannah about it."

"I wouldn't do that, Ed," Cupie said.

48

Eagle looked up a number in his address book. "Hang on," he said to Cupie and Vittorio. "I need to make a call to a guy I went to law school with, who works in the State Department now."

Eagle dialed the number, a direct line that was picked up by a secretary.

"Mr. Abbott's office," she said.

"This is Ed Eagle speaking. I'm an old friend of Mr. Abbott's, and I'd like to speak to him, please."

"One moment, Mr. Eagle," the woman said. "I'll see if I can locate him." Eagle pressed the speaker button so the two PIs could hear.

"Ed?"

"Bob, how are you?"

"I'm very well, and you?"

"I'm well and getting better." He told Abbott about the attack on him.

"Wow," Abbott said. "I guess the practice of criminal law is more dangerous than I thought."

"In this case, Bob, the danger is in whom you choose to marry. This is the third attempt on my life, and my ex-wife was behind all three."

"Didn't I read something about her being arrested in Mexico?"

"Yes, and she was sent to prison there, but she escaped."

"Is there some way I can help, Ed?"

"I hope there is, Bob. I have reason to believe that the warden of the prison from which she escaped has not reported that fact to his superiors, so there is no police search on for her."

"How could that happen?"

"My assumption is he just kept her on his books, and nobody outside the prison knows she's gone. What I need is for somebody from the Mexican Ministry of Justice to go there and demand to see Barbara Eagle. When they learn she's gone, she'll officially be wanted."

"Do you have any idea where she is now?"

"Two private investigators I've employed tell me she's at the home of some people she knows, near Los Alamos."

"Why don't you call the New Mexico State Police?"

"Because she's not wanted for any crime in the U.S.

If the Mexican government makes a request for extradition, then she can be arrested here and sent back. It'll take time, but she'll at least be in jail while we're waiting. Right now, we're pretty sure she's plotting another attempt on my life."

"Ed, this is the worst thing I've ever heard. I have a solid contact in the Mexican foreign ministry, and he will certainly know someone at Justice. I'll call him and see if we can get an investigation going."

"Thank you, Bob," Eagle said. "You can understand that time is of the essence."

"Certainly, Ed. I'll get back to you when I know something."

"Thank you so much, Bob." Eagle hung up and turned to Cupie and Vittorio. "All right, we're moving on that front. Now I suggest, Cupie, that you call whoever you can in LA and see if you can get them to issue an arrest warrant for Barbara. I know we're light on evidence, but I'd like her off the street."

"So would we, Ed," Cupie said. "I'll get right on it."

"You can use the phone in the living room," Eagle said.

Cupie went into the living room, dialed the number in Burbank and asked for Dave Santiago.

"Detective Santiago."

"Dave, it's Cupie Dalton. I'm going to give you an opportunity to turn that lunch I owe you into a dinner, with a very expensive bottle of wine."

"You have my attention, Cupie."

"I know who killed Bart Cross."

"Are you going to share that name with me?"

"It's two names. Got a pencil?"

"Always."

"Her name is Barbara Eagle, and she also uses the name Eleanor Keeler."

"Wait a minute," Santiago said. "Isn't that the woman who was tried and acquitted of the murder of some Mafioso at the Hotel Bel-Air?"

"One and the same."

"And she was married to that guy, Keeler, the electronics zillionaire, who drove his car into a gasoline tanker?"

"It sounds as though you've been introduced to the lady."

"No, but I read the tabloids like everybody else. Tell me why you think she killed Cross."

"Evidence that she knew him is in the airplane logbook you're already in possession of. The next-to-last page in the logbook."

"Wait a minute," Santiago said. He came back a moment later. "Okay, I've got it: a flight from Acapulco to Yuma?"

"That's it. That's proof that she knew him. The guy she was traveling with is James Long."

"Movie producer?"

"Righto."

"Motive?"

"She hired Cross to kill my client, Ed Eagle, and he very nearly got it done, cut the man's throat. When Barbara heard Eagle was still alive, she killed Cross and burned her bridges."

"Is Long involved in this?"

"I can't prove that he knew she was going to kill Cross, but he certainly introduced the two, and he told me that he kicked her out of his house when he heard about the murder. Cross worked for him out at Centurion."

"What *can* you prove?"

"I'm afraid that's up to you and your guys, pal, but trust me, she's your perp."

"Any idea where she is?"

"As a matter of fact I do. Long told me she knows some people in Los Alamos, and my partner and I tracked her there this morning, saw her car parked at their guesthouse. Their name is Holroyd." Cupie gave him the address.

"Cupie, I've been through the murder book, and we don't have anything that can place anybody in that house on the night Cross was killed."

"Well, you know *somebody* was there, Dave."

"Sure, we do."

"You need to go back to that house and find something—*anything*—that can put her at the scene. Her prints and DNA are in the system."

"I can get that done," Santiago replied.

"In the meantime, can you get a warrant and get her off the street before she makes another attempt on Ed Eagle's life?"

Santiago was silent for a moment. "Cupie, I'd like to help you, but all we can prove is that she knew Cross, and that's not enough for an arrest warrant. The DA would throw me out of his office."

"I'll give you odds she's still got the gun," Cupie said. "And that would be all you need."

"Cupie, she's in New Mexico."

"I know that."

"Haul James Long in and grill him. Maybe he'll give her up."

"Guy like that is going to lawyer up instantly."

"I'll bet you he'd sell her out for immunity."

"It's a thought. I'm going to have to get back to you, Cupie."

"Make it soon, Dave. You've got my cell number."

"Where are you now?"

"In Santa Fe, at Eagle's house."

"When I know something," Santiago said, and hung up.

Cupie went back and reported to Eagle.

"All right," Eagle said. "Now all we can do is wait: me for my guy, you for yours."

Vittorio spoke up. "Ed, we've involved the U.S. government and the Burbank police in this, and that means that we can't do anything, ah, extracurricular, to Barbara."

"I understand that," Eagle said, "and we're all better off not being tempted."

49

Barbara was watching *Morning Joe* on MSNBC, as Joe Scarborough, in a generous mood, was saying something nice about Barack Obama.

"Pinko!" she shouted at the screen as her cell phone rang. Barbara found it under a pile of clothes and picked it up. "Yes?"

"Barbara, this is Ralph Waters, in Palo Alto."

"Yes, Ralph."

"I've made some real progress here," the lawyer said. "I've located Margie, the secretary, and she's given me copies of the two pages that were changed in Walter's will, along with copies of the two replacement pages. I've taken it to a judge, and he's going to schedule a hearing as soon as he can appoint a new executor to represent the estate."

"Why does he have to do that?"

"Because Joe Wilen was the executor, and Ms. Hight was the backup, and they're both dead."

"Oh. How long is this going to take?"

"I can't say. I've pushed the judge as hard as I can to move this along, and I'll call his clerk tomorrow to remind him."

"Once the hearing date is set, how long will the process take?"

"If everything goes smoothly everything could be decided at the hearing, and I'll ask the judge for expedited probate."

"All right, Ralph. Call me the minute you know something."

"Do you want to come to the hearing?"

"Not unless I have to."

"No, you don't. I can represent you."

"Thank you, Ralph, and please continue to keep this quiet."

"I'll do the best I can."

They both hung up.

She tried not to hope, lest she be disappointed. She watched television for another two hours and was about to get into a shower when her cell phone rang again.

"Yes?"

"Barbara, it's Ralph Waters."

"Hello again, Ralph."

"I've got something incredible to tell you: The judge

has appointed a new executor. He's an underemployed crony of the judge, who will do whatever he's told. We've got a hearing tomorrow, and Margie is going to be there with the original pages of the will!"

"That's fantastic, Ralph! I don't know how you got this done so quickly!"

"It was a matter of knowing which judge to take this to," Waters said.

"What about the other heirs?"

"There'll be no dispute there. They'll inherit as per the will, so they'll have no beef. The only entity that will lose on this is Walter's personal charitable foundation, and Walter's old secretary is the head of that. What sort of relationship did you have with her?"

"I met her only once, and we got along very well. After that, I spoke to her when I was calling Walter, or he was calling me, and that's all."

"Then I hope she won't be a problem," Waters said. "One thing: The judge wants you at the hearing, and I think your testimony will be valuable."

"I'll be there. If the hearing goes our way, do you think you can get the new executor to release Walter's airplane for my use?"

"I'll try, Barbara."

"You call me the minute that hearing is over, Ralph. What time is it set for?"

"Eleven a.m. The judge is a late sleeper."

"I'll look forward to hearing from you," Barbara

said, then hung up and fell to her knees. "Dear God," she prayed, "I'm sorry I've been such a bad person, but if you'll let me have this money, I'll never kill anybody again, not even Ed Eagle!"

IN TRES CRUCES, Pedro Alvarez was sitting at his desk, speaking to his bookie about a soccer game in Mexico City that weekend, when there was a knock on his door.

"Come in!" Alvarez shouted, and went on with his conversation. The door opened, but he paid no attention. "One hundred pesos on Mexico City," he was saying.

"Capitán," the female guard said.

Alvarez turned and looked at her, and there were two men in suits and a federal police officer standing next to her. "I'll call you back," he said to the bookie, and hung up.

"Capitán Alvarez," the taller of the two civilians said. "I represent the minister of justice."

Alvarez's mouth dropped open. This did not sound good, and the presence of the policeman was even worse. He got to his feet and saluted. "Good morning, señor," he said. "How may I be of service?"

The man handed him a document. "This is an order, signed by the minister of justice," he said. "It demands that you produce your prisoner Barbara Eagle forthwith."

Alvarez's mouth went dry, his head began to spin and he fainted. He woke up when someone threw a glass of water in his face. He raised a hand to wipe away the water and discovered that it was handcuffed to his other hand.

ED EAGLE ANSWERED his ringing phone. "Hello?"

"Ed, it's Bob Abbott, in Washington."

"Hello, Bob. I didn't expect to hear from you so soon."

"I spoke to my friend in the Mexican foreign ministry after you called, and he spoke to his contact in the Ministry of Justice. Apparently, there was a Justice official in Acapulco for a conference, and yesterday morning he and an associate visited the women's prison in Tres Cruces and confronted the warden, a Captain Alvarez."

"That's good news, Bob. What was the outcome?"

"They demanded that he produce Barbara Eagle, and he passed out on the floor."

Eagle laughed. "That must have been a rude shock for the man."

"Apparently so. When they revived him he confessed that he had not reported her escape because he was embarrassed."

"I expect he was."

"In any case, the official called Mexico City, the minister of justice signed an arrest warrant for Barbara

Eagle on a charge of escape from prison, and he faxed the warrant to me. I have it in my hand."

"That's wonderful news, Bob. What's the next step?"

"I have to messenger this over to the attorney general, who will issue an order to the director of the FBI, directing him that the U.S. government has acquiesced to extradition. The director will then instruct the agent in charge of the Santa Fe office to see a federal judge and apply for an extradition warrant. Once that's signed by the judge, then agents will go to the address in Los Alamos and arrest her. There'll be an extradition hearing soon after that."

"I don't see how she can beat extradition," Eagle said.

"Neither do I. It's going to take several days to penetrate all these layers, but I'll move it along as well as I can."

"Thank you, Bob," Eagle said. "I owe you a very nice vacation as my guest in Santa Fe, just as soon as this is over."

"I'll take you up on that, Ed."

Eagle thanked him again and hung up. "Susannah!" he shouted. "Good news!"

50

Ralph Waters called Barbara back half an hour later. "I've spoken to the executor, and he's released the airplane for the round-trip. I've spoken to the FBO, and they can have the airplane in Santa Fe by five o'clock, at Santa Fe Jetcenter. You'll be home by dinnertime."

"Wonderful!" Barbara said. "See you tomorrow morning!" She packed everything and called the live-in maid at the San Francisco apartment and warned her of her arrival. She then announced her departure to the Holroyds, who were sorry she was leaving and invited her back anytime. She was at the airport by four thirty and watched the beautiful airplane land and taxi in.

The captain came into the FBO, introduced himself and directed the loading of her luggage. There was no need to refuel, so he escorted her aboard the airplane immediately.

Barbara stood in the aisle and looked around her at the gleaming leather and walnut interior. "It's wonderful," she said to the stewardess. "What kind is it?"

"It's a Gulfstream Four," the young woman replied. "Haven't you flown on it before?"

"No. Walter had a CitationJet when we were married, and he bought this airplane immediately after that. He died before we could fly in it together."

The stewardess helped her choose a seat and brought her a drink and a snack while they were taxiing to the runway. As the big airplane roared down the runway Barbara smiled and thought to herself that this was the only way to travel.

They landed at San Jose two hours later, after bucking a headwind, and the FBO had arranged a car to meet her. An hour later she walked into the San Francisco apartment and found it exactly as she had left it. She ordered dinner and began going through her wardrobe to select the perfect courtroom outfit.

THE JUDGE CALLED the court to order and asked Ralph Waters to present his case.

"I call Mrs. Walter Keeler," Waters said, and Barbara took the stand and was sworn. She was wearing a black Chanel suit and appropriate jewelry.

"Mrs. Keeler, how long did you and Mr. Keeler know each other before you were married?"

"Only a few weeks," Barbara replied. "We fell in love almost on sight."

"Do you remember the day Mr. Keeler died?"

"Very well."

"Can you tell us what occurred that day before his death?"

"We had breakfast together on the terrace. Walter said that he wanted to go down to Palo Alto to close up his old apartment, and that he wanted to see Joe Wilen and make a new will."

"Did he tell you what would be in the will?"

"Yes. He told me he had a few bequests to make, including one of a hundred million dollars to his foundation, and that the rest would come to me. In fact, he had made notes to that effect, and he showed them to me."

"And after Mr. Keeler's death, when did you hear from Mr. Wilen?"

"He called me that afternoon to tell me about the accident, but I had already heard about it on television. He said he needed to see me and made an appointment for the next day."

"And what did he have to say to you at that time?"

"He told me that my inheritance was use of the apartment and a monthly allowance for life, nothing else. He also told me that Walter had put a clause in the will saying that anyone who contested it would have their inheritance reduced to one dollar, and he advised me not to contest it. I told him what Walter had said to me the previous morning, but he said that was not what was in Walter's mind. He gave me a copy of the will and showed me the relevant pages."

"Thank you, Mrs. Keeler," Waters said. "That concludes my questioning. Your Honor, do you have any questions for my witness?"

"No," the judge said.

Waters called the secretary, Margie, to the stand and asked her to give her version of events on the day Walter Keeler had died.

"Mr. Keeler had come into the office that day to sign the will that Mr. Wilen had prepared from his telephone instructions," she said. "He also instructed Mr. Wilen to disperse funds to pay for an airplane he had bought."

"Did Mr. Keeler read the will?" Waters asked.

"Yes, and very carefully. He took his time; then he signed it and Ms. Hight, another office worker, and I witnessed it, and I notarized his signature."

"What did you do with the will at that point?" Waters asked.

"I made two copies for Mr. Keeler and his wife, and I put the original in our safe, at his request."

"Can you give us a brief summary of Mr. Keeler's bequests in the will?"

"He left bequests for his alma mater and several

friends, and a bequest to his personal charitable foundation. The remainder of the estate he left to his wife, Eleanor Keeler."

"How much was the total of the bequests left to others?" Waters asked.

"Approximately four hundred million dollars," Margie replied.

"And how much was the residue left to Mrs. Keeler?"

"Approximately one billion two hundred million dollars in liquid assets," she said, "plus the San Francisco apartment; the Palo Alto apartment, which he planned to sell; the new airplane he had just bought; and several pieces of commercial real estate, including a hangar with an apartment in it at San Jose Airport."

"What was Mr. Keeler's mood during his visit to your law firm?"

"He was quite cheerful and happy. He had just been married, and he was very happy about that."

"What time did Mr. Keeler leave the firm?"

"Around three in the afternoon," she replied. "He wanted to beat the rush-hour traffic back to San Francisco, and he took the two copies of the will with him."

"And do you remember what happened after that?"

"Yes, vividly. Half an hour after he left the office, someone had a local TV station on our office set, and they reported that a car driven by Walter Keeler had collided with a gasoline tanker truck on the interstate, and that he had been killed and his car destroyed by the flames."

"What happened then?"

"Joe Wilen called Ms. Hight and me into his office and read us a letter from Mrs. Keeler's ex-husband, which said some bad things about her. I didn't think much of it, since people who've been divorced often say terrible things about each other, but Mr. Wilen took it very seriously. He told us he had shown the letter to Mr. Keeler and urged him not to leave so much to Mrs. Keeler, but that he had refused to even read it and said the will reflected his desires, something he also said when the witnesses were sworn."

"What happened next?"

"Mr. Wilen told Ms. Hight and me that he despised Mrs. Keeler and was determined to see that she did not get the bulk of Mr. Keeler's estate. He told us about his plan for doing her in and asked if the two of us would cooperate with him. He warned us that what he was doing was unethical, and that if it was ever found out, all of us might go to prison."

"What was the reaction of Ms. Hight and yourself?"

"Ms. Hight agreed immediately, as she shared Mr. Wilen's opinion of Mrs. Keeler, but I was reluctant because although I had met her only once, I thought Mrs. Keeler was a very nice lady."

"But you agreed to join them in this?"

"I felt under a great deal of pressure," Margie said.

"I had worked for Mr. Wilen for more than twenty years, and he had been very kind to me, so, to my regret, I went along."

"Tell us how the will was changed, please."

"It was very simple: Mr. Wilen removed the two pages of the will that dealt with bequests and dictated changes to me which reduced Mrs. Keeler's inheritance to the use of, but not the ownership of, the San Francisco apartment, and an allowance of fifty thousand dollars a month, both for life. I typed up the new pages and Mr. Wilen forged Mr. Keeler's initials on them with the same pen he had used to sign the will, and he instructed me to destroy the original pages."

"Did you do so?"

"I did not. I could foresee a time when I might have to reveal what Mr. Wilen had done."

"And did you do so?"

"Yes. Mr. Wilen was murdered a couple of weeks later, and a few weeks later Ms. Hight was diagnosed with advanced breast cancer. She died a couple of months later. Since they were both gone, I felt I should reveal what had been done to the will, so I wrote to the Ethics Committee of the California Bar Association and told them what had been done to the will."

Waters picked up four pieces of paper from his table and handed them to Margie. "What are these papers?" he asked.

Margie held up two pages. "These are the original pages from the will, as Mr. Keeler had instructed them to be drawn." She held up two pages with her other hand. "These are the two pages that Mr. Wilen dictated to me, eliminating nearly all of Mrs. Keeler's inheritance."

The judge spoke up. "Hand them to me," he said. He read all four pages carefully. "I understand that the chairman of Mr. Keeler's foundation is here with her attorney."

A lawyer stood up. "I represent the foundation, judge."

"Have you read these four pages?" the judge asked.

"Yes, Judge, both the chairman and I have read them."

"Do you have an opinion as to the veracity of this witness's testimony?"

"Judge, we believe her testimony is accurate, and although accepting it reduces drastically the amount due to the foundation, we feel we must accept it."

"Is there any other person in the courtroom who has any objections to raise or wishes to contradict this lady's testimony?"

There was silence in the courtroom.

"In that case I rule in favor of Mrs. Keeler and order that the original pages be restored to the will, and that it receive expedited probate. Mr. Waters, do you have any requests?"

"Yes, Your Honor," Waters said. "We request that the executor immediately transfer the sum of one hundred million dollars, or securities in that value, and that she be given the free use of Mr. Keeler's airplane and its hangar, and that bills for the support and fuel of the airplane be paid by the executor until the will is probated and all the funds dispersed." Waters held up a document. "I have prepared an order to that effect."

"So ruled," the judge said. "Give me the order." He signed two copies and gave one to the executor and one to Waters. "This court is adjourned."

BARBARA HAD TO SIT DOWN, and she had to work very hard not to pee in her pants.

Waters sat down beside her and handed her the court order. "Are you all right?" he asked.

"I'm very well, thank you. I just need a moment."

"Take your time."

The executor walked over and introduced himself. "Mrs. Keeler, if you will give me a voided check on your bank account, I will transfer the funds in cash immediately."

Barbara ripped out a check, wrote "VOID" across it and handed it to the man.

"And as soon as I get back to the office I'll fax a letter to the FBO ordering that you control the airplane and that bills are to come to me, until the estate is settled."

"Thank you so much," Barbara said, giving him a winning smile.

51

Half an hour passed before Barbara could collect herself enough to allow Ralph Waters to walk her out of the courthouse and put her into a cab.

As Waters held the door for her, she grabbed him and gave him a huge, wet kiss. "Send me a big bill," she said, "and on top of that, I owe you the best blow job of your life."

She got into the cab, and the stunned lawyer mustered enough control to close the door and wave her off.

Barbara gave the driver the address of her apartment building, but as they were driving toward home, she saw an important sign hanging in front of a plate-glass window. "Stop!" she said, and the cab skidded to a halt before the premises.

"What's the matter, ma'am?" the driver asked, alarmed.

Barbara handed him a hundred-dollar bill. "Absolutely nothing," she replied, opening the door and getting out. "Have a wonderful life!" She opened the door to the business and walked inside.

A distinguished-looking, middle-aged gentleman, clad in a double-breasted blue blazer with brass buttons, approached her with a welcoming smile. "Good morning, madam," he said smoothly in a mid-Atlantic accent. "How . . ."

"That is the most beautiful thing I have ever seen," Barbara said, interrupting and pointing. "Exactly what is it?"

"That," the gentleman said, "is the brand-new Bentley Mulsanne, and this is the first of its kind to reach the San Francisco market. By the way, my name is Charles Grosvenor," he said, handing her an engraved and embossed card.

"How do you do? I am Mrs. Walter Keeler. I don't suppose this one is for sale," Barbara said.

"Actually, it was a special order by a regular customer, but we received word only this morning that he has suffered a serious illness and will be unable to complete the sale."

"How very sad," Barbara said, looking through a window at the gorgeous interior. "I'll take it."

"This example is in Aspen green with an interior of

saffron and green leather, and trim of burled English walnut."

"I'll take it," Barbara said.

"It has a twin-turbocharged, twelve-cylinder engine rated at six hundred horsepower."

"I'll take it," Barbara said.

"The base price of the car is two hundred and eighty-five thousand dollars, but this particular Mulsanne is equipped with every option available for the car, bringing the total price to three hundred and forty-five thousand dollars, plus sales tax of nine-point-five percent, making a total of three hundred seventy-seven thousand, seven hundred and seventy-five dollars."

Barbara sat down at the salesman's desk and withdrew her checkbook from her purse. "To whom would you like the check made?" she asked.

"Bentley of San Francisco," Grosvenor replied.

Barbara wrote the check, ripped it out and handed it to the man. "I'm going to need a driver," she said.

"We will be pleased to supply you with a uniformed chauffeur until such time as you are able to hire your own person," he replied. "May we arrange automobile insurance for you? We recommend Chubb."

"That's fine. They insure my apartment. My address and phone number are on the check. Tell them to add the car to my policy."

"Do you require a personalized number plate?"

"Yes. Make it KEELER."

He wrote down the name. "We will be happy to make that application for you. Will you excuse me for a very few minutes while I have the ownership paperwork prepared for your signature?"

"Of course," Barbara said, walking over to the car, opening the driver's door, seating herself inside and closing the door with a satisfying thud. The man was calling her bank, of course.

She explored the car's interior, opening the glove box and the center console, running her fingers over the leather and walnut. She adjusted the seat and steering wheel, switched on the ignition and tried to figure out the radio. Soon she had a soft flow of lovely classical music playing through hidden speakers.

Ahead of her along the showroom wall a door opened and a small man in a sharply cut black suit with a peaked cap under his arm emerged and walked toward the car and stopped outside the open driver's window.

"Good afternoon, Mrs. Keeler," he said in a cockney accent. "My name is Stanley Willard, and I have been assigned as your driver."

"What do you like to be called?" Barbara asked.

"Willard is the usual term of address," he replied. "No title is necessary."

"Willard it will be," Barbara said.

"May I give you a tour of the car's controls?" Willard asked.

"Thank you. Yes."

Willard walked around the car and got into the front passenger seat, and for the next ten minutes he took her carefully through each control and showed her how to operate the many systems that displayed on the car's navigation screen.

As they completed the tour Charles Grosvenor entered the showroom with a file folder under his arm and escorted Barbara back to his desk. "Ownership requires a few signatures," he said. "You will receive a temporary dealer's tag and registration. Your vanity plate and permanent registration will be mailed to your home address."

Barbara signed all the papers, and Grosvenor tucked them into a heavy cream-colored envelope embossed with the Bentley logo and handed it to her. "Is there anything else I may do for you, Mrs. Keeler?"

"Yes, there is," Barbara replied. "I would like to buy Stanley Willard."

Grosvenor smiled. "Willard is a free agent, Mrs. Keeler, and you may negotiate directly with him." He leaned in closer and lowered his voice. "You may like to know that he is currently paid five hundred dollars a week."

Barbara stood up and offered him her hand. "Thank you, Mr. Grosvenor, for handling this transaction with such dispatch."

"It has been my very great pleasure, Mrs. Keeler, and I hope that I may continue to be of service. Please call me at any time for any reason."

"Are you married, Mr. Grosvenor?" she asked.

"I was widowed two years ago," he replied.

"Would you like to have dinner this evening?"

"How very kind of you, Mrs. Keeler. I would be delighted to join you."

"Drinks at my home at seven, followed by dinner at Boulevard? I'll send Willard for you."

"Perfect. Willard knows my address."

"Now, how do we get the car through the plate-glass window?" Barbara asked.

Grosvenor pressed a button on the wall next to him, and the window rose like a garage door. "There we are."

"I'll drive, Willard," Barbara said, sliding into the car and adjusting her skirt. "You ride shotgun."

"You may put the ignition key in your purse, if you wish," Grosvenor said. "The starter button will operate any time you're in the car, and the doors will lock or unlock as you arrive or leave."

Barbara settled into the seat, pressed the start button and was greeted with a sound like a distant Ferrari. She put the car in gear, drove across the sidewalk and turned toward home.

"Willard," she said, "I'd like you to come to work for me. How's seven hundred and fifty dollars a week, paid vacation and medical insurance sound?"

"I am delighted to accept, Mrs. Keeler," Willard replied, fastening his seat belt as Barbara rounded a corner with a roar and squealing of tires.

52

Lieutenant Dave Santiago pulled up to the Beverly Hills address, stopped at the curb and switched off the engine. "Jeff, let's get something straight before we go in there," he said to the FBI agent, Jeff Borden, in the passenger seat.

"What's that, Dave?"

"This is my investigation, and I take the lead in the questioning. Got it?"

"In our book," Borden said, "a murder in the United States takes precedence over a prison escape in Mexico."

"Good."

"Dave, I don't have to tell you how thin the ice is that you're skating on, do I? I mean, given the lack of direct evidence against Barbara Eagle in the murder of

Bart Cross, you may have to settle for letting us send her back to Mexico. At least she'll be off the streets of LA"

"I understand that, Jeff, but this guy is our best shot for hanging the homicide on her, if I can turn him. I'm going to be the good cop here—then, if it looks like I'm not getting anywhere, I'll defer to you, and you can explain his other liabilities to him, okay?"

"Okay. I'm good with that," Borden replied.

As they opened their car doors a big BMW swung into the driveway and stopped. James Long unfolded himself from the car and started up the walk toward the front door.

"James Long?" Santiago called.

Long stopped and looked at the two men in suits, their jackets unbuttoned, a badge showing on the belt of the one who had spoken to him.

"Yes?"

"I am Detective David Santiago, and this is Special Agent Jeff Borden of the FBI. We'd like to speak to you, please. May we go inside?"

"Sure," Long said. He unlocked the front door and set his briefcase on a table in the foyer, then led them into the living room and waved them to seats. "Would you like a drink?"

"On duty, I'm afraid," Santiago said, "but thanks for the thought."

"Mind if I have one?"

"Certainly not," Santiago replied. He didn't mind questioning a man who was drinking.

Long walked to a bar built into a bookcase, poured himself a shot of something, downed it, then put ice into his glass and poured another, then returned to where the two sat and took a chair. "What can I do for you?" he asked, taking a tug at his drink.

He was trying to look calm, Santiago thought, but he wasn't making it. "My department is investigating the murder of your former employee, Barton Cross."

"Good. I'm glad to hear it. I was very upset when I heard of Bart's death. He was a good man."

"I'm sure he was, Mr. Long. Specifically, I want to talk to you about your relationship with Barbara Eagle."

"Okay," Long said. "What would you like to know?"

Mistake, Santiago thought. He should have asked how Barbara Eagle was related to the death of Cross. "When did you last see Mrs. Eagle?"

"About a week ago," he said. "She stayed here for a couple of days, and then I drove her to the airport."

"To LAX?"

"That's right."

"Where was she going?"

"She didn't say, and I didn't ask," Long replied. A light film of sweat had appeared on his forehead.

"That seems odd, Mr. Long. You drive an old friend to the airport, and there's no conversation about where she's going?"

"Well, Barbara is kind of odd about her privacy," Long said, seeming to grope for an answer.

Santiago took his notebook from his shirt pocket, opened it to a blank page and stared at it for a moment. "Let's see," he said, "the day you drove her to the airport was the, what, twenty-eighth?"

"That sounds about right," Long said.

"What time of day?"

"Afternoon, I believe. I had just come home from work, and she said she had to leave."

"That would be the day after Mr. Cross was shot in the head in his living room, wouldn't it?" Santiago asked.

"I don't see the connection," Long said, wiping his forehead with the back of his hand and taking another pull from his drink.

"Well, Mr. Long, we know that Barbara shot Bart Cross. The question now is how much help you gave her."

"Help?" Long asked, wiping sweat from his upper lip.

Santiago glanced at his notebook again. "For a start, you introduced Barbara to Bart, didn't you." It was not a question. "In Acapulco, it's says here. That's so, isn't it."

"That doesn't mean I'm connected to anything."

"It means that Barbara is connected to Bart, and you made the connection," Santiago said, careful to sound reasonable, to keep accusation out of his voice. "And you're right, there's nothing wrong with introducing two people. You and Bart dropped her off at Yuma International, didn't you? I'm just trying to get the sequence of events established."

"Well, yes, and I didn't see her for a couple of weeks after that."

"She asked you how to get in touch with Bart, didn't she?" Santiago asked. "I mean, you were her only connection to him, weren't you? Seems logical that she would ask you for his number."

"She may have," Long replied, wrinkling his brow as if trying to remember.

"So, here's how it went after that, Mr. Long," Santiago said. "She hired Bart to kill Ed Eagle, and he did his best, but Eagle survived the attack. Barbara killed him so he couldn't connect her to the attempt."

"Look here," Long said. "Do I need a lawyer?"

"You're certainly entitled to a lawyer, Mr. Long. I'd be happy to explain your rights in detail, if you wish. Whether you *need* a lawyer is another matter."

"I have a law degree," Long said, pulling himself upright in his chair. "I don't need to have my rights explained to me."

"Duly noted," Santiago said, scribbling something in his notebook. "Do you need a lawyer, Mr. Long?"

Long stared at him. The booze was obviously taking effect now, and his thinking must be affected.

"Mr. Long," Santiago said gently, "I'm not after

you. I know you didn't kill Bart Cross, just as I know that Barbara did. What you have to decide now is how much you want your future to be affected by what Barbara has done. Surely you know that this is not the first time she has hired a killer. There was a fellow named Jack Cato, who also worked for you from time to time as a stuntman. She hired him to kill a lawyer in Palo Alto, remember?"

"I don't know anything about that," Long said emphatically.

"Mr. Long," Santiago said slowly. "If you cooperate with my investigation now, answer questions freely and agree to repeat your answers in court, I don't see why you should be placed in jeopardy for what Barbara has done. You're not a target of my investigation now, but from here on in, the story could change, depending on your truthfulness. Do you understand?"

Long stared into his drink. "I think I want a lawyer," he said.

"If you make that a formal request, then this questioning will end right here," Santiago said, "but I need to explain to you that a lawyer will instruct you not to answer any other questions about your relationship to Barbara and her decision to kill Bart. He will advise you to stand on your rights under the Fifth Amendment of the United States Constitution, but frankly, that would be a very big mistake. Don't you think so, Jeff?"

Borden took his cue and leaned forward in his chair.

"I should tell you, Mr. Long, that in Mexico, you may not have the same rights as you do in the United States. We now know that Barbara Eagle escaped from a Mexican prison and met you in Acapulco—perhaps you even drove her there—and that you assisted her in entering the United States."

"She has a passport. She had a right to enter the country."

"But the Mexicans are going to say that you abetted her escape from prison and in fleeing the country. And on this side of the border, well, Homeland Security will have to get involved, and frankly, I don't think you're going to have time to produce movies while you're trying to stay out of prison in two countries."

Long was breathing harder now.

"I should tell you, too, that the Mexican Ministry of Justice has requested the extradition of Barbara Eagle to Mexico, and the attorney general of the United States has agreed to extradite her, and a federal judge has issued a warrant for her arrest."

Long drained his glass and set it down on a table next to him. "That woman is the best piece of ass I have ever had in my life," he said, "but I am *not* going to go to prison for her."

"You've made the right decision, Mr. Long," Santiago said. He removed a pocket recorder from his jacket pocket, pressed a button and set it down on the coffee table in front of Long. "Now, let's start again."

53

Todd Bacon was watching a football game on television when the phone rang. "Hello?"

"Hi. It's Dolly. How are you?"

"I'm good, Dolly. I've been waiting to hear from you."

"I was trying to reach Ellie, but she didn't answer her cell phone right away. When I finally got her, she was in San Francisco, so she can't join us."

"That's too bad," Todd said, with genuine regret.

"Can you make do with just me?"

"You bet I can," he replied with feeling.

"Tell you what—why don't you come out here to the house?"

"Okay. Give me directions."

She told him how to get to Las Campanas and to the house.

"Take the second drive to the guesthouse," she said. "That way I won't have to worry about my boss coming home and rousting us."

"Sounds good. Can I bring anything?"

"Nope. Right now is good. See you soon?"

"I'm on my way," Todd said, switching off his TV.

Todd had been holed up in his room for a day and a half, hoping Holly Barker and Lance Cabot would think he was working. His plan now was to fuck Dolly's brains out, then pack up tomorrow morning and leave, maybe try Sedona, in Arizona. Teddy could be there just as well as anyplace else.

He got to the garage and drove out.

AT HOME, Teddy's little GPS unit made a chiming noise, and he picked it up. Todd's car was on the move. Teddy had begun to think he had locked himself in his room and committed suicide.

"I've got to go out for a while," he called to Lauren, who was starting dinner. "I'll call you when I'm on the way home."

"Okay," she called back. "Don't be too late, or I'll be drunk!"

"I'll catch up," he said, laughing. He unplugged the GPS from its charger and got into the Tahoe. Todd's car was moving north toward the road to Espanola, but it turned west, then north again. Teddy followed, not having to see the Toyota, just following the dot.

TODD FOLLOWED the directions to the golfer's house, then passed the driveway and made the next turn. He stopped at the small guesthouse and rapped on the door.

Dolly came to the door naked, grabbed him by the belt and pulled him into the house, towing him toward the bedroom. She stripped him and pulled him into bed with her. "I want you inside me," she said, helping him perform that task.

TEDDY MADE HIS way north, passing the sign for Las Campanas, turned into a driveway and stopped. He could see the large house ahead of him, and there were no cars parked out front. He backed up and drove a little farther down the road until he saw another dirt track, then pulled over and left the car.

The sun was just sinking below the horizon as he approached the guesthouse, and lights came on, as if on a timer or a light sensor. He had a look through a window into the living room and saw no one, so he walked slowly around the house. No one in the kitchen, either, but then he came to a bedroom window and was transfixed momentarily by the sight of a young woman on top of Todd Bacon, riding him like a rodeo pony.

Teddy waited until he heard the noises of orgasm; then the woman got off Todd, went to the bathroom for a minute, then came out. He could hear her say, "Don't you move. I'm not through with you yet. I'm just going to get a drink." She exited the bedroom.

Now, knowing the layout of the house, Teddy let himself quietly inside and peeked around a corner to see her doing something at the kitchen counter. He walked silently to her and chopped her across the back of the neck with the edge of a hand, then caught her and led her easily to the floor. Then he walked toward the bedroom.

As Teddy turned a corner he got a look at the rumpled bed, which was empty. He heard water running in the bathroom and stood by the door, his back pressed against the wall. He removed the nine-millimeter pistol from the holster on his belt and waited. The toilet flushed, and Bacon walked out.

Teddy pressed the barrel of the pistol to the back of Todd's neck. "Stand perfectly still and listen to me," he said. "Cross your arms in front of you." Todd did so. "I'm leaving Santa Fe tonight," Teddy said, "and if you follow me, if I ever lay eyes on you again, anywhere in the world, I'll going to kill you immediately, if not sooner. Do you understand what I'm telling you?"

"You can't run forever, Teddy," Todd said. "They'll keep sending people until they find you."

"You're out of your league, Todd. Remember what I said." He rapped Todd on the back of the head sharply with the barrel of his pistol, and the young man sank to the floor in a heap.

Teddy left the house and walked back to his car.

DOLLY CAME TO FIRST. She didn't understand immediately what had happened to her, but she put a hand to the back of her neck and found it sore. That son of a bitch! Why had he done that? She grabbed a butcher knife and walked back to the bedroom, staggering a little. Todd lay crumpled at the foot of the bed. "What the hell?" Dolly said aloud.

Todd stirred a little, and she turned him over and pinched his cheeks. "Wake up!" she yelled at him.

Todd's eyelids fluttered, and he focused on her face. "What?" he said.

"Somebody's been here," she said. "What's going on?"

Todd struggled up onto one elbow and felt the back of his head, which was damp. He looked at his hand and found blood on it, then got to his feet and sat down heavily on the bed. "Get me some ice in a towel," he said.

She went to the kitchen and returned, and he held the ice pack to the back of his head.

"Did you see anyone?" he asked.

Dolly sat down beside him. "No. I was getting some ice out of the fridge for a drink, and the next thing I knew I woke up on the floor."

"Are you hurt?"

"No, but I'm going to have a hell of a headache tomorrow morning," she said.

"That makes two of us," Todd replied, looking at the towel, which had only a little blood on it. "That was expert," he said to no one in particular. He started looking for his clothes.

"What has happened here?" she demanded.

"I can tell you only that it's work-related."

"Where are you going?" she asked.

"Back to the hotel. I want to wake up in my own bed. I'm leaving town tomorrow."

"I'm leaving here pretty soon myself," Dolly said. "Give me your cell phone number."

He recited the number, and she wrote it down.

"It's been fun," he said, "up until a few minutes ago."

TEDDY GOT HOME in time for a drink and a good dinner; then before he turned in, he went to his computer, logged on to the Agency mainframe, making his location Moose Jaw, Saskatchewan, and addressed and composed an e-mail message.

TODD GOT BACK to his hotel room, took three aspirin and sent Holly Barker an e-mail. "He's gone. I'm moving on to Sedona tomorrow."

54

David Santiago worked late, finishing up his notes and filling out his application for a warrant. Finally, he locked everything in his desk and made a phone call.

"It's Cupie."

"Hey, Cupie. It's Dave Santiago."

"You working late, pal?"

"You know the drill."

"How'd you do with Jim Long?"

"A lot better than I expected. I turned him. I got everything on tape, in exchange for a guarantee of immunity for anything our girl Barbara has done, plus for any testimony he gave at her previous trial."

"That's great news, Dave."

"I'm going to the DA first thing tomorrow morning. You got any idea where the girl is, Cupie?"

"First of all, it's dangerous to think of her as a girl. Think monster."

"C'mon. How tough can she be?"

"Well, the first time I ever set eyes on her I followed her out of a hotel, and she turned into an alley. I called out to her, and she turned around and shot me."

"No shit?"

"None at all."

"I assume you recovered."

"A couple of inches lower and this would be a very long-distance call," Cupie said. "Then there's what she did to Vittorio."

"What'd she do?"

"We had her on ice, taking her back to the States. We were on the top deck of a ferry across the Sea of Cortez, leaning against the rail, basking in the sunshine, when I had to go to the can. In the two minutes I was gone, I later found out, she hustled Vittorio into giving him a blow job, and while she was at work, she grabbed the bottoms of his jeans and tossed him into the drink."

"Holy shit."

"Worse than that—did I mention that Vittorio doesn't swim?"

"How'd you get him back?"

"He found something to hang on to, and a few minutes later a fishing boat picked him up. You see what you're dealing with now?"

"I think I'm getting the picture. Any idea where she is?"

"She'll end up here in Santa Fe," Cupie said, "because she's got this wild hair up her ass about killing Ed Eagle. She might be in Los Alamos."

"Nah. The Feds went to the Los Alamos house to serve the extradition warrant, and she was gone. They claimed not to know where."

"Well, she won't go back to Long's house," Cupie said. "He threw her out, and she's already taken care of her LA business, so she could be anywhere. Remember, she uses the Eleanor Keeler name sometimes."

"Yeah, that's on my aka list. You got any other names for her?"

"She's used a lot, but I don't remember any of them right now."

"How come you're still in Santa Fe, Cupie?"

"Vittorio and I are still on the Ed Eagle thing. We screwed it up once already, when Bart Cross got to him, but this time we've got the local cops to help."

"If she turns up there, shoot her for me, will you?"

"It would be my pleasure, Dave, but she's very, very smart, and I wouldn't give you odds."

"Well, I'll start all over tomorrow," Santiago said. "Good night, Cupie."

"Night, Dave." Both men hung up, and Santiago went home.

THE FOLLOWING MORNING Todd Bacon got up early, went to his computer and did a flight plan for Sedona, then called Flight Services, got a weather report and filed.

He ordered some breakfast from room service. Then, as he was about to start packing up his laptop, he thought he'd check his Agency e-mail. There were two messages, the first from Holly Barker.

Message received. Good luck in Sedona.

Then he clicked on the second message, which was from Lance Cabot.

Report to this office Monday, nine a.m., for reassignment.

Apparently Lance and Holly had disagreed on what his next step was. He started to compose a message to Lance requesting more time, but then he thought better of it. If he got more time and failed again, that could reflect negatively on his future at the Agency. After all, he was dealing directly with the DO.

Todd's instinct was to go on to Sedona. The events of last night had not put him off. Indeed, they had added anger to his motive for finding Teddy. Still, one did not ignore a direct order from the DO. Todd started packing his things.

TEDDY AND LAUREN were having a good breakfast at their new Santa Fe home.

"You're humming," Lauren said.

"Am I?"

"You only hum when you're very happy," she said. "Why are you happy? Does it have something to do with whatever you were doing last evening before dinner?"

"You might say that," Teddy replied. "I was out neutralizing Todd Bacon."

"Do you really think you can neutralize him?"

"I worked it from two angles," Teddy said. "I sent him an e-mail from Lance Cabot, recalling him to Langley for reassignment."

"Well, that might get him out of Santa Fe for a few days, but do you really think that they will stop looking for you?"

"They just might. I sent Lance a note about that very thing a few days back, and by now he's had time to see the wisdom of my suggestion. Lance is a practical fellow. When I used to equip him for missions, he always displayed that. Some of the boys and girls who went out were dreamers, but not Lance."

"I hope you're right," Lauren said. "I like it here, and it would be nice if we didn't have to leave."

"I know you do, sweetheart, and I'll do everything I can to see that we stay here."

She leaned over and kissed him on the forehead. "That's good enough for me," she said.

55

Barbara slept late and had breakfast in bed. She felt wonderful, having had a good dinner and a fine roll in the hay with Charles Grosvenor the evening before, but something was nagging at the edges of her brain, something she couldn't put a finger on. She didn't feel safe.

Mexico, she decided. At some point Pedro Alvarez was going to screw up. It was in his nature, and sooner or later someone above his pay grade was going to find out that she had flown that particular coop. She put aside her breakfast tray, picked up her new lawyer's card, called his number and was immediately connected to him.

"Good morning, Mrs. Keeler," Waters said. "I hope you're feeling well today."

"I am, Ralph," she replied, "but I have a question for you."

"Anything I can do," he said.

"Who would be the best lawyer, besides yourself, to fight an extradition to Mexico?"

"For whom?"

"For me."

"I don't understand."

"Is this conversation covered by attorney-client privilege?" she asked.

"Of course."

"Some months ago I was falsely accused of a crime in Mexico, and after a sham trial I was sent to a women's prison there. I managed to get out and back to this country, but eventually they may come after me. Now, please answer my question."

"We have a partner in this firm who would be ideal to handle that," Waters said.

"If you were in my position, would you choose him above all others?"

"I would, most certainly," Waters replied.

"What is his name?"

"Raoul Estevez. He was born in Mexico and has been a naturalized citizen for more than thirty years, and he has the advantage of the Spanish language, which can be helpful in these matters. He also has a number of contacts in the Mexican government."

"Would you ask him to come and see me this afternoon?"

"At what hour?"

"Four o'clock would be convenient."

"I will see that he is there," Waters replied. "Is there anything else I can do for you?"

"This is less urgent, but I have reason to believe that someone in this country wishes to charge me with a crime. I hope that won't happen, but if it does, then I will need the best criminal lawyer in this city."

"I believe Raoul Estevez would fill that bill as well."

"Good. I'll see him at four." She went to Walter's computer and fired it up, and in a very few minutes she had opened an online brokerage account. She wrote the account number on a card and tucked it into her purse.

She picked up the phone and called her bank. "This is Mrs. Walter Keeler," she said. "Who is the president of the bank?"

"That would be Mr. Evan Hills, Mrs. Keeler," the operator said. "May I connect you?"

"Thank you. Yes."

There was a click. "Mr. Hills's office," a woman said.

"This is Mrs. Walter Keeler. I would like an appointment to see Mr. Hills at the earliest possible time."

"One moment, please."

Within a satisfyingly short time a male voice said, "Mrs. Keeler? This is Evan Hills." They exchanged brief pleasantries; then Hills said, "May I offer you lunch today in my private dining room?"

"That would be lovely," Barbara said.

BARBARA ARRIVED at her bank in the Bentley, chauffeured by the trusty Willard. He gave her a card with his cell phone number. "I'll be in the bank's garage," he said. "Please call if you need me." He held the door for her.

Barbara swept into the bank and was immediately greeted by a man who appeared to be in his midthirties.

"Good day, Mrs. Keeler," he said, "My name is Morton Johns. May I take you up to Mr. Hills's office?"

"Thank you," she replied. She was whisked into a private elevator. They emerged on a high floor and walked past two secretaries and into the office of the bank's president.

Hills leapt to his feet and shook her hand warmly. "I'm so sorry for your loss of Mr. Keeler," he said, "and I was delighted to read in this morning's paper that you had successfully solved your problems with Walter's estate. I know he would be pleased to see his wishes honored."

"Thank you, Mr. Hills."

"I've asked Mr. Johns to join us, since he is the senior vice president who will oversee the day-to-day work on your account and who will be available to you twenty-four hours a day."

"I'm pleased to hear that," Barbara said, accepting Johns's card.

"Would you like to go straight in to lunch?"

"Thank you, but first I'd like to do a little business."

Hills offered her a chair and went behind his desk. Johns took a seat next to her. "What may we do for you?" Hills asked.

"You should have received a wire transfer into my account this morning," she said.

"Yes, Mrs. Keeler, we have had a deposit of one hundred million dollars from the executor of Mr. Keeler's estate."

"You will be receiving a great deal more in the course of events," Barbara said, "and we will discuss over lunch how investments are to be handled. Right now, though, I would like you to wire twenty million dollars to this brokerage account." She handed Johns the card with the account number on it.

"Of course, Mrs. Keeler," Hills replied. "Morton will be happy to do that at once."

"And I would like a cashier's check, payable to me, for twenty million dollars," Barbara said.

Hills appeared to gulp. "Of course," he finally managed to say. "Morton, will you attend to those two transactions immediately, then join us for lunch?"

"Certainly," Johns said. "Mrs. Keeler, are there any other transactions you would like to make at this time?"

"Well, I wrote a check yesterday for three hundred

and seventy-seven thousand dollars to the Bentley people. You might see that it is paid upon presentation."

"Of course. I'll be back shortly." Johns vanished, as
if in a cloud of smoke.

HILLS AND BARBARA were already seated at a beau-
tifully set table in the next room with a fabulous view
of San Francisco Bay and the Golden Gate Bridge.
Hills said, "I'd like you to know that Mort Johns is the
brightest and most capable man at this bank, and I do
not exclude myself from comparison. He is destined to
have my job when I go, and I think you will be very
pleased with him."

"I'm sure I shall be," Barbara replied.

Johns rejoined them and handed Barbara an envelope. "Your cashier's check for twenty million dollars
and your receipt for the wire transfer to your brokerage
account," he said, then seated himself.

"Thank you, Morton," Barbara said. "Now, let's talk
about what we're going to do with the more than one
billion dollars in cash and liquid assets that will soon be
sent to the bank."

Barbara issued instructions while the young banker
made notes and two waiters served them a lunch of
caviar and salmon. When they were done, Hills asked if
there was anything else they could do for her.

"I'd like to make an acquisition," Barbara said. "A

business. I would be grateful if you would research its soundness and availability, and ascertain what price I should offer for it and what I might expect to pay."

This request was received as if it were an unexpected gift.

56

E d Eagle sat at his desk, munching on a sandwich
and reading *The Wall Street Journal*. His eyes fell
on a news story on page two that caused him to begin
choking.

WIDOW OF WALTER KEELER BREAKS WILL

*When avionics billionaire Walter Keeler died in
a car crash, he left a will that severely restricted
the inheritance of his new wife, Eleanor Keeler, to
a monthly allowance of $50,000 and the lifetime
use, but not ownership, of their apartment in San
Francisco. The remainder of his estate went to a few
charitable bequests and to support his foundation.*

Earlier this week, on the testimony of his late attor-

ney's secretary, two pages illegally excluded from the will were restored, and the bulk of Keeler's $1.5 billion estate reverted to his widow. Today, the newly appointed executor is to turn over to Mrs. Keeler more than $1.2 billion in liquid assets, plus her apartment and extensive other real estate holdings.

The lawyer who took it upon himself to change Walter Keeler's will was subsequently murdered outside his home, and an associate who participated in the fraud has died of breast cancer. The secretary, who had typed the original will, had kept the original pages and, freed from the threat of retribution by her former boss, disclosed his actions to the Ethics Committee of the California Bar Association. She has been rewarded by Mrs. Keeler with a substantial whistle-blower's reward.

Eagle cleared his throat with a gulp of iced tea and pressed a button on his phone. "Find Cupie Dalton and Vittorio and get them in here," he said.

CUPIE AND VITTORIO SAT across Eagle's desk from him and read the *Journal* article. "I don't believe it," Cupie said.

"Who could believe a story like that?" Eagle asked. "What does this mean to us?"

"I think it means," Cupie replied, "that Barbara is

going to be too busy spending her money to have time to try to kill you again."

"Well, should she get caught at that, she certainly has a lot more to lose now than ever before," Eagle said.

"And she has a murder charge and an extradition warrant to deal with," Cupie said. "She'll soon be out of our hair."

"I'm not so sure," Eagle said. "Now she can afford any attorney in the United States to defend her. I'll bet she's working on that right now."

BARBARA WAS SITTING ON HER terrace overlooking San Francisco Bay when the maid led Raoul Estevez outside and announced him.

Barbara held out a hand and waved him to a chair. "I'm very pleased to meet you, Mr. Estevez," she said. She found him handsome and well tailored.

"And I you, Mrs. Keeler. Ralph Waters has asked me to inform you that your husband's estate has cleared probate, and the executor has begun to transfer cash and stock accounts to your bank."

"That is very good news indeed," Barbara said brightly.

"Now, Mrs. Keeler, how may I be of service to you?"

"I'll be as concise as I can," Barbara replied. "Two or three years ago I and my sister were on a vacation in Acapulco when we met a charming young man. In the course of events we took him into our bed, but he became violent and abusive, and in order to defend our lives, my sister grabbed a steak knife from a room-service cart and stabbed him, killing him. She also, in a rage, took it upon herself to, ah, remove a part of his genitalia.

"We managed to leave the country undetected, but the young man turned out to be related to an important captain in the Federal Police. My sister subsequently met her death in Santa Fe, and I married a man there, an attorney named Ed Eagle. Do you know him?"

"We've never met, but I know him by his formidable reputation," Estevez replied. "Go on, please."

"I left Ed, and divorce negotiations became difficult. He hired two private detectives to lure me aboard a yacht out of San Diego for a dinner cruise. Later that evening, unbeknownst to me, the yacht sailed into Mexican waters, where it was met by a police boat. I was arrested and subsequently received a brief, extremely unfair trial and was sentenced to twenty years to life in a women's prison at Tres Cruces, east of Acapulco.

"There I was repeatedly sexually assaulted and raped, on almost a daily basis, by the warden, a Captain Pedro Alvarez. Finally, after several months of this abuse, I was able to slip a dose of Valium into his tequila, and I escaped through a window in his apartment, which adjoined the prison. A friend drove me to Acapulco, then we were both privately flown back to the United States."

"I understand, Mrs. Keeler," Estevez replied. "I take it you have not read this morning's *Examiner*?"

"No, I have not."

"There is a story that the United States attorney general has acquiesced to a request for extradition from the Mexican minister of justice, and that a federal judge has issued a warrant for your arrest."

"I was not aware of that," Barbara said.

"I will leave for Mexico City tonight and begin to try and right this wrong that has been done to you," Estevez said. "I understand that you have access to a private jet aircraft."

"That is so."

"I suggest, entirely off the record, that you leave the country immediately and wait for me to contact you."

"Would the Bahamas do?" Barbara asked.

"Very nicely," he replied.

"I will follow your advice, Mr. Estevez."

"Mr. Waters mentioned another legal concern?"

"That will have to wait," Barbara replied.

"If I am to be successful in Mexico one or more bribes will have to be paid. The total could come to as much as a million dollars, perhaps even more."

"I will leave that entirely to your judgment," Barbara replied.

"Very well. Please arrange with your bankers to be

able to wire-transfer funds on a moment's notice to accounts in Mexico or other countries, the numbers of
which I will supply you with."

Barbara wrote down her cell number and the number
of the satphone on the airplane and handed them to him.
"Thank you, Mr. Estevez. Now, if you will excuse me, I
have some calls to make and some packing to do." She
stood up, shook his hand and waved him off.

Barbara sat down again and called Morton Johns at
her bank and explained that she was leaving town immediately and about the need to wire funds. He gave
her his cell number.

"Call at any hour of the day or night and I will attend
to it," he said. "Incidentally, I have researched the business investment you wish to make, and we here consider it to be an attractive proposition." He mentioned
the price. "There is one owner, and he is prepared to
close immediately. I will send the report to you in San
Jose," he said.

"Please proceed with all speed," Barbara said. "You
may use the power of attorney I gave you. Keep in
touch with me by phone, as I will be traveling. You
have the numbers."

"Of course, Mrs. Keeler. And I have some good
news for you: Your husband's estate has transferred
eight hundred million dollars to your account here, and
there is more to come, I am assured."

"Wonderful news," Barbara said. She thanked him

and instructed him to initiate the procedures they had discussed at lunch. She hung up and called the FBO in San Jose and ordered the airplane to be prepared for an immediate departure to Nassau, then made another call.

"Bentley Motors," the operator said.

"Charles Grosvenor, please," Barbara said.

"Please hold."

"This is Charles Grosvenor."

"Charles, it's Ellie Keeler."

"How nice to hear your voice."

"I have an invitation for you," she said. "You've said that you enjoy travel."

"Yes, indeed, Ellie."

"Do you have your passport handy?"

"Yes. It's in my briefcase."

"Here's what I'd like you to do. I'd like you to go directly to the San Jose Airport and meet me there." She gave him directions to the FBO. "We will be departing immediately for the Bahamas."

"I'll have to get time off," Grosvenor said.

"Please don't worry about that. Just walk away now. I'll explain later."

"But my job."

"Don't worry about it, and don't worry about clothes. We'll get you a new wardrobe in Nassau."

"Whatever you say, my dear," he replied. "I'll look forward to seeing you in an hour."

"I'll look forward to it as well," she said, then ran to pack a small bag.

AS WILLARD DROVE HER away in the Bentley, a government car drove up to Barbara's apartment building, and two FBI agents got out and went inside. They were told by the maid, as per Barbara's instructions, that she had flown to Rome earlier in the day.

57

Lieutenant David Santiago was shown into the office of the chief deputy district attorney and asked to sit down and be quick with his report.

Santiago handed the man his completed request for an arrest warrant for Eleanor Keeler. The deputy DA, whose name was Warren, opened a copy of *The Wall Street Journal* and handed it to Santiago. "Does your request for a warrant refer to *this* Mrs. Eleanor Keeler?"

Santiago read the article quickly. "I believe so," he said.

"Play me the tape recording," Warren said, placing his feet on his desk and leaning back in his chair.

Santiago played the recording.

Warren smiled. "I compliment you on the thoroughness of your questioning and the quality of your recording," he said. "I did not see any reference to the discovery of the murder weapon or any physical evidence connecting Mrs. Keeler to the murder of Mr. Cross," he said. "Did I miss something?"

"No, sir. I believe Mrs. Keeler may still be in possession of the weapon, though, and a search warrant might bring it into our possession."

"Lieutenant, are you aware that the Feds have procured an extradition warrant for Mrs. Keeler, and that as soon as she is arrested, she will be returned to prison in Mexico?"

"Yes, sir."

"Well, rather than involve this office in what would be an incredibly long and hideously expensive trial against the kind of defense team that only large sums of money can provide, and without the weapon or any physical evidence, I think it is in our best interests to let the Feds return Mrs. Keeler to Mexico to serve out her sentence. Perhaps during her twenty years to life there you will develop other, stronger evidence that can be used to prosecute her here when she gets out, should either of us still be alive when that occurs."

"Yes, sir," Santiago replied, getting to his feet.

Warren stood and shook his hand. "Good day."

ON HIS ARRIVAL in Mexico, Raoul Estevez checked into his hotel, dined in his suite with the beautiful young woman associate he had brought with him, screwed her thoroughly and got a good night's sleep.

The following morning, having phoned the previous day for an appointment, he breakfasted with the deputy minister of justice, a civil servant who had run his ministry with an iron hand through many governments over many years, and who was routinely deferred to by the political appointees above him, who were happy to deal with the trappings of office instead of the responsibilities. Their conversation took place in the garden of the deputy's home in a Mexico City suburb and was conducted in elegant and nuanced Spanish.

"Raoul, it is good to see you," the deputy said, embracing the lawyer warmly.

"Benicio, it has been too long."

A large breakfast was brought by servants while the two men chatted amiably about fast horses and brave bulls. When the garden had been cleared of servants the deputy sat back, folded his hands and simply nodded.

"Benicio," Estevez said, "I wish to bring to your attention a very serious matter which could cause a great deal of trouble both domestically and internationally for your ministry."

The deputy made a concerned face and nodded again.

"More than three years ago two American women made the acquaintance of a young man who subsequently beat and raped both of them. One of them got her hands on a knife and killed him, then removed the penis from the corpse."

"Ahhhh," the deputy said, nodding.

"I knew you would know of this, Benicio. The woman who wielded the knife is now dead, but her sister, in the midst of an angry divorce, was kidnapped by operatives of her husband and taken aboard a yacht into Mexican waters, where it was met by a police boat. After a brief and highly prejudicial trial the woman was convicted and sentenced to a prison term at the El Diablo prison in Tres Cruces, run by a Capitán Pedro Alvarez.

"There she was raped and otherwise sexually abused by Alvarez on nearly a daily basis. Finally, unable to bear further ill treatment, she managed to drug the capitán and escape through a window from his apartment. She eventually made her way back to El Norte, and now her former husband, who has political influence, has intrigued to have her extradited from the United States and returned to prison.

"The woman, formerly known as Barbara Eagle and now as the recent widow of Walter Keeler, a very wealthy man from San Francisco, has inherited his wealth and is in a position to fight the extradition in the most public and time-consuming manner. Once her story is told and retold ad infinitum by the media on both sides of the border, both our countries will be faced with the worst sort of publicity, and in the end, she might well avoid extradition.

"I believe it would be to the advantage of both your ministry and Mrs. Keeler if you could suggest a discreet resolution to this affair. Mrs. Keeler understands that such a resolution would involve considerable expense and would see that your ministry does not suffer the costs." Estevez sat back in his chair and waited for the deputy to speak.

"Where is the woman at this time?" the deputy asked.

"It is my understanding that she has left the United States, possibly for Italy."

"So, that would complicate even further any attempt to return her to Mexico." It was not a question.

"I am very much afraid that it would."

"The prison warden, Alvarez, has already been dealt with," the deputy said. "He is now supervising a prison work program in the jungles in the south of the country, and all records relevant to the woman have been removed from his former office. It is as if she was never there."

"I see," Estevez replied.

"I believe the simplest solution to our mutual problem would be if our president issued a pardon."

"My client would be *extremely* grateful if that could be effected, Benicio."

The deputy produced a notebook. "What is your client's full name?" he asked.

"Eleanor Eagle Keeler," Estevez replied.

"What time is your flight home?" the deputy asked.

362

"At one p.m. from the general aviation terminal," Estevez replied.

"And the aircraft registration number?"

Estevez gave it to him.

"I calculate that the costs of this transaction will come to"—the deputy did some quick counting with his thumb against his fingers—"two million seven hundred and fifty thousand dollars." He wrote something on a page of his notebook, tore it off and handed it to Estevez. "Here is an account number."

"Will you excuse me for a moment while I telephone?" Estevez asked.

"Of course. I will go and put on a necktie for the office while you call."

Estevez made the call and waited for the deputy's return.

"The funds will be in the account by the time you reach your office," he said.

"Oh, good. Upon verification the pardon will be prepared, signed and delivered to your aircraft in time for your departure. Come, walk with me to our cars."

Estevez fell in step with him, and the two men linked arms. "There is one further step I would be very grateful for," Estevez said.

"Please."

"If you could telephone the United States attorney general, explain that Mrs. Keeler has been pardoned and is no longer a fugitive in the U.S. and that her extradition warrant should be canceled, then she could resume her normal life immediately."

"Consider it done, Raoul." The deputy stopped at his open limousine door and offered his hand. "It is always good to see you, Raoul, and, of course, always a pleasure to do business with you. Go with God."

Estevez shook his hand and got into his own limousine, where his associate waited.

"How did it go?" she asked, placing a hand on his thigh.

"Perfectly and profitably," Estevez replied, adjusting his position so that her hand could better reach its target.

58

Barbara put down the telephone at the pool of her cottage at a private club in Nassau.

Charles sat beside her on the double chaise. "You're smiling. Good news?"

"Very good news," she replied. "For us both."

"Ellie, I don't think I can receive good news properly until I understand why you are unconcerned with my employment status. I do need the job, you know, and I can't relax here while worrying about it."

"Would you like a promotion at your firm?" she asked.

"I'm already the top-producing sales manager for the firm," he replied. "Anything else would be a demotion."

"How do you get along with your general manager?" she asked.

"He's an ass, but there's nothing he can do to me, except for cause, and I've never given him cause, until I walked out of that showroom yesterday."

"Would you like his job?"

Charles thought about that. "Only if I could continue to render service to my clients, and only if I could have the pleasure of personally firing my general manager and throwing him out of his office."

"Then do so," Ellie said. "Yesterday, I bought the firm."

Charles turned and stared at her. "My God, are you *that* rich?"

"I am," Barbara said. "Charles, I know this will seem sudden, but I think it would be very much to our mutual advantage if we married."

Charles fell back onto the lounge. "You are breathtaking, Ellie."

"If you accept my proposal I will make you a gift of the dealership and provide working capital for it. In return, you would sign a prenuptial agreement limiting your settlement, in the event of a divorce, to the firm and any money I have invested in it."

"That is a very generous proposition, Ellie," Charles said. "And I think we could make each other very happy."

"Then why don't we start the honeymoon right now, my dear," Barbara said, snuggling up to him.

————

ED EAGLE TOOK the phone call from his friend in the State Department. "How are you, Bill?"

"I'm okay, Ed, but I have some rather startling news for you."

"Go ahead and startle."

"I've had an e-mail from the attorney general's office. The general received a phone call today from a highly placed officer of the Mexican Ministry of Justice."

"They've extradited Barbara?"

"No, the president of Mexico has pardoned her."

Eagle was dumbstruck.

"Ed? Are you still there?"

"Just barely, Bill," Eagle replied. "Have you any idea how this happened?"

"I don't have any details, only deductions. Have you seen the piece in *The Wall Street Journal?*"

"Yes, I have."

"You must know, Ed, that when the sort of money she has inherited comes into play, things can happen in a hurry, especially in Mexico."

"Are you telling me that Barbara *bribed* the president of Mexico?"

"Of course not. That isn't how it works."

"How does it work?"

"My best guess is Barbara got herself a lawyer who knows people down there, and he passed a large sum of money to someone in the Ministry, who then took care of things and distributed the funds accordingly, probably in cash. That's only a guess, mind you, but I've heard of other cases where this sort of thing happened."

"I could sue her for injury resulting from her attempt on my life, I guess," Eagle said.

"Come on, Ed. What would you say to a client who walked into your office and wanted to sue a billionaire?"

"All right, all right."

"Ed, I'm awfully sorry about this. I did what I could."

"Bill, you did more than I could ever have expected. Thank you." Eagle hung up and sagged in his chair.

THE FOLLOWING MORNING, Barbara called a number at the Nassau Airport and chartered a twin-engine airplane for the day. She instructed the company to file a flight plan to Georgetown, Cayman Islands, and to file a return flight plan for later in the day.

BARBARA TOOK A CAB from the Georgetown airport to a large bank on a principal street and walked in. She approached a man at a desk in the lobby.

"Good day, madam. May I help you?" he asked.

"Yes. I'd like to open an account."

"Please be seated," he said, holding a chair for her. "What kind of account would you like to open?"

"A very private account," she replied. "One with a number, not a name."

"Of course, madam." He looked at his computer, selected a new account number and printed a document. "Please sign here," he said, indicating a line at the bottom.

"I don't wish to sign anything," Barbara said. She took the twenty-million-dollar cashier's check from her purse and handed it to him.

"Of course, madam," the man said. "There is no necessity for a signature. Would you like a card that can draw on the account from anywhere in the world?"

"What a nice idea," Barbara said.

He typed a few more keystrokes on his computer. "The card will be ready momentarily," he said. "Would you like us to invest the funds for you, or would you prefer an interest-bearing account? Currently the rate is three percent."

"The latter, please."

He printed another document. "This will tell you how to view your account and statements online. Nothing will be mailed, since we don't have your name or address."

Barbara received the credit card and her deposit receipt, put them in her purse, shook the man's hand and left the bank. She got into her idling taxi, went to the airport and was flown back to Nassau. Upon entering the country she used the false passport she had had made in California.

"What did you do with yourself today?" Charles asked.

"I built an escape hatch from my life," she replied.

He looked at her oddly but did not question her further.

The following day they were married. Then the Gulfstream flew them back to San Jose.

59

T ip Hanks stood in front of the cameras and received his silver cup and a dummy check for nine hundred eighty-nine thousand dollars. The amount would automatically be wired to his account.

During the past few days he had set a course record and won the tournament by four strokes. He gave an interview to a television journalist, then returned to the clubhouse, showered and changed, and gave another, longer interview to a woman from The Golf Channel.

That night he had a steak dinner, watched TV, then turned in early. He slept late the following morning, and it was noon before he got to the airport. He drove up to his Santa Fe home at four thirty that afternoon, noticing that Dolly's car was not parked out front. She must be running an errand, he thought.

He walked into his home, unpacked his clothes, put the dirty things into a laundry hamper, then walked to his study next door. The room seemed oddly messy. He looked into Dolly's office and found drawers pulled out and papers scattered around the room. His first thought was a burglary, and he went back into his study to phone the police, but he found a pink message slip stuck to the phone.

Bye-bye, sweetie. It's been fun.

He was still puzzling over that when the phone rang, and he picked it up. "Hello?"

"Tip, it's George Herron." Herron was his accountant.

"Hello, George. Did you see I won the tournament yesterday?"

"Yes, I did, and congratulations. I'm afraid I have some troubling news, though."

"What's wrong?"

"I looked through your accounts online today for some tax information, and I saw that your prize money had been wired into your account this morning."

"That is as it should be, George."

"The problem was that it was wired out of your account only a few minutes later to an account in Singapore, as were another seven hundred thousand dollars from a bond fund in your brokerage account. Do you have a bank account in Singapore, Tip? Because if you do we haven't been reporting that to the IRS, as the law requires."

"No, George, I don't have an account in Singapore, and I don't know what you're talking about."

"Who else is a signatory on your accounts?"

"Well, my assistant, Dolly . . ." Tip stopped and looked at the pink message slip. "Oh, shit," he said.

CUPIE ANSWERED THE TELEPHONE.

"Cupie, it's Dave Santiago."

"Hey, Dave. How are you?"

"Not so good."

"Did you pick up Barbara?"

"No, I didn't. The DA wouldn't sign the warrant. Not enough evidence and too much money."

Cupie's face dropped. "I saw the newspaper piece. He was scared off by the money?"

"Of course, he was," Santiago replied. "Think about it. If you were the DA would you issue a warrant on a woman with that much money, without a murder weapon or physical evidence? You'd be looking at another O.J. trial against the best lawyers in the country. It would cost the county millions."

"I see your point," Cupie said. "Thanks for trying, Dave."

He hung up and turned to Vittorio.

"No warrant, huh?" Vittorio asked.

"No warrant."

"I guess you'll be going back to LA, huh, Cupie?"

"I guess," Cupie replied woodenly.

"It doesn't have to be over," Vittorio said. "She'll do something outrageous again, and maybe we'll be in on the takedown."

"Yeah," Cupie said, brightening. "She'll do that, and we'll do that."

60

Todd Bacon landed at the Manassas, Virginia, airport on Sunday night and left the keys to the Bonanza at the FBO desk for pickup by the Agency the following day. He checked into a nearby hotel for the night. Then, the following morning, he was at the Langley headquarters by eight thirty. He killed a little time in the lobby, then checked in with security and took the elevator up to the executive floor.

HOLLY WALKED into Lance Cabot's office.

"What do you hear from our man in Santa Fe?" Lance asked.

"He's our man in Sedona now," Holly replied. "I had an e-mail from him."

"Why Sedona?"

"He didn't say. I suppose he had some trail to follow."

There was a knock on the open door, and both Holly and Lance looked that way. Todd Bacon stood in the doorway.

"Good morning," he said. "I'm reporting as ordered."

Lance stared at him, uncomprehending. "Reporting for *what*?"

"As ordered," Todd said. "For reassignment." He took a folded sheet of paper from his inside pocket and approached Lance's desk.

Holly took the paper from him and read it, then handed it to Lance. "Something you want to tell me, Lance?"

Lance read the e-mail, and his face fell.

"That's the e-mail you sent me," Todd said.

"Oh, my God," Holly said.

"I thought you were in Sedona," Lance said.

"Well, I was going there, but then I got your message. It was in my Agency mailbox."

Lance had turned quite red. "Have you got any vacation time coming?" he asked.

"Yes. I've got two weeks," Todd replied.

"Take it," Lance replied. "Go. Report for reassignment when you get back."

Todd looked at Holly questioningly.

Holly made a shooing motion with her hands.

"Can I keep the Bonanza for my time off?"

"Yes," Holly said.

Todd watched as Lance fed the e-mail into his desk-side shredder; then he got the hell out of there.

"Well?" Lance said to Holly. "What are you looking at?"

"Absolutely nothing," Holly said, rising.

"None of this ever happened," Lance said.

"Of course not," Holly replied.

She went back to her office and started looking for something to take Lance's mind off Teddy Fay.

ED EAGLE GOT DOWN a suitcase from the top shelf of his dressing room and started packing.

Susannah entered the room and watched for a moment. "Going somewhere?" she asked.

"I've got some business to take care of," Eagle said.

"Where?"

"It's better if you don't know."

"I want to come with you," she said.

"I'm sorry, no."

"Ed, if you're going to do this you'll have a better chance of bringing it off if there are two of us."

Eagle closed his suitcase and stared at her. "Listen to yourself. Where do you think I'm going?"

"San Francisco," she replied.

"Why San Francisco?"

"Because that's where Barbara is."

"Do you think I'm going to Barbara?"

"I think you're going *for* Barbara."

Eagle thought about that for a moment. "No. You have to stay here."

"What makes you think you can tell me what to do?" she asked, her hands on her hips.

"I don't know," Eagle said. "I never tried before."

She walked over and put her arms around his waist and her head on his shoulder. "And don't you ever try again," she said.

Eagle sighed and kissed the top of her head. "All right," he said. "Pack a bag."

She ran to her dressing room.

Eagle went back into his dressing room and opened his safe. There was an old .45 in there, one he hadn't fired for years, one somebody had given to him, one that couldn't be traced back to his ownership. He checked the magazine, pocketed another, then put the weapon into a holster and threaded it onto his belt.

When he came back into the bedroom he saw Susannah about to close her suitcase. Her little Smith & Wesson Ladysmith was lying on top of her clothes. "You ready?" he asked.

"More than ready," she said, zipping the bag shut.

Eagle called the airport and asked that his airplane

be pulled from its hangar and refueled; then he and his wife got into his car and headed out.

TEDDY CRADLED LAUREN in his arms. They had just made love, and this was the time he liked most.

"Teddy," Lauren said, "do we live in Santa Fe now? Is this our home?"

"It is," Teddy replied. "Until it isn't."

AUTHOR'S NOTE

I am happy to hear from readers, but you should know that if you write to me in care of my publisher, three to six months will pass before I receive your letter, and when it finally arrives it will be one among many, and I will not be able to reply.

However, if you have access to the Internet, you may visit my Web site at www.stuartwoods.com, where there is a button for sending me e-mail. So far, I have been able to reply to all my e-mail, and I will continue to try to do so.

If you send me an e-mail and do not receive a reply, it is probably because you are among an alarming number of people who have entered their e-mail address incorrectly in their mail software. I have many of my replies returned as undeliverable.

AUTHOR'S NOTE

Remember: e-mail, reply; snail mail, no reply.

When you e-mail, please do not send attachments, as I never open these. They can take twenty minutes to download, and they often contain viruses.

Please do not place me on your mailing lists for funny stories, prayers, political causes, charitable fund-raising, petitions or sentimental claptrap. I get enough of that from people I already know. Generally speaking, when I get e-mail addressed to a large number of people, I immediately delete it without reading it.

Please do not send me your ideas for a book, as I have a policy of writing only what I myself invent. If you send me story ideas, I will immediately delete them without reading them. If you have a good idea for a book, write it yourself, but I will not be able to advise you on how to get it published. Buy a copy of *Writer's Market* at any bookstore; that will tell you how.

Anyone with a request concerning events or appearances may e-mail it to me or send it to: Publicity Department, Penguin Group (USA) Inc., 375 Hudson Street, New York, NY 10014.

Those ambitious folk who wish to buy film, dramatic or television rights to my books should contact Matthew Snyder, Creative Artists Agency, 9830 Wilshire Boulevard, Beverly Hills, CA 98212-1825.

Those who wish to make offers for rights of a literary nature should contact Anne Sibbald, Janklow & Nesbit, 445 Park Avenue, New York, NY 10022. (Note: This is not an invitation for you to send her your manuscript or to solicit her to be your agent.)

If you want to know if I will be signing books in your city, please visit my Web site, www.stuartwoods.com, where the tour schedule will be published a month or so in advance. If you wish me to do a book signing in your locality, ask your favorite bookseller to contact his Penguin representative or the Penguin publicity department with the request.

If you find typographical or editorial errors in my book and feel an irresistible urge to tell someone, please write to Penguin's address above. Do not e-mail your discoveries to me, as I will already have learned about them from others.

A list of my published works appears in the front of this book and on my Web site. All the novels are still in print in paperback and can be found at or ordered from any bookstore. If you wish to obtain hardcover copies of earlier novels or of the two nonfiction books, a good used-book store or one of the online bookstores can help you find them. Otherwise, you will have to go to a great many garage sales.

Read on for a sneak peek
at the next Stone Barrington novel by
New York Times bestselling author
Stuart Woods

STRATEGIC MOVES

Available in hardcover from
G. P. Putnam's Sons.

E laine's, late.

Stone Barrington was uncharacteristically late in meeting his former partner at the NYPD, Lieutenant Dino Bacchetti, for dinner, and Dino was not alone at the table. Dino ran the detective bureau at the 19th Precinct. Stone's other dinner partner, Bill Eggers, managing partner at the prestigious law firm of Woodman & Weld, pretty much ran Stone, who, working from his home office in Turtle Bay, handled cases and clients of Woodman & Weld that they did not wish to be seen to handle.

"You're late," Eggers said.

"I'm late for dinner with Dino," Stone said, "but since I didn't have a date with you, I prefer to think of myself as right on time for our meeting."

Eggers managed a chuckle. "Fair enough," he said. "I'm buying tonight."

"For me, too?" Dino asked.

"For you, too, Dino," Eggers replied.

A waiter set a Knob Creek on the rocks before Stone; the other two men already had glasses of brown whiskey before them. Stone raised his glass, but Eggers put a hand on his arm.

"No, I'll do the toasting tonight," he said, raising his own glass. "To Stone Barrington, who has earned more than a night out on my expense account."

"Hear, hear," Dino said.

"I'll drink to that," Stone offered, raising his glass and taking a pull from it. "Is there an occasion, Bill, or are you just feeling magnanimous?"

"A little of both," Eggers said, taking an envelope from his pocket and handing it to Stone.

Stone saw, through a window in the envelope, his name, which indicated to him that it might be printed on a check. "Bill, have you taken to personally delivering payment of my bills to the firm?"

"Open it," Eggers said.

Stone lifted the flap and pulled open the envelope far enough to see the amount of the check, which was one million dollars. His mouth worked, but no sound came out.

"Don't bother to thank me," Eggers said. "After all, you earned it, and may I say that this is the first annual bonus the firm has ever paid to an attorney who is 'of counsel'?"

Stone recovered his voice. "Why, thank you, Bill, and please thank anyone else at the firm who had anything whatever to do with this."

"This event is occurring because you were substantially responsible for bringing in Strategic Services as a new client, and they have turned out to be a very good client indeed. The death of Jim Hackett has increased their need for your counsel and ours."

Jim Hackett had been the founder and sole owner of the firm, which served many corporations around the world in security matters of all sorts. He had been shot to death while in Stone's company, on an island in Maine, by a sniper employed by two senior members of the British cabinet who had believed Hackett to be someone else.

"Thank you again," Stone said.

"I want you to know—and I realize I'm saying this in front of a witness—that if the growth of the Strategic Services account continues as I believe it will, then by this time next year I may very well be recommending you for a partnership at Woodman and Weld," Eggers said.

Stone was once more dumbstruck. That this might happen had never, in his years of service to the firm, entered Stone's mind. Furthermore, he knew that a partnership in Woodman & Weld would bring an annual income that would be a considerable multiple of the check in the envelope he held. Stone had always been an outsider at the firm, only occasionally visiting its offices and listed as "Of Counsel" only at the bottom of its letterhead.

"I will take your silence as evidence of shock," Eggers said.

Stone nodded vigorously and downed half his drink while signaling for another.

"Make it three," Eggers said to the waiter, "and let me see the list of special wines."

Stone had seen the list of special wines, but he had never once ordered from it, because the wines started at five hundred dollars a bottle.

"Well," Dino said, raising his glass again, "I'm happy I could be here on this special occasion."

"Dino," Eggers said, "you've done Stone many favors on our behalf over the years, so I'm happy you could be here, too."

"Feel free to add me to the bonus list," Dino said wryly.

"Only should you die in our service," Eggers said pleasantly.

"I figured," Dino replied.

Eggers opened the wine list, glanced at it, then closed it. "Order something that will go well with a Château Pétrus 1975," he said, opening his menu.

Stone turned to the waiter, who was braced beside

the table, holding his pad and pencil ready. "I want one of Barry's secret steaks, medium rare," Stone said, "and I'll start with the French green bean salad. Hold the peppers. Use truffle oil."

"Same here, rare," Dino said.

"Make it three," Eggers echoed, "and mine medium."

The waiter dematerialized.

"Tell me," Eggers said to Stone, "have you figured out why Jim Hackett was murdered?"

"I've never said this to anyone before," Stone replied, "but I am under the constraint of the British Official Secrets Act and am, therefore, unable to respond to your question."

"You're shitting me," Eggers said.

"I shit you not," Stone replied. "You will recall that my client, at that time, was an arm of Her Majesty's Government. They made me sign the Act."

More specifically, Stone's client had been a lovely redhead, who also happened to be the head of MI6, the foreign arm of British Intelligence.

"And," Eggers said, "I perceive that your work for them resulted in the resignation and arrest of the British foreign secretary and the home secretary."

"I cannot either confirm or deny your perception," Stone said, "but just between the three of us, I would be very much surprised if those two gentlemen ever came to trial."

"I suppose, if that happened, too much embarrassing information would come to light," Eggers said.

"That is what I suppose, too," Stone replied, "though no one has said as much to me. The government managed to keep it out of the British newspapers by employing the Official Secrets Act."

"It made the *New York Times,*" Eggers said.

"All copies of which were banned for sale that day in the UK," Stone said. "I don't think that sort of thing has happened since the abdication of Edward the Eighth."

"I'm glad your name was kept out of it," Eggers said. "The firm would not have liked that sort of publicity. Our London office has too many clients who might have been embarrassed by your participation."

"I'm glad, too," Stone said. "Believe me."

Dinner arrived, and the bottle of Pétrus, which Eggers tasted with some ceremony. "We'll drink it," he said to the waiter, and they did.